I0524193

Tommie W. Whitener

TOM & LEONE
Star-Crossed Lovers

San Francisco 2019

ISBN: 978-0-9986815-4-2

Cover design by Keith Song and Vanya Akraboff

ACKNOWLEDGEMENTS

My deepest appreciation to the following people without whom this book would be much less than it is now:

In Arkansas: Timothy G. Nutt and his staff at the University of Arkansas in Little Rock, Twyla G. Wright, George Lankford and Kyna Stys.

In California: Penny Dufficy, Larry Gail, Margi Stuber, Vanya Akraboff, John Byrne Barry, Susan Keller, and Joel Blackwell.

INTRODUCTION

Tom and Leona were real people who lived in northeast Arkansas about one hundred years ago. They were my paternal grandparents. Many of the other people mentioned in the book were real also. Most of them were my ancestors. However, some of the characters are completely fictional. I made them up and developed them as realistically as I could so as to create an interesting story.

I never met any of these people. Their personalities (and of course all dialogue) were entirely invented by me.

As much as I could, I wrote the book using as many actual dates, places and documented actions as possible. Thus, almost all dates of birth and death are true, as are the various places the Whitener, Bailey and other families lived in Independence, Sharp and White counties. However, not all is factual

Sometimes I embellished. For example, in 1927 there really was a huge flood that inundated and devastated the states along the Mississippi River. But the floodwaters never reached so far as the area where my ancestors lived. Similarly, Leone really was confined in the mental institution in Little Rock. However, all I describe as happening to her there, as well as the other patients, were products of my imagination.

Sometimes I made things up. Was Tom really a moonshiner? It seems likely, but I have no evidence of that. Did Tom and Leone really create a huge fiery barrier to save their farm from millions of locusts? Maybe, but again I have no proof.

Sometimes I used hearsay. Leone is described as suffering from pellagra. This was told to me in person and in letters from people who actually knew her. Yet pellagra is properly described as a deficiency disease often linked to overdependence on corn as a staple food. Leone's family was not overly poor, nor was Tom's. Thus, it is unlikely that she would have suffered from a dietary malady. My personal belief is that "pellagra," as that description was used in Arkansas at that time, was a sort of catch-all term to describe mental illness when no other diagnosis seemed entirely appropriate. However, I have used the term in spite of not believing it accurate because Leone and those around her at the time used it, and because I do not have facts which would make some other diagnosis more suitable.

THOMAS A. WHITENER
b. 7 Feb 1876
d. 8 Jun 1943

LEONE N. WHITENER
b. 13 Aug 1886
d. 17 Dec 1960

PROLOGUE

In the spring of 1919 when Tom Whitener took the witness stand to testify at his wife's commitment inquest, every available seat in the small Batesville, Arkansas, courtroom was taken. Leone had recently attempted to burn the couple's farmhouse with their four children inside and the judge had to decide whether she should be sent to the, as it was known then, insane asylum.

One of the hottest days of the year, even the open windows and churning ceiling fans didn't alleviate the oppressive heat. In almost every hand was a constantly waving hand fan or newspaper. The faint smell of spring flowers occasionally made its way inside and combined with body odor to produce a musky, not wholly unpleasant, aroma.

Tom and the judge were very different individuals. Tom's excited demeanor and quick movements were in sharp contrast to the judge's slow deliberate manner. Even the two men's attire emphasized their differences. Tom had on clean, if worn, farmer's denim overalls, underneath which he wore a freshly washed white shirt with the right sleeve rolled up to his bicep, past the missing forearm he had been born without. For his part, the judge's tweed suit, starched wing-tip collar and black necktie made it clear that there were huge social and economic distances between him and the others in the courtroom.

Two court-appointed psychiatrists, known as alienists, had already testified that they had examined Leone and found her to be insane.

Both recommended her commitment. Now, as expectant silence dominated the courtroom, it was Tom's turn to answer the gray-headed jurist's questions.

Judge: And what was the first thing you saw when you got back from town?

Tom: Well, I didn't see nothing at first, but as soon as I came around the woods next to the pond, I could hear the young'uns yellin'. Especially Loyce, him being the oldest and all. He was screamin' like a banshee.

Judge: Did you see Leone? What was she doing?

Tom: Sure I seen her. She had a fire going up against the side of the house and was pilin' kindlin' against the front door. Had our big kerosene can sittin' next to her, fixin' to pour it on.

Judge: What did you do?

Tom: Why, I jumped down off the wagon of course and ran up on the porch. I almost knocked her down getting to the door. She had a rope tied around the handle so the kids couldn't open it, but I yanked that right off. Soon as I flung the door open the kids came flyin' out, all coughin' and wheezin' and cryin' and eyes runnin'. Loyce was carryin' little Allen. Smoke was just a pourin' out.

Judge: Remind us again how old they are.

Tom: Loyce's seven, Clifford's five, Otto's three and Allen's two.

Judge: What did you do then?

Tom: I got 'em all down off the porch and made sure none of 'em wasn't burnt or anything. They wasn't. Just still cryin' pretty good. They was real scared.

Judge: What was Leone doing then?

Tom: Well at first, she was just standin' there looking at me, all wild-eyed. She kept sayin', "Burn 'em. Got to burn 'em." Over and over. "Burn 'em. Got to burn 'em". Then, when I got the well pump goin' and got a couple of buckets poured on the fire, she started helpin'. She started pumpin'. She'd pump a bucket full and I'd pour it on. It was hard on account of me only having one arm, but pretty soon we got it out. We was sure lucky the well was right there next to the front of the house.

Judge: And, then what happened?

Tom: Why, Leone started actin' like she hadn't had nothin' to do with it. Loyce and Clifford didn't want anything to do with her, but she picked Otto and Allen up and started cooin' to 'em, tellin' 'em everythin' was goin' to be all right, and how precious they were. I ain't never seen such a sight.

Judge: How long had you been gone from home?

Tom: Oh, five, seven hours. I'd left early to go to town to pick up some supplies and groceries. By the time I got back it was early afternoon.

Judge: Did you have any idea she was going to do something like this?

Tom: Nope. None at all. Course she's always acted a little strange sometimes, but never nothin' like this.

Judge: What happened then?

Tom: Fred Thompson and his boys down the road had seed the smoke and came roarin' up in their wagon to help, but by the time they got there the fire was out and we was all just settin' on the ground lookin' at each other. Fred had sent his youngest boy, Marcus, for the sheriff and it wasn't long before he showed up.

Judge: What did the sheriff do?

Tom: First he talked to me and I told him what happened, just like I just told you. Then, he asked Leone if all I said was the God's truth and she started cryin' and sayin' she didn't remember nothin'. That's when he arrested her and took her to jail.

Judge: I think I've heard enough. Anything else you want to say, Tom?

Tom: No, sir, I believe I done told everythin' there is to tell.

Judge: Tom, think about it long and hard for a minute and tell me what you think I should do. She's your wife and these are your young'uns. What do you think I should do?

Tom: I don't rightly know, judge. I just don't. She seems fine now. I know she loves those young'uns with all her heart. But, I just can't forget what she did. If I hadn't come home when I did, she would've burned 'em up.

Judge: Alright, Tom, compose yourself and sit down. Leone, you quit crying too, and if there's anything you want to tell me, now is the time to do it. Is there anything you want to say?

Leone: I don't remember none of that what Tom said. I love my young'uns and wouldn't hurt 'em for anything in the world. I can't believe I would do anything like that. I wanna go home. Please, judge, can I go home?

Judge: Well, Leone, from the evidence presented to me today it seems that you did exactly what Tom says you did. The neighbors saw the smoke and the burned house, and when the sheriff got there, you was all sitting there looking at it. The evidence is one hundred per cent against you.

Leone, I've known your family and Tom's ever since I was a little shaver. Both families, Tom's and yours, are some of the most honest, hardworking, God-fearing people I've ever had the pleasure to know. They settled this rocky land and made it produce when it wasn't nothing but Indian country. But, that don't excuse what you did. And, my first duty is to protect your children. I have to think first about the children and their safety.

As required by the laws of this state you have been examined by two alienists, both of whom have written reports which I now have in front of me. They both conclude that you are insane and that you are presently a danger to yourself or others. I find no reason to disagree with those conclusions.

Therefore, as much as I hate to do it, by the power vested in me by the State of Arkansas, I hereby adjudge you insane and direct the sheriff to transport you to the State Hospital for Nervous Diseases, formerly known as the Arkansas State Lunatic Asylum, at Little Rock. You shall be confined there until the superintendent certifies that you are no longer a danger to yourself or your children, or anyone else for that matter.

"No, judge, no," Leone screamed as the sheriff's deputy approached, reaching for his handcuffs. "I got to go home and take care of my young'uns."

The judge had stood up and was about to leave the bench when out of the corner of his eye he caught sight of Tom, red in the face and about to come forward.

"Tom, the judge said, "you sit back down and stay out of this. It's out of your hands now."

"But judge," the distraught husband and father said, "you just gonna send her to Little Rock just like that? What about me and the kids? We need her."

"Tom, apparently you don't understand. She's going to the State Hospital and you just got to do what you got to do. Them kids is your responsibility now."

Tom slumped back into his chair and watched Leone's wide-eyed stare as the deputy led her through the rear doorway.

CHAPTER ONE

After the deputy hurried Leone out the door to catch the afternoon train to the asylum in Little Rock, I thought about how Leone and I had met twelve years before.

I was thirty-one then and wasn't getting no younger. More and more I was feeling the lack of a wife and young'uns. That's when I started socializing more. Going to church dances seemed like the best way to meet someone, and so I was doing that as much as I could.

I would of gone to the Baptist church in Sidney. That's the closest one. But they didn't allow no dancing. So I started going to the Methodist Church down by Cave City. It was a piece further, but they had regular Sunday night dances. That's where I met Leone.

For the dances, a couple of the fellas would get to the church early and get everything ready. They would shove all the pews back against the walls, hang some bunting the women had made special for decoration and set up a couple tables for punch and cookies. They even had a special little platform for the musicians. By the time the fifty or sixty of us showed up, you almost never would have known it was a church.

I'd been going there for a while and I knew most of the young single gals. They was all nice enough, but none of them really suited my fancy. And, well, to tell the truth, some of 'em was put off by my lack of an arm. Then one evening Leone showed up. Walked in with her cousin Lena Wilcox that I knowed from some place or other. Lena lived there in Cave City, and Leone was up from Floral staying with her for a few days.

Leone was pretty as a picture. I noticed her right away. When Lena went to get some punch, Leone was just standing there on the gals' side of the room and soon as I could I caught her eye and gave her a big smile. She smiled back a little, and that's all I needed. I crossed right over to ask her to dance. But as soon as I got close, her eyes got wide and she said: "What happened to your arm?"

"I don't rightly know," I said. Something must have happened while I was in my mama. That's the way I came out. My name's Tom Whitener. Would you like to dance?"

"I never danced with a one-armed man before. Is your other one all right?"

"Why, sure. It's just fine, probably the strongest one this side of the Mississippi."

"Well with one of your arms gone, how can we dance?"

"I done it a bunch of times. With my left hand I'll hold your right hand, like normal. But my right arm won't reach all the way around you, so I'll just put it as far around as it will reach, right up against your side."

"OK, I'll try it."

"Don't worry, it will work out. I use it for plowing and everything."

"So, you're a farmer? We farm some, but mostly my folks is traders and run businesses. We're from south of Batesville, down by Floral."

"Nothing wrong with being a farmer. Me and my brother, Jim, he lives with me, we got a little piece of ground down towards the river. We're way up in the woods, kinda off the beaten track, so to speak, but we do all right. We ain't getting rich, but who is?"

"Is Jim your older brother?"

"No, he's two years younger. Except for my sister, Mary, me and him is the oldest young'uns in our family."

"Has he got both his arms?"

"Why, sure, of course he does. All Pa's young'uns does, except me. Jim's kind of a quiet fella, but he's strong as an ox and twice as hard-working."

By this time the music was going pretty good and we went to make up a square out on the dance floor. I do OK with the dancing, except sometimes, like with the "hand over hands" and the "dosey does." With them I have to skip a touch or two. I like clogging better; especially when there's a banjo. I don't like it when there's just fiddle and guitar. But old timey music ain't my favorite. It's waltzes I like. With the waltzes I can hold the gals real close.

After that first dance, I told Leone I would be right back and went out back to have another pull at that jug I'd brought. They was a couple good ol' boys there that had brought they own jugs and we got to talking and comparing products, and the first thing I knowed, I'd had a little more to drink than I'd intended. When I went back in, Leone looked at me a little funny, as if she noticed, but she didn't say nothing, and after I shooed off a couple eager bucks, we started in dancing again.

One dance led to another, and before you knowed it we'd danced every dance. Of course, there was other fellas wanting to horn in, but I wouldn't let 'em. When they'd come over to Leone, I'd just get between 'em so they mostly couldn't see her. A couple of 'em tried to talk to her over my shoulder, but she ignored 'em. We was pretty much a couple beginning right then. I did take a couple breaks to go back out back and have a couple more swigs, but mainly I was just with her.

And, talk. Land o' Goshen. We just talked and talked. We had a whole passel of things to talk about. Nothin' in particular. Just one thing and another. She did tell me she was twenty-one years old and had two sisters and three brothers. And they all helped out some with the farming and in the store.

She asked me about my farm and crops, and was our place subject much to flooding, all kinds of things like that. I told her my daddy had a farm up by Ash Flat, but she didn't say anything about it. Then, I told her he was on his third wife and already had seventeen kids and maybe wasn't done yet. She thought that was pretty good.

But, when I told her my grandpa that had just died down in Texas was a preacher, her eyes really lit up. She said she had always been partial to preachers because they always seemed so kind. And, when I told her he had had two wives and twelve children, she thought that was just the cat's meow. So, I went on and added that my pa was an elder in the Presbyterian Church and that seemed to please her even more.

Pretty soon the dance was over, and it was time to leave. I wanted to ride her home, but she'd come with Lena, and said she better keep her pa happy and go back with her. I probably shouldn't have had so much to drink and then maybe she would have let me.

By the time I got home, it was way past midnight. Too late to wake Jim and tell him about her. I was bustin' a gut to do it though, and it was only by bitin' my tongue real hard that I let him sleep.

Jim and me has been farming together for quite a spell now and it's working out real well. When I thought I was going to be able to buy this piece of ground, I asked him if he'd go in with me. He said he didn't have no money to put in, but that he'd like to go in on his labor. He's a real hard worker, smart as a wagon load of teachers and honest as the day is long. He don't talk a whole lot, but when he does, it always makes a lot of sense. I think it's called having good judgment. So, I was real glad to take him in. That was more than seven years ago and we ain't had more than a couple little dust-ups between us the whole time.

Next morning, soon as we woke up, I started in telling him about Leone:

"Jim, I think I met her. I think I finally met the woman I'm going to marry."

"How do you know?"

"Well, first of all, she's pretty as a June bug on a string. Short black hair. Cute round face. Big brown eyes and long lashes. Just perfect. Secondly, she's just as sweet and nice as a man could ever want. Me and her danced every dance, and talked and talked. Seemed like she was real interested in me and I knowed I was interested in her.

"And one of the things I liked best about her was her voice. It was so soft and sweet. Kinda reminded me of a little kitty who's lost her mama. You know, a little ball of fur you want to pick up and hold real close and give her a saucer of milk. That's the way I feel about this gal. Right away I wanted to take her in my arms and protect her, just like you would a little kitty mewing for its mama."

"Ain't that a little strong? You just met her. What did she say about your arm?"

"Why, nothing. What could she say? It ain't there that's all. And we danced just fine."

"She from a farm family?"

"Nope. Says they farm some, but mainly her daddy's got a store in Batesville."

"She a Bailey? Seems like there's a John Bell Bailey runs one there."

"Sure is. John Bell is her pa. She's Leone Bailey."

"Well, ain't you moving up in the world!"

"Them owning a store ain't got nothing to do with it. I couldn't care less if her family didn't have a pot to piss in, nor a window to throw it out of. It's her I like. There's just one thing that's a might troubling. Sometimes she says things that don't quite make sense. Nothing big or important things you understand, but on occasion what she says don't seem to match up with what we was talking about."

"Like what, for example?"

"Well, we was talking about her pa, and all of a sudden she started talking about one time when she was little and her older sister, Hattie, chased her with a buggy whip. Didn't seem to be no connection between her pa and Hattie with the whip. And then she got back to talking about her pa and what a big shot he was, and nothing more was said about Hattie or the whip. A little strange."

Jim's about two years younger than me. Seems like all Pa's kids are about two years apart. Jim's a good lookin' fella, and big and strong. He's got a kind of bony face with real noticeable cheekbones and kinda setback eyes. We been told we look quite a bit alike. I don't know how I could get by without him.

"And what's her family going to say about you?" Jim said. "You think they'll have you courting their high-toned little daughter?"

"She said she didn't care what they think. She said she was going to tell them all about me, and say I might come calling. They's another dance in two weeks and she's going to tell me then when I can come by on a Sunday afternoon for tea or lemonade. And, we might be able to get together before then. She's working on something with her sister Mabel. If Mabel will help out, we can fix up a meeting for next week."

"Tom, I don't want to rain on your parade or nothin, but don't you think you better see how things work out before you start hiring a preacher? Been my experience that a strong pa has a powerful influence over his young'uns, and over his womenfolk in particular. I'm sure it's all going to work out for you, but just don't go getting your hopes too high before you know which way the wind blows."

And that's how Jim and I left it for then. Raising cotton and corn to sell and vegetables and fruit for us to eat, to say nothing about the hogs and chickens, was a real busy job and we had lots to do and talk about besides Leone. Not that I didn't think about her. Of course, I did. Constant. I almost couldn't wait 'til the next dance.

• • • • • •

For her part, Leone returned from the dance just as excited as Tom, just dying to tell her sister about him:

"Mabel. Mabel, wake up. I've got something I've got to tell you."

"Shush, you'll wake the whole family. What is it?"

After Leone had traded her dress for her nightgown and slid between the flour sack quilts to join Mabel in the bed the two shared, Leone eagerly continued. "I met this boy. Well, he's not a boy, really. He's thirty-one. But he's got a sweetness about him. Me and him really hit it off."

"OK, tell me about him."

"He's handsome, tall. He's got his own farm. Name's Tom Whitener. His brother, Jim, farms with him. His pa's a farmer, too."

"I ain't never heard of no Tom Whitener. Where's his farm?"

"He said north of Sandtown, up by Sidney. He said his farm's back up in the woods a ways. I don't think he gets to town too often. I told him about daddy's store, but he didn't seem to know it. I think he's just about the nicest, most polite man I've ever met. He must have got it from his mama. Looks like she brought him up real good."

"Has he got young'uns?"

"Nope. Never been married, he says."

"He wasn't into the shine there at the dance was he? I know some of them boys keep a jug out back, and before the evening is over they're actin' pretty silly."

"Well, some. But he wasn't no worse than any of the rest of 'em."

"What does he think about you?"

"Said he wants to see me again as soon as he can."

"Did he notice your affliction?"

"If he did, he didn't say nothin'."

"Maybe you didn't do nothin' to let it show. Did you do anything to let it show?"

"I don't think so. But, I don't always notice."

"Well just be careful. I can't count the number of boys you've been interested in, and every one of them hightailed it as soon as you started acting funny. I don't want to be trying to comfort you no more after some boy quits you. You just be careful."

"Oh, Mabel, I do so want to have a man and a normal life and kids. I want that so bad. And, it always feels so good when it starts. And, I'm so depressed when it don't work out."

"Well, twenty-one ain't too old and I guess you've got lots of time. Just take it slow. Just take your time. If it happens it happens and if it don't, it don't."

"Mabel, one more thing. He's got a funny arm. His arm ain't all there."

"Ain't all there?"

"He says he was born like that, with one arm that don't reach but to his elbow. He told me he farms just fine, but I don't know how he could handle a plow. I'll ask him about that when I see him next."

"Oh, Leone."

"Mabel, you've got to help us. I just got to see Tom. I can't wait until the next dance. We got an idea. Will you help us?"

"If it involves going behind Pa's back, I ain't gonna do it. I don't mind helping, but I ain't telling no lies."

"No, nothing like that. Just a little detour when we take the wagon over to pick up that foal at the Jefferson's on Friday. All you got to do is go a mile or two out of our way over by Huff and drop me off. Tom says he's gonna be there, regardless. Then, you go on for the colt. Tell 'em I was with you but you dropped me off to gather some berries and that you'll pick me up on your way back. I'll even pick some berries. You don't have to tell no lie. You pick me up on the way home and I'll have a basket of berries and no one will be the wiser."

"And you and Tom will have had two or three hours out there in the woods by yourselves?"

"We ain't gonna do nothing. Just talk, that's all. Just talk."

"You promise me that's all you're gonna do, is just talk? You do something with him you're not supposed to, and Pa will shoot the fella just as sure as God made little green apples. You understand?"

"I promise, Mabel. I promise."

"How will Tom know you're coming?"

"When we was at the dance on Saturday I told him about picking up the foal. That's when he hatched this detour plan. He said he would be there waiting whether I was or not."

"Well, OK, but it better not git back to Pa."

I sure hope I'm doing the right thing, Leone thought to herself as she turned away from her sister to try to go to sleep. *I like that boy, but I do wish he hadn't had so much to drink.*

CHAPTER TWO

There was no sign of Tom when Mabel reined the wagon horse to a stop at the intersection of the two dusty country roads, one leading north to Sidney and the other east and then south to Floral. However, the dust had not yet settled when he stepped out of the thick woods. Wearing a bright smile and a sparkling white shirt with the sleeves rolled up to his biceps, he enthusiastically waved at the two women with his good left arm.

"Hello, Leone. And, Mabel, I am very pleased to make your acquaintance. How y'all today. Mabel, I feel like I know you already 'cause Leone done told me a lot about you. I sure appreciate you bringing her out here. Much obliged. We both do, don't we Leone?"

"And, I am pleased to meet you, too, Tom Whitener. Leone tells me you been farming up north of here. Says you told her your pa's got a farm up that way, too."

"Yes, ma'am. I made a pretty good crop of corn and cotton this year. That April flood put about two inches of silt on my fields and you know how crops love that. Soon as it dried out, I got my seeds in and they never quit growing."

"Well, the Bailey's ain't big farmers so I wouldn't know too much about it. But Tom, I'm gonna tell you something, just like I told Leone. I'm gonna drop her off. But I'm only gonna do it because she told me you was a true gentleman and that there wasn't gonna be no fooling around. Just talk, right? That's all you're gonna be doing, right, is just talking?"

"Yes, ma'am, that is for sure. That's all there's gonna be. We'll just be gabbing."

"Well, it better be. I'll be back here in about three hours and you better both be here then. And, no fooling around."

As Mabel cried out "gee" and reined the horse to the left to the road leading to the Jefferson's, Tom thought, *Now, why would she have it in her head that there might be fooling around? She shouldn't be thinking about me like that.*

After a silence during which Tom and Leone nervously looked at each other, he was the first to speak:

"I sure like your dress. My sisters ain't got but two dresses each— one regular one and a go-to-meetin' one. But you, you got more than two, probably. And this one is even prettier than the one you wore to the dance."

"Why, thank you, Tom. I'm glad you like it. But, I only got one."

"Only got one? Why, that ain't true. You've had a different one on both times I've seen you. You had the pink one on at the dance and now a green one."

"I only got one, " she replied turning her gaze to the ground.

Puzzled, but not wanting to pursue the matter, Tom changed the subject.

For both Tom and Leone the next three hours fully lived up to their expectations. As they walked and sat and talked and gathered berries, each of them was fully absorbed in the other.

"Leone,"Tom was saying, "I already told you about my grandaddy, the preacher in Texas, and the Whiteners startin' out with the Old German in North Carolina before the Revolution. But, what about the Baileys? Where your people originally from?"

"Most recently, before Arkansas, from Tennessee. But before that they's all from Virginia. Been Bailey's and Powell's, that was my mama's name before she married my daddy, Powell, in Virginia since before there was a United States. Still a whole passel of 'em there, I guess. But, Tom, you didn't tell me you mama's name. What was she before she was a Whitener?

"She was a Suttle. Mary Susan Suttle. I think her people go back to Tennessee and before that to North Carolina."

"My mama's name," Leone responded, "is Margaret Winifred Powell. Everybody calls her Maggie. I reckon you already know about my pa, John Bell Bailey. Everybody calls him John Bell. His pa was a John, too, so they call my pa John Bell."

As Tom talked and listened, his thoughts were partly on the many disappointments he had known with regard to finding a wife:

I got to keep remembering what Jim said. Can't be getting my hopes too high. More than ten years of trying to find a gal to marry, and I surely don't need another one to cause me grief.

"Tom," Leone asked after a short pause, "reckon you're always going to be a farmer?"

"Why, I don't know what else I'd do. I only went but to the third grade and I don't know nothing but farming. I'd sure like to get me a better piece of ground, though. Even with floods every few years, it's hard to make a decent crop. That's a pretty rocky patch I got. Not like down by the Mississippi where you could put a stick in the ground and grow a tree."

"You don't have to want to do anything else, of course, but lots of people do other things. Lots of people live in cities and have jobs."

"And, why would I want to live in a city? I like living in the country."

"I'm just asking. Well, for one thing in the city you wouldn't have to work so durned hard. You could have a job and when you was done you could relax. Seems like on a farm the work is never done. And in cities they've got theaters and museums and cultural stuff."

Tom didn't respond. Instead, his mind had become fully occupied by thoughts of how attractive this young beauty was. He thought:

She is just about the cutest gal I ever met. I have never seen such pretty eyes.

"Tom," Leone changed the subject, "can I ask you something, something personal?"

"Why, of course. Ask me anything you want."

"What do you think about young'uns? You want some?"

Breaking into a wide smile, he answered: "Do I want some? Why, of course I do. Didn't I tell you about my daddy and my granddaddy and all the young'uns they had? Big families is a Whitener feature. And, you got two sisters and three brothers. I want at least that many."

Why this boy is right conversational, Leone thought, *and saying the right things, too.*

"Me, too," she said. "About a dozen. Need 'em on to take care of you when you get old."

And then in spite of his earlier promise to Mabel, he heard himself saying: "Now I need to ask you something. Leone, can I kiss you?"

"Why, Tom Whitener. You promised Mabel there wouldn't be no fooling around. Of course, you can't kiss me. Well, maybe just a little one on my cheek. But, that's all."

And, that's all there was.

As the sun's rays began to soften, the snort of Mabel's horse interrupted the young people's non-stop conversation.

"Leone," Tom took her willing left hand to say, "this has been just about the best afternoon I have ever spent in my life."

"Me, too, Tom. Me, too," she looked up at him to say.

As Leone climbed up and Mabel clicked her tongue to start the horse, Tom thought:

I love you Leone. I already do.

● ● ● ● ● ●

Sunday morning after church the Bailey girls, now only Leone and Mabel since Hattie's recent marriage to John Newton and move to Searcy, helped their mother, Maggie, in the kitchen with supper preparations. When there were guests, as there usually were, John Bell, depending on the weather, liked to take the male guests either to the parlor or to the sprawling porch which extended the entire length of the front of the home. And, notwithstanding frequent denunciations of strong drink in Sunday morning sermons at the nearby Cedar Grove Church, he made sure a full jug of white mule was close at hand.

Owing to John Bell's prominent position in the county (he was the owner of one of its largest businesses) an invitation to these Sunday suppers was much sought after. Few were the locals who did not want to recount their previous weekend's activities by beginning, "I was at John Bell's house for supper yesterday and . . ."

While the conversation in the kitchen usually focused on

housekeeping, children and health issues, the men made politics, farming and the "late difficulty between the states," their main topics. Lincoln haters and avid Democrats to a man, the outcome of the "difficulty" was lamented long, hard and repetitiously.

This day, John Bell had invited Homer and Sara Maxwell, as well as William and Martha Suggs. Homer was the mayor of Batesville and William was the owner of the local bank. The three of them, John Bell, Homer and William, formed an informal triumvirate and pretty much ran Batesville and Independence County. Many important decisions with far-reaching consequences for the people of the area were made on one of John Bell's verandas.

Summoned to table by Maggie, John Bell gave the blessing. It was loquacious and long, calling down the higher power's favor and protection on all present, as well as their sundry endeavors. The table was filled to capacity with the usual Sunday fare—fried chicken, pork chops and pork roast, fried okra, two kinds of beans, yams and sweet potatoes, most of it drowned in lard-based gravy. For dessert there were two different kinds of pies, berry and apple.

After all had eaten their fill, John Bell pushed his chair back and stood up to announce:

"Ladies, that was just about the best supper I have ever had. You really outdid yourselves. What fine use you have made of the great crops and bounty we have here in Arkansas. But now, ladies, if you'll excuse us, the menfolk will retire to the porch for cigars and, perhaps a glass of something to complement that fine meal."

"Not so fast, John Bell," Maggie interrupted. "Mabel has a poem she wants to recite and you said she could do it."

"I'm sorry. Maggie, you are so right. I completely forgot. Mabel, what are you going to recite for us, Honey?"

"It's called 'Helen of Troy' by Sara Teasdale."

Whereupon, with insightful inflection and deeply felt emotion, Mabel flawlessly recited the lengthy Teasdale masterpiece. When finished, she was rewarded with sincere and enthusiastic applause.

"Not bad for my all-growed-up little girl," John Bell complimented as soon as the applause quieted. "Thank you, Honey, that was beautiful. Where did you learn it? In school?

"No, Daddy. I learned it on my own. I liked it and so I learned it by heart."

"Well, you did a fine job and we thank you. And now, gentlemen, for those cigars. Once again, ladies, please excuse us."

The stench of the men's sulfurous matches on the veranda had hardly subsided when a rider appeared down the road.

"Who's that?" Homer asked, straining to make out the man.

Coming off the main road and reaching the short road leading to the home, the man reigned his mule to the right and approached. As he got nearer, he dismounted and walked the last few feet to look up at the porch where the men were sitting.

"Howdy, I'm Tom Whitener. And which of you fine gentlemen is Leone's father, John Bell Baily?" Tom's tone was bright and friendly, as if he expected a warm reception. He was starting to tie his horse to the hitching rail post in front of the porch, when Leone's father answered:

"I'm John Bell Bailey. What's this about Leone?"

"Sir, I've come to introduce myself and ask your permission to court Leone. We met at the dance a while back and I've really taken a fancy to her. With your permission, I would like to be able to spend some time with her."

John Bell didn't say anything, but turned to the left to look at his friend Homer Maxwell and then to the right to William Suggs. Returning his gaze to Tom, he started:

"Son, I don't know you and I don't know nothing about you. I only know what I see and that's a one-armed man on a broken-down mule, come up here talking crazy stuff about wanting to court my daughter. Where you from?"

One of the children had gone to the kitchen and told the women that there was a man out front asking about Leone, causing her to excitedly come to the door and shyly peer out.

"Tom, I think I know you," Homer joined in. "You're Dan Whitener's boy, ain't you? Dan and Mary that got that farm up in Sharp County, almost to the river.

"Yes sir, that's me. Dan's my pa."

"You farmin' with your pa?" John Bell scowled at Tom.

"No, sir. I got my own place. Me and my brother, Jim, got us a place up the Cave City Road. Doing just fine, we are."

"You own your place?" John Bell asked.

"Yes, sir, I do. I got a little mortgage still, but I'll soon have it paid off. I'm doin' plenty good enough to take care of Leone, if ever she would have me."

At this, the more than six-foot tall, 300-pound John Bell imposingly rose from his rocker to glare at Tom. Jutting out his chin menacingly, he spat out:

"Well, son, there ain't gonna be no havin' you. You are not gonna be courtin' Leone, or my other daughter for that matter. Just get your ass back on that nag you rode in on and ride back to wherever it was you came from. The sooner we're shut of you the better."

Tom caught sight of Leone coming to stand in the dim doorway behind John Bell and ignored the big man to say:

"What about you, Leone? Ain't you got no say in this? What do you say?"

"Boy, I done told you once. She ain't got nothing to say about it. Now git! Maggie, bring me my shotgun."

Tom's pounding heart and suddenly sweaty palms told him it would be a very bad idea for him to be present once John Bell had a gun in his hands. He quickly untied his mule and headed back down the road.

"Leone," John Bell turned to say to his daughter, "git back in the kitchen and help the other womenfolk. Ain't gonna be nothing more between you and this Tom Whitener. Just forget about him."

• • • • • •

A few days later when Leone and Mabel walked into the Grange dance, Tom and Mabel's beau, Herbert, were waiting for them. Mabel and Herb had known each other for a while and most all who knew them assumed their marriage would be happening sometime soon.

With wide smiles and animated conversation, the two couples immediately paired off. Seemingly not caring if the music ever started, Tom and Leone looked at each other and talked, while Herb and Mabel talked nearby on their own hay bale.

"Just wait til it gets back to your pa that we was holdin' hands," Herb said, smiling at Mabel.

"And what if he does say something. That's just too blamed bad. I'm almost 19 years old and I guess I'll do as I please," she responded with more assertiveness than she actually felt.

"What about Leone? Do you suppose it's gonna get back to your pa that she met Tom here?"

"Yes, I reckon it will. Too many tongue-waggers for it not to. And then there'll be hell to pay. Pa will surely come down hard on her. She knows that. Told me she didn't care. She's even older than me and says she doesn't care what pa says."

"Well, I don't know about that," Herb replied. "John Bell is a pretty imposing individual. I hope I don't never cross him."

"Herb, have you been into that sour mash whiskey again?" Mabel suddenly changed the subject.

"Me and Tom had us a little snort. Yes. Just a little one. It ain't nothin'."

"Well, I sure don't like it none. I wish you wouldn't do that."

"Don't worry about it. Tom brought it. You know he's got him a little still back in the woods behind his house."

"I didn't know that. I'll bet Leone don't either. You think Tom told her?"

If Herb was able to answer, Mabel wasn't able to hear it because not ten feet from where they were sitting, the band suddenly launched into "Cotton Eyed Joe." Further thought of conversation was immediately abandoned as all made for the middle of the straw-strewn hall to dance. "Soldier's Joy" followed "Cotton Eyed Joe," and song followed song as the perspiring couples twirled and whirled. Finally, though, the fiddler announced that the hard-working musicians had to have a break.

"That is just about the best banjo player I ever did hear," Tom said to Leone as he escorted her to an unoccupied bale. The guitar picker ain't bad, either. I'll get you some punch."

Returning to the bale a few seconds later, he handed Leone her punch and announced that he needed to step outside for a minute.

He didn't return in one minute and he didn't return in two. After more than twenty minutes when he finally did return, Leone recoiled in shock. There was blood on his face, his right eye was almost swollen closed and his shirt was torn. More than that, he reeked of whiskey and was swaying from side to side.

"Tom, what on earth happened," she was finally able to muster.

"Nothin'. A couple of them boys from Calamine said something I didn't like, and we got into it, that's all. It's nothin'."

"Tom, you been drinking more, too, ain't you?"

"I had a little taste, that's true. But, I'm OK."

"What was y'all fighting about?"

"You don't need to worry your pretty little head about that. It was nothin'."

When the band started again and the dancers returned to the floor, Tom and Leone didn't join them. He was in no condition to dance and she sat next to him dabbing at his cut face with a kerchief she had dampened.

Much later, and when the band was packing up, Tom and Leone were still seated on their bale. Herb and Mable approached them.

"Tom, you shouldn't have hit that cracker," Herb said. "I know you think it ain't my business, but I saw what happened. You just walked over and slugged him. You got back just exactly what you deserved. A one-armed man pickin' a fight. If that ain't the craziest thing I ever heard."

"Well, he was lookin' at Leone. He shouldn't a been lookin' at her like that."

"He didn't mean no harm. Besides, Leone's a pretty girl. Everybody looks at her. And, another thing: you'd be better off if you'd leave that shine alone. You're a mean drunk and everybody knows it. Come on girls, I'll walk outside with you."

"Good night, Tom," Leone said as she got up to accompany her sister and Herb to the door.

"Good night, Leone. I'm sorry," he responded as he watched her walk away and then thought:

I don't mind that I got beat up, but I sure hope I didn't ruin my chances with her.

"Oh, Mabel," Leone said to her sister on the way home," what am I gonna do? When he's not drinking Tom is just the sweetest, most likable fella. But when he gets to drinking, he gets mean."

"So you want me to tell you whether or not one is worth the other? Whether you should put up with his drinking? Well, I can't do that. That's a decision you've got to make for yourself."

CHAPTER THREE

"Leone, come here. I want to talk to you," John Bell called for his daughter from his easy chair a week or so after the Grange dance. "I got something I want to talk to you about."

Leone and her father had not talked since Tom had been run off, but Leone knew John Bell was not one to let sleeping dogs lie.

"Sit down there," John Bell directed as she entered the parlor. "Take Ma's chair for a bit."

Ma's chair was next to a small table on which sat a kerosene lamp providing the sole source of light for the comfortably furnished parlor, or sitting room as they sometimes called it. The room had been made particularly cozy with last year's addition of new wallpaper and a large oval rug Leone and Mabel had braided from rags.

A picture of John Bell's parents, John and Sarah, were prominently displayed on the left of the glowing fireplace. On the right, where one might have expected to find a similar picture of Maggie's parents, there was nothing. As a matter of fact, Maggie's parents were something of a mystery and Maggie never talked about them. All that was known about Maggie's origins was that she was born in Missouri. More than that she wouldn't say, and neither would John Bell.

Leone had never before been afforded the honor of sitting in her mother's parlor chair. Thus, she sat uncomfortably on the front of it, staring expectantly at her father.

"Leone, I heard about you seeing that Tom Whitener at the Grange dance. Seems like you was quite the center of attention. Especially after he got drunk and started a fight. Didn't you think I'd hear about that?"

"I supposed you would."

"Well, then why did you do it? I run him off once and I don't want you having anything to do with him."

"Pa, he's a real nice man."

"I don't care how nice he is. I got you a husband all lined up. I got you a man I've convinced to marry you. It took some doing, but he said he's pretty sure he'll do it. I told him all about your pellagra and he still says he'll marry you."

"Pa, I like that Tom Whitener. Who you wanting to marry me to?"

"His name's Browning. Van Browning. He ain't the sharpest knife in the drawer, but you ain't exactly a prize yourself. I think it would be a good deal for you both."

"Pa, I really cotton to Tom Whitener. He's a nice fella and says his farm's doing real well."

"Honey, you know I only want the best for you. I want you to marry someone who's gonna do right by you and provide you with a decent home. That Tom Whitener don't show me nothing. I don't think he's ever gonna make a real man. How could he, only having one arm? How old is he, anyway?"

"He's thirty-one."

"He ever been married before?"

"Nope. Says he's been waiting for the right gal to come along. He thinks that right gal is me. Please daddy, I don't want to marry Van Browning."

"More likely no one would have him and that stump for a right arm. But it don't make no difference, you ain't gonna marry him. You're marrying Van Browning and that's all there is to it."

"I'm tired of this one and that one coming around and you getting your hopes up and then we never see him again. Mr. Browning's coming on Sunday and you two can get acquainted. He's a real decent sort and I think you'll like him. You know I wouldn't choose someone who wasn't right for you. After you get married, Ma said you can have her sewing room. We'll fix it up real nice for you. Then, in time, you can find your own place."

"Please, Pa, no."

"I done said it's what's gonna happen. Mr. Browning will be here on Sunday."

Leone ran to the bedroom and threw herself on the bed sobbing. She didn't notice Mabel seated on the chair in the corner and her younger sister's words startled her:

"Daddy told us he was going to talk to you. He told us all about Van Browning. He said Mr. Browning's coming for supper on Sunday."

Abruptly raising her head, Leone responded: "I don't know no Van Browning. Never even heard of him til today and I sure don't want to marry him."

"Pa says Mr. Browning is a hard-working, honest sort, and that he'll make a good husband. Pa should know. You know Pa's a fine judge of character."

"I only wanna marry Tom Whitener."

"Well, you ain't a gonna marry Tom Whitener. Pa said you ain't and so you ain't. You're gonna marry Van Browning," Mabel announced decisively. "You're gonna marry Van Browning and be happy about it."

Mabel wanted to tell Leone how sorry she felt for her and how she believed that even with his drinking Tom Whitener was a better choice for her than the simpleton Van Browning. But she didn't say that. Owing to her respect for their father and in the interest of not causing further division in the family, she held her tongue. Instead, she softened her tone and said:

"Honey, Mr. Browning will make you a fine husband. And, you can live right here in town. You can have a whole group of young'uns and we can visit all the time and everything. And with that Tom Whitener, and his one arm," she couldn't resist saying, "you'd probably wind up doing the plowing."

"That ain't true," Leone responded. "He tells me he drives a team just fine. He's strong as an ox with his good arm. He had me feel it. His brother does most of the plowing, of course, but that ain't nothing."

"Well plowing or no plowing, what Pa said goes," Mabel tried to close the matter.

"What about me?" Leone questioned, the tears resuming. "What about what I want? I got wants, too, you know. I got dreams, too, you know. I want a husband and a house and some kids. I want those things, too, you know. Hattie's already got two young'uns. And you're gonna have a husband and kids and a place to call your own right soon."

"Leone, you can have all those things. You're just gonna have 'em with Van Browning, that's all."

"I don't want 'em with Van Browning. I want 'em with Tom Whitener. He's the only man that's ever treated me half decent for more than a day or two. He's the only one that's ever treated me like I wasn't crazy. Van Browning won't treat me right, I just know he won't. He'll start treating me mean just like all the others. Tom Whitener is a good man. He'll treat me right and I'm gonna marry him."

"We'll see, Leone," Mabel said with quiet assurance. "We'll see about that."

• • • • • •

"Leone," John Bell said as he ushered a tall, thin young man into the parlor where he had previously seated his daughter, "this here is Mr. Van Browning. Mr. Browning, this here is my second oldest daughter, Leone."

"How do you do," Leone said as rose to greet the man, distracted by his flourishing acne and one particularly ripe pimple square in the middle of his left cheek.

"How do you do, Miss Leone," he responded as he excitedly took her hand and began jacking it.

"That will be enough, Mr. Browning," John Bell finally said. "She ain't a water pump. Now, I want you two to get to know each other. Both of you have a seat and start talking. Ma's making some lemonade and she'll be bringing it in after a bit. In the meantime, you can just sit here and talk. Ain't nobody gonna bother you. And, Mr. Browning's staying for supper, so if you don't git all your talking done, you can come on back in here afterward and visit some more. Leone, you hear me. I want you to be getting to know each other. That means talking."

As the door closed behind her father, Leone looked nervously at Van Browning. He grinned back at her like a Cheshire cat.

"Leone, you wanna hear about that big ol' rattlesnake I killed last week? I was telling your pa and he thought it was real interesting. Probably the biggest rattlesnake ever killed in Independence County."

Taking silence for, yes, the young man went on.

"Well, me and my friend, Bob, was down on Black Slough fishing. We was just sitting there watching our bobbers and here he come, just slithering along like he owned the whole durned world. He didn't notice us because we was just sitting there, not even talking. I saw he was gonna cross right in front of us, and so real sly-like I reached over and got a grip on a big 'ol dead branch lying next to me. When he got close enough, up I come, swinging that limb like Samson and his jawbone. I whacked him and kept on whacking til he was dead. Oh, he was striking at me all right, but my branch was long enough so's he couldn't get me. And, I got the rattle right here in my pocket to prove it. Wanna see it?"

Leone stared at the man, thinking:

How could he possibly think I'd be interested in him killing a stupid snake?

"And, you know what else? They's a man down by Johnson City give me three cents for the skin so's he could make a picture frame out of it. I ain't never seen a snake skin picture frame, but he give me the three cents and that's all I care about."

Leone's eyes were fixed on the pimple which seemed to grow even as they spoke.

"Mama said I should ask you if you can cook. You can cook, can't you?"

"Yes, I can cook. I cook and help Ma in the kitchen most every day," she matter of factly answered.

"Well, that sure is good, 'cause I love to eat. Eatin's probably my favorite thing."

"You don't look like you eat a lot."

"Well, I do. I may be skinny as a bean pole—always have been—but I eat a lot. Don't know why I don't never gain no weight."

"Mr. Browning, can you read and write?"

"Why sure I can. Not real well mind you. I only went to the sixth grade. But I learned enough. Besides, I don't put a lot of stock in book learnin'. Reckon I know all I need to know."

"Did you know I graduated high school and can read and write, and do my numbers, real well?"

"That ain't nothin'. A woman don't need no learnin' so's to cook and bring up young'uns. I aim to have a passel of kids and book learning just gets in the way."

Why this man don't want a wife, Leone thought, still focusing on the acne, *he wants a cook and baby maker, that's all. Oh, Papa, how could you do this to me?*

The arrival of her mother with a pitcher of cold lemonade gave Leone the opportunity she needed to excuse herself for a minute and go to her father, who was in one of his favorite reading places, a rocker next to the stove in the kitchen. He put down a scarcely-begun copy of the current best seller, "The Iron Heel," by Jack London, as she started:

"Daddy, that man is dumb as a board."

"Honey, I know he ain't no genius, but he'll be all right. He's a hard worker and I think he'll make you a solid husband."

"Daddy, I do not want to marry him."

"Well, you are. And, don't forget about your pellagra. You're lucky he'll marry you. Ain't none of them other fellas that would. You and him will make a fine couple."

"Papa, you're always talking about my pellagra, but that's just a small part of me that sometimes happens. Most of the time I'm right as rain."

"All the same, we'll start getting ready for the wedding."

●●●●●●

After his final examination of Maggie, Doctor Webster existed her bedroom to tell the anxious family:

"Y'all can go in now and say your good-byes. The Lord works in mysterious ways and in spite of our prayers, she ain't gonna make it."

"She's gonna die?" the thirteen-year old John Henry involuntarily cried out. "Pa, say it ain't so."

"I'm sorry, son," John Bell, barely able to stifle a sob himself, put his hand on his son's shoulder to say. Then, speaking to all six of his children:

"I don't want no crying in there. You got any blubbering to do, do it out here. When we go in to Mama, she don't need to see none of you squalling."

"Olin, you hear that," Hattie leaned down to say to her snuffling six-year old brother. "You can't be crying in there where Ma can see you."

The tears running down his cheeks, the boy could scarcely be heard as he murmured:

"I'll try, Hattie. I'll try, but I don't know if I can."

After taking a few seconds to finish their sobbing and compose themselves, the family solemnly trooped into the bedroom and surrounded the tall feather bed John Bell and Maggie had slept in for the last twenty-four years. With half-opened eyes the wife and mother looked up at them and transferred her gaze from one child to another. Too weak to make herself heard, she mouthed the words, "I love you." Six times she did it, each time eliciting "I love you, too, Mama" in return. When she got to John Bell, she didn't say anything. Instead, just the flicker of a smile crossed her face and an almost imperceptible nod told him all that needed to be said.

"I can't see," Olin suddenly cried out, holding up his arms to be picked up. "I want to see Mama."

Without words, Leone reached down and hoisted the boy onto the bed, where he looked at his weakening mother to say:

"Ma, don't die. I don't want you to die."

Maggie struggled to say something, but the words wouldn't come. She tried to reach to comfort the boy, but her arm refused to move. In desperation she willed her thoughts to console, but before she could think of a way to try to communicate in a different fashion, her eyes quivered and closed for the last time.

• • • • • •

The next day Hattie deftly switched from helping to plan Leone's wedding to arranging for her mother's funeral. With her husband, John, looking after their own two small children, Hattie again proved to be the wisest and most able of John Bell and Maggie's six children.

One of her first actions was to try to assuage the family's grief by assigning tasks. *Keep 'em too busy to wallow in their morning,* she thought to herself.

The girls of course continued to be responsible for cooking and household chores, while the boys helped their father out at the store and with their small farming operation. On top of this, Hattie made sure to assign some portion of the funeral arrangements to each one of them. There were to be more than one hundred people at the house after the funeral and there was a lot to do.

To Mabel she assigned the task of reminding Parson Wyatt of Maggie's favorite hymns and several relevant facts about her life. To the sixteen-year old Luther, Hattie gave the job of installing a new and larger hitching rail in front of the house. Even little Olin was told he had to be on the look out for flowers he could pick on the morning of the funeral.

As to the memorial service, it would of course be held at the Cedar Grove Methodist Church. Parson Wyatt would take care of arrangements there, but Hattie told Leone she should also find some nice wild flowers and greenery to place on the altar.

Rather than next to his own parents in another cemetery adjacent a church the family no longer attended, as a grave site John Bell carefully selected a spacious area in the cemetery across the road from the church. Also, he initially thought he would have his sons, Luther and John Henry, dig the grave, but after talking with Hattie, decided he would spend the few dollars to hire workers to do it.

For the reception, Hattie assigned to herself the task of making sure there would be sufficient food and drink. This was by far the biggest job and it wasn't made any easier by the fact that the day after Maggie's death well-wishers began dropping by to pay their respects. Even though some of them came bearing gifts of fried chicken, hams, pies and the like, Hattie would have preferred not to have had the interruptions. Even so, one evening she finally found time to approach her father.

"Pa," she said, closing the parlor door behind her. "There's something I've got to talk to you about."

Ignoring what his daughter had said, John Bell voiced concerns of his own:

"Hattie, I just don't know how I'm going to go on. I truly don't. Your mother was just about the most wonderful woman who ever walked the face of the earth and even with God's help, I'm not sure I can do it. Why would he take her? Only forty-seven years old."

Kneeling next to his chair and putting her arm over his shoulders, she responded:

"I know, Pa, I know. But we'll get over it. All families do. Remember when your ma and pa died. That wasn't so long ago. But we got over it. We'll get over Ma's death, too. But Pa, I need to ask you about Ma's people. Don't you think we should try to tell her folks she died?"

"No need, Hattie. Don't worry about them."

"I'm sorry, Pa, but this time I'm not going to take no for answer. We been asking you and Ma about her people most all my life and it's time you told what happened. Something terrible bad must have happened for her never to see them and us to never even know their names."

John Bell didn't respond right away, but after a few seconds he turned his head to look at her and said:

"All right, Hattie. You ain't gonna think no better of me for it, but here goes:

"It was 1883 and times was hard here in Arkansas, real hard. I was still living at home with my ma and pa. The South was still recovering from the war and it come a draught. Didn't hardly rain all summer. We was trying to get a store going and farm some and we was hardly making it. Then, we heard they was hiring miners up in Missouri around St. Joe, a place called the Old Lead Belt.

"So, I went up there and quick as a wink I was a lead miner. Pay wasn't too bad, and the company provided vittles and a place to sleep, so I was able to send almost all my pay home.

"We had the Sabbath off, so every Sunday I'd clean up best I could and go to church. About the fourth or fifth time I was there me and your mother got to making eyes at one another and before you knowed it, we was talking. One thing led to another, and it didn't take long until we was meeting on the sly. Finally, I got up nerve enough to ask her to marry me and she said she would. Wasn't but one problem—her pa. I guess he had noticed me and Maggie winking at each other, and he wasn't happy about it.

"It was a known fact that he didn't like miners in general—thought they was low class—and now me, in particular. So when she told him about me, his predictable response was, 'You're going to marry you a respectable man, not no gol-durned Arkie lead miner'.

"So we eloped. We high-tailed it out of there and back here to Arkansas and got married. Got married up at Evening Shade. She was twenty-two, so wasn't nothing anyone could do about it. We wasn't proud of what we did, but under the circumstances, we didn't know what else to do.

"Maggie tried to stay in touch with her folks, but they ignored her. She sent 'em letters and messages and even one time saved up and sent a telegram. They never answered. Never even got back to her when she sent a letter telling 'em you was born. You was born almost nine months to the day after Maggie and me was married and they never even acknowledged their own granddaughter.

"So we give up on 'em. Been nigh on to twenty-five years and I don't know whether they're dead or alive. Surely, some of the brothers and sisters are, but they never bothered to contact us either, so we just didn't bother. We decided to try to forget about them. Never told you kids about them and acted like they was dead."

"So, I might have kinfolk and even a grandpa or grandma up in Missouri?"

"Might."

"Pa, would you mind if I tried to get in touch with 'em?"

"No, I guess not. They're your kin. And, I guess they should know Maggie is dead."

••••••

After Maggie's death, many people suggested that John Bell allow his wife's death to "settle a bit" before putting on a big wedding for Leone, but he was adamant. An April wedding had been planned and it would take place. To acquaintances he would say, "Well, life goes on," while to intimates, it was, "I ain't taking a chance on this Van Browning getting away. If he's willing to marry her, I'm going to make it happen as soon as I can."

And, reflecting John Bell's status as one of Batesville's most influential citizens, it was to be a grand one. Three years previously Hattie had married John Newton and their wedding was still being talked about as one of the biggest and best ever. Those who had been invited, virtually every important person from three counties around, were still raving about the band John Bell had hired all the way from Memphis, as well as the way he had spared no expense in laying on a lavish spread of food and drink.

For reasons probably related to John Bell's suspected political ambitions, he was determined that even if Leone was a reluctant participant, her wedding would be even grander than Hattie's. Not only would he hire a fiddle, guitar and banjo band from Little Rock, but he would also arrange for a small waltz combo of local prominence.

Notwithstanding the fact that preparations continued apace, Leone continued to express her objection to the marriage. Due to her father's resoluteness, she had given up complaining to him, but to anyone else who would listen, she adamantly affirmed that she was not going to marry "that man." No one paid the slightest bit of attention to her.

Ma was hardly buried before decisions were being made about which Leone was not consulted. Hattie came up from her home in Searcy to bark orders, direct a thorough cleaning and repainting of the home and shrewdly bargain with purveyors. Dresses were sewn for Leone and for Mabel, who was to be Leone's maid of honor, and a hairdresser hired especially for the occasion. Decorations for the house were purchased, seating arrangements for the crowd were decided upon, and sleeping arrangements for out of town guests were discussed. Even flowers for the ladies were decided upon without Leone's input.

"Hattie, I don't like what she's done with the sleeves," Leone complained to her sister one day as the dressmaker flitted about with a mouthful of pins. "It's not what we told her to do at the last fitting."

"Why, sure it is. It looks just fine. Now, if we can just get that bow like we want it."

"I told you I didn't want a bow. Why do I have to have a bow? It's my wedding."

"Of course you have to have a bow. It wouldn't look right without it."

Outside, John Bell and his boys laid out the dimensions for a large new barbecue pit and pig smoker, as well as for five sets of horseshoe pits. The family's two-holer outhouse was closed up and two new three-holers built, one for women and one for men. And, for some reason to Olin's particular delight, lines festooned with colorful streamers were strung for suspension of kerosene lanterns.

However, it was Hattie that brought everything together, smoothed petty jealousies and made sure her father's dream of the best wedding in Batesville ever came true. Hattie's strong character and organization skills were only slightly impeded by the constant presence of her three-year old daughter, Ruby, and her still nursing son, Charles. Only John Bell himself possessed the ability to rein in Hattie, a reigning in he seldom utilized; he rarely needed to. He and Hattie were the main doers and organizers in the family, fully respected by all the others.

The next Saturday the wedding was held in the Cedar Grove Methodist Church, the very same church where just days before most of the same people had gathered for Maggie's funeral. Parson Wyatt conducted his standard wedding ceremony and, except for "I do's" by a hesitant Leone and then by Van, he was the only one who spoke. The attendees had heard his words, or ones very similar to them, dozens of times before. Only an incident with Leone's dress made this wedding remarkable.

Leone and Van had been pronounced man and wife and were stepping down the outside stairway to leave the church when the groom somehow got behind his bride and stepped on the train of her dress. When she attempted her next step forward, all of his weight was on it and she was abruptly brought up short. Had it not been for a bystander grabbing her arm, she would have fallen. Looking the other way and oblivious to it all, Van continued past her and down the path. Even though she didn't say anything when she caught up to him, she thought:

I might as well not even be here. He don't even know what he did. Such a self-centered man I never did meet.

The party that afternoon and evening was every bit as grand as John Bell had planned. Until the wee hours of the morning the revelers enjoyed the father of the bride's music, food and liquor. Even John

Bell himself, usually just a social drinker, was quite tipsy by the end of the evening. In the next edition of the Batesville Daily Guard it was reported the party was the grandest that Independence County had ever known and that "a good time was had by all."

But a good time that night was not had by Van Browning. Having had far too much to drink, by the time he and Leone retired for the night he was barely conscious. She had little trouble fending off his feckless attempts to grab her breasts and announced in no uncertain terms that she was sleeping on the pallet she had made on the floor. Even the next night, and the next and the one after that, he was no match for her when she said she would continue to sleep on the floor and that she would scratch his eyes out if ever he came at her.

CHAPTER FOUR

The little unpainted farmhouse Tom and Jim shared sat on an upslope in front of a large stand of hardwoods. When Tom had taken out a mortgage to buy the farm several years before, the house had been a simple two-room shotgun shack. However, every year, mostly in the winter when the farming was done, he had made improvements and added rooms. Even now one would not call the home commodious, but both the men had their own bedroom, and, after the addition of a dining room, there was even space to have guests for dinner.

To the home's front and down the slight incline, in most years prospered a well-tended garden. Depending on the time of year, there were strawberries, tomatoes, beets, carrots, okra, peas, beans and other vegetables. Beyond the vegetables was the wagon road. Turning left took you to Evening Shade. A right turn was the way to Cave City and Batesville. Both ways quickly disappeared as they swung around behind thick groves of oak and hickory. Beyond the road there were cotton and corn fields, as well as a small patch of tobacco grown for personal use.

It was almost dark and a few fireflies were beginning to show when Jim circled the bend in the road from Batesville and pulled the wagon up next to the house. Tom was at the well, just finishing washing his hands after a full day in the fields. As Jim began to take the bridle off Milly, Tom glanced into the wagon and said, "Looks like you got most all of it, but I don't see no salt. Did you get the salt?"

I'll tell him I got the salt alright, Jim thought to himself, *but I sure hate to tell him about Leone. He going to take it real hard.*

"Course I got the salt. It's right there under the axle grease," Jim answered. "I got it all. But, Tom, I got some news you ain't gonna like. Leone done got married. Married that Van Browning fella. Wasn't hardly no one in town. They was all out at the Bailey place for the reception. And, not only that, Leone's ma died. She died a week or so ago, but because the wedding was already planned, they went ahead with it any way."

Tom dropped his towel, half-heartedly kicked at a chicken and stared at his brother: "Jim, I feel like I been hit in the stomach with a sledge hammer. She wasn't supposed to marry him. She was supposed to marry me. Who is he anyway? I don't know no Van Browning. And, her ma. I didn't know she was sick. How did she die."

"Browning is one of John Bell's employees, works in his store. And Leone's ma died of that Spanish flu. Just come down with it all sudden like, and a couple days later she was dead."

"How did they get married so fast? John Bell didn't say nothing about her getting married when he run me off."

"I don't know. Probably if we wasn't so blamed far back up here in the woods we would have heard about it. But, it's true. They got married in the Cedar Grove Church this morning. No doubt John Bell bought a whole barrel of whiskey for all those thirsty freeloaders. By this time the whole passel of 'em is probably drunk as skunks."

Me, busting my tail every singled blessed day, Tom thought, *building and improving and getting everything ready for the right gal, and when she comes along, she ups and marries some fella I ain't never heard of. It just ain't fair.*

"I know she ain't quite right in the head," Tom said, "but I cotton to her real strong. She was partial to me, too. Why did she go and marry him?"

"Unless I miss my mark real bad, her pa had something to say about that, figured he'd get her married off to someone he could keep an eye on and keep her away from you. Didn't you tell me he called you "no account"?

"I don't remember if he called me "no account" or not, but it was sure plain as day he didn't like me none. And I never did anything for him not to like me. We never had one cross word between us before he started yelling at me to get off his property. He just don't like me cause I only got one arm. I got to see her. I'm gonna see her and find out why she married him."

"No, you ain't Tom Whitener. No, you ain't. She done married that other fella and you ain't gonna have nothin' more to do with her. Now, git over here and help me unload this wagon."

"Unload it yourself," Tom glared at his brother to say. "I'm getting a drink."

• • • • • •

As Tom and Jim went through their daily chores growing their crops and tending their animals, Tom's thoughts of Leone were mostly driven out of his head by work. Six days a week the young men labored, normally from sunrise to sunset, or, as they said, from "can see to can't see."

The seventh day was, of course, the Sabbath. However, their observance of it was pretty much a hit and miss affair. If there was nothing pressing on the farm and they could afford the luxury of a day off, they sometimes attended church. More likely however, they would sleep in and spend the day relaxing, chewing tobacco and maybe a little earlier than usual, a little white mule. But these quiet Sundays were few and far between. As Tom said, "I'd love to spend the Sabbath in observance or doing nothing, but there's always so blamed much work to do."

On the lazy Sundays when Tom thought Jim was sleeping in, Tom sometimes wasn't sleeping at all. Instead, he would lie in bed, staring at the ceiling, thinking of Leone. Again, and again his mind would replay being with her at the dance, at their secret meeting, even seeing her peeking out from her father's doorway. He remembered and re-remembered the sound of her voice and her every gesture.

After work during the week he thought of her, also. The boys' routine was that after they had eaten the simple dinner one of them had fixed, they got the whiskey jug down from its shelf and sat, saying little. Jim rarely had more than a small glass of the fiery liquid, while Tom almost always had several. During these quiet times he thought mostly about Leone.

However, he was not so obsessed with her that he became unaware of the fact that she was now a married woman and he once again began to attend the local dances. He met no prospects. He already knew most of the eligible girls, and either they were put off by his deformity, or comparisons with Leone got in the way of him pursuing any of them.

More than ten years, he often thought to himself, *and I ain't never come close to getting married. I surely didn't expect that it was going to be like this. Am I going to die without never having a wife of children? God, please don't let that happen.*

But farming and a few social activities weren't all that occupied Tom. He and his brother were increasingly concerned with making whiskey. Up the hill and into the woods behind the house their still ran pretty much full time. The shine they made was described by some as the best this side of Kentucky. It wasn't a large still, but it met Tom's thirsty needs, as well as his brother's much more modest requirements. There was sometimes even a quart or two extra to be eagerly purchased by friends and neighbors.

• • • • • •

As spring lapsed into summer and summer slid into fall, a particular event occurred which troubled Tom for weeks afterward.

One Sunday morning he was in charge of getting breakfast and was frying a large skillet of bacon. The bacon had been cooking for a while and was almost crisp, the way Jim liked it, when Tom tilted the skillet a bit too far. A few drops of grease spilled into the flames below, igniting the entire pan. The erupting flames reached almost to the ceiling. Dropping the roaring skillet, Tom quickly grabbed the box of baking soda they kept on hand for just such an occasion and immediately extinguished the fire. This sort of thing was an occasional occurrence and barely worthy of comment. Other than the ruined bacon and the expenditure of a few ounces of baking soda, there was no harm done. But for some reason, Tom couldn't get the image of the roaring skillet of flames out of his mind.

There was a face in those flames, he thought. *A damned face. There was a man's face looking out at me. I ain't going to say nothing to Jim, or he'll sure enough think I'm crazy. But, if it happens again, I'm going to tell someone. That was real spooky.*

More to get his mind off the face and the fire than anything else, when the boys finally sat down for breakfast Tom asked Jim:

"Do you know all Pa's children's names?"

"I sure do. I know all seventeen of 'em, including their birthdays. He had thirteen with Ma, three with Louella and now one, Hubert, with Sallie. Why do you ask?"

"Oh, nothing. I was just thinking. What about Sallie? She's crazy, ain't she?"

"She's a little strange, that's true. But I don't know if you could call her crazy."

Suddenly changing his mind about the face in the fire, Tom asked:

"Would you think I was crazy if I told you a saw a face, a distinct man's face, in those flames a minute ago."

"No, not all. Everyone sees all kinds of things in flames sometimes. Like sitting around a campfire and you can stare until you're seeing images and shapes and even people. Or looking at clouds and seeing all manner of things."

"This wasn't the same. I know exactly what you're talking about, but I saw something evil, real evil."

"If it wasn't morning, I would think you'd been hitting the jug. But, since it ain't, I just think you were imaging things."

"I reckon," Tom said, unconvinced.

•••••••

As usual, Tom had risen with the chickens this particular morning and was on his way to the little tarped structure over a hole in the ground the boys called an outhouse. In the dim light provided by an about to rise sun, he almost stepped on a shapeless form lying on his dewy porch. It was only on closer inspection that he was able to discern that the large lump was a person, covered with a blanket. Poking with his big toe, he called out:

"Hey, you there. What you doing on my porch?"

As the "lump" stirred and looked up, he was shocked to see that it was Leone.

"Leone, what you doing here?"

"Morning, Tom," she softly murmured, the sleep still evident in her voice.

"Leone!" he cried dropping to his knees. "Why are you here?"

"I done run off, Tom. I run off from Van and I came to be with you."

"You what? Well, I swan. Is that the truth? You come to be with me? Does your pa know about this?"

"Don't nobody know. Not pa and not even Van, unless he already woke up."

"How did you get here?"

"We was up spending the night with my cousin in Cave City, and as soon as everyone was asleep I just left. I walked most all night."

"You walked the whole nine miles?"

"Yes, I did. It was a full moon, so I could see, and I walked all the way. But now I sure am tired. I need to sleep."

"Well, ain't this a lick. Who could have imagined it? But, ain't they going to come and get you?"

"Nothin they can do. I'm a grown woman and I'll do what I want. I'm gonna divorce Van, and if you'll still have me, I'll marry you?"

"Are you sure, Leone?"

"Why, sure I'm sure. Will you have me, Tom? Please say you'll have me."

"Of course I will."

"I ain't going back to Van, or back to pa's, for that matter. If you won't have me I don't know what I'll do, but I ain't going back there."

"What are you talking about? I already said I would do it."

"Hi, Leone," Jim interrupted, his bare feet making no sound as he joined them. "I heard you talking. What are you doing here?"

"I hope Tom and me is gonna get married."

"That right, Tom? You and Leone gonna get married? What about her husband?"

"She's gonna divorce him, and then me and her is gonna get hitched.

Yep, we're gonna get married as soon as she can divorce him."

At that, Leone fairly flew up to throw both arms around Tom's neck and shower his cheeks with kisses.

"Oh, Tom, I am so glad. Tell me you love me."

"Of course, I do. But now there's something I've got to tend to."

Still entwined with Leone, Tom turned his attention to Jim:

"Jim, Leone's gonna stay here and sleep. I'm going to town. A couple people I got to talk to. Will you come with me?"

"Of course, Tom. Let me get dressed."

• • • • • •

"Well, that wasn't as hard as I thought it was going to be," Jim said to Tom as the two mounted the wagon for the trip back from seeing Leone's father. "I thought John Bell was gonna bust a gut or something at first, but he calmed down after a bit. But, what was that he was saying when he called you aside? I heard something about an accident and Leone being crazy?"

"He said Hattie and Leone was canning a mess of peaches one fall and something exploded. Said something on the stove blew up and a piece of glass or metal flew into Leone's head. He said she healed up OK, but she ain't never been quite right since, that every so often she gets these spells."

"That true? She ain't quite right in the head?"

"I don't know about that. She seems fine to me. Oh, sometimes she's a little different, but she's not crazy or anything. She's fine."

"Van don't think so. He says he's gonna divorce her because she's crazy. Isn't that what John Bell said?"

"Don't pay Browning no mind. He's just jealous because Leone loves me and not him."

"How did he get Leone to marry him anyway?"

"I reckon it was pressure, just too much pressure. Pressure coming from John Bell and Leone's ma and Hattie and the whole bunch of 'em. They told her if she didn't marry Van she wouldn't get nothing from them and she'd wind up at the poor farm or the insane asylum, without anything."

"She can't be too crazy. I've talked to her and she seems almost normal to me."

"And, Van says she never would have sex with him. According to John Bell, she made her a pallet next to the bed and every time Van tried to touch her, she'd run out the door. Van said he begged and threated and everything he could think of, but nothing he said or did made her be a wife to him. When she run off, that was the last straw. 'Good riddance,' John Bell said he said."

"Well, then, how do you know she's gonna be a wife to you?"

"Don't worry about that. I know. I just know it. She's gonna make a fine wife."

"Be careful, Tom. I sure ain't no expert on loving, but I've heard there are some women just can't tolerate it, don't want it no way."

"That ain't her. I just know it ain't."

"And, John Bell? He going to make a fine father-in-law, like she's going to make a fine wife?"

"Well, I think he will. I think after a while he'll begin to see how good I'm taking care of her and then the two of us will get along just fine. He really ain't got no reason to be against me except my lack of an arm. Once he sees how good she's making out on the farm with us, I think he'll come around. Might take a little time, that's all. But that's OK, I got time. And, Mabel's already pretty much on my side. I heard she didn't like Van much, anyway. Sooner or later I'll get all of them to like me."

With only the creak of the wagon and an occasional snort of the bay to break the silence, the boys rode on, lost in their separate thoughts.

As ecstatic as Tom was to finally almost be married to the girl of his dreams, Leone's conduct and what had been said about her did give him pause. He had personally observed enough of her "not quite right" behavior to know that the allegation that she was a bit touched was not entirely groundless. And, notwithstanding what he had told Jim, the claim that she had not been willing to enter her husband's bed was disconcerting to him in the extreme. Loving and children of his own were at the very top of the list of things he needed from a wife.

As to Jim, he had very much enjoyed the past few years farming with his brother, and while he didn't begrudge Tom a bride, he was somewhat apprehensive about how bringing a new person in the house would affect their relationship. Jim looked up to Tom with respect and admiration and, didn't want anything to jeopardize what they had. And since he had not yet given up on getting married himself, he thought that if Tom already had his wife on the farm, he could hardly object to another one being there.

•••••

Even before Jim turned the mule around the south of the hardwoods, the boys smelled the cook stove. As their house came into view, they could see a long, lazy curl of whitish gray smoke rising from its chimney. Jim guided the mule up next to the house and Tom leaped off the wagon."

"Leone," he called out, "we done it. We talked to your pa and lived to tell about it."

Meeting him on the porch before he had a chance to come inside, Leone responded to Tom's glee:

"You didn't tell me you were going to talk to Pa. What did he say?"

"Not much. First, he said he didn't approve, and that if he had his druthers, you would make up with Van. When I said you were a grown woman, and would do what you pleased, he got pretty sour for a bit. But then it was like he thought it over and changed his tune. He started talking about how I better take care of you and if he ever hears about me mistreating you, there will be God's own hell to pay."

"What did he say about Van?"

"Oh, yeah, I forgot. He said Van's gonna get divorce papers filed as soon as his lawyer can do it. He's claiming grounds of failure to consummate the marriage."

"Failure to consummate the marriage, what does that mean?"

"It means you wouldn't have marital relations with him."

"That's true enough. I slept on a pallet every blessed night."

As the couple walked inside, they were joined next to the stove by Jim, returning from putting the mule away."

"Boy," he said, lifting the lid from their large black stew pot, "that sure smells good. I sure hope it's almost done. I'm so hungry

I could eat a horse."

"Leone," Tom suddenly blurted, spinning his head to look around the previously unkempt interior, "what have you done? You've cleaned the whole place. Everything looks great."

"I got everything straighted up and put away. You probably won't be able to find stuff, but I know where everything is. Just ask me. I'll get some curtains sewed soon as I get a chance. And, you won't have long to wait for dinner, either. I got ham hocks and white beans with okra and biscuits. And for dessert I got an apple pie. It's cooling there in the window. Now, you boys wash your hands real good, and your dinner will be on the table when you come back."

At table, the brothers hashed and rehashed all that had happened with John Bell, and after they had consumed almost all Leone had prepared, she brightly said, "I know you boys is hankering' to have a chew and take a pull at that jug. Why don't you go out on the porch and do that and I'll clean up here?"

"Why, thank you, Leone," Jim answered. "That's a fine idea. Ain't it Tom?"

A few minutes later, Leone had just finished drying the last of the dishes when Tom returned from his white mule and chewing tobacco. Jim had gone to the barn. With obvious trepidation he asked, "Are you sleeping on a pallet tonight, Leone?"

Leone laid her towel and the dish she had been drying down, slowly turned to face Tom and took the two steps needed to close the distance between them. "Tom, I didn't make love to Van because I didn't love him. I love you and I don't reckon I'm gonna need a pallet."

Reaching up to wrap her arms around his neck, the couple kissed their very first real kiss, long, tender, and loving. However, before it could resolve into passion, Jim's cough and words interrupted them:

"Well, look at you two love birds."

Flushing, Leone turned back to the dishes.

After the dishes were done and the dish towel hung on the counter to dry, the three of them seated themselves in the living room, where Tom announced he would like to read from the Bible. He said he thought Ephesians Five, Verses 25 through 33, would be appropriate and started:

"Husbands, love your wives, even as Christ also loved the church, and gave himself for it."

However, before he could go further, Leone interrupted him:

"Tom, how did you know that passage? I think I heard it a long time ago, but I didn't remember it until you started reading."

"I'm not rightly sure," he answered. "I reckon I run across it now and again, and then when you came, I looked it up. Seemed like exactly what we should be reading at a time like this. Now listen to how it ends:

"Nevertheless, let every one of you in particular so love his wife even as himself; and the wife see that she reverence her husband."

"Why, Tom," Leone commented when he was done, "you are a regular Bible scholar. That was so sweet."

• • • • • •

Notwithstanding a lot of hard work, the next months passed pleasurably for the young people. There was no sign of Leone's "impairment" and she pitched right in to uphold her end of the unstated labor bargain. While Tom and Jim did the farming and tended the larger animals, she did the housework, cared for the vegetable garden and minded the chickens. Any possible discomfort on account of having a female in the house had been solved by Jim's decision to move his bed to the barn, where he avowed to have a stove before winter came.

However, it didn't take Leone long to realize much was lacking in both Tom and Jim's educations. Although both men could read and write, neither of them had progressed beyond grade school.

"We were OK with the schooling until it was time for the spring plowing and planting, and then Pa said farming was more important than book learning," Tom explained. "Then we got behind and wasn't no way we could catch up. So we just quit. Pa couldn't read or write so good himself, and if he minded, he never said nothing."

And so Leone set out on a plan to improve at least their three Rs. Every evening after she had finished the dishes and could get Tom and Jim back to the dinner table, a kerosene lantern illuminated the reading, writing and arithmetic lessons she drilled into them.

Somehow she had obtained "The Elementary Spelling Book" and a well-worn McGuffey's Reader, and despite Jim's objections (Tom seemed to enjoy the learning) took them from page one to the end in both. She desperately wanted to teach them some geography and show them places in the world she dreamed of visiting someday, but didn't have an atlas or globe.

Then one day, on a Saturday afternoon, the sheriff's deputy came riding up just as the three were finishing their noon meal.

"Howdy, Clarence, what you doing way out here?" Jim greeted.

"Hello, Tom. Hello, Jim. Leone, I got papers for you. They's divorce papers. It's all over. Van divorced you. Your pa asked me to run 'em out to you."

"Yippee," Tom shouted. "Clarence, that's the best news I've heard all year. It calls for a celebration. Ain't that right, Leone? Let's have a drink."

"Thanks, anyway, Tom, but I've got to get back. I guess you folks will be getting hitched yourself now, ain't that right?"

"It most certainly is, Clarence," Leone said with a grin.

The next morning the trio attended the Baptist Church in Sidney, but made no mention of Leone's new status as a single women. They figured everyone had learned of Leone's divorce before the judge's ink was even dry, and thus they saw no reason to bring it up. Also, Tom thought that bringing up the divorce would bring to mind the fact that he and Leone were "living in sin," a status about which the local God-fearing folks heartily disapproved.

However the day after, the three of them dressed in their best clothes and headed for the justice of the peace in Evening Shade. When they hit the main road north and south, Jim had to "haw" Milly twice to get her to take the unfamiliar road north to Evening Shade rather than the usual "gee" south to Cave City and Batesville.

"Like I said last night," Tom said to no one in particular, "I ain't taking no chances. We ain't getting married in Batesville because John Bell knows everyone there, the justice of the peace included. Likely that justice up in Evening Shade don't know us and he'll be glad to get his two dollars to marry us."

"Tom," Leone said, "there ain't been no problems with Pa and I don't think he's gonna say anything. Matter of fact, now that I'm divorced from Van, he's probably glad you're making an honest woman of me."

"All the same," Tom answered, "we're getting hitched in Evening Shade. It's in Sharp County."

When they reached the few buildings that constituted the town of Evening Shade, Jim rang the bell at the one with a "Justice of the Peace" sign. The justice's wife answered the door, ascertained that Tom and Leone wanted to get married, and started filling out paperwork. Descending the stairs while pulling his suspenders over his shoulders, the justice did what he needed to do and ten minutes later the wedding party was back on the road, Tom holding a freshly signed marriage certificate.

"Tom, you have made me the happiest woman in the world," Leone said, looking admiringly at the groom.

"And, you have made me the happiest man in the world," Tom responded, taking his bride into his arms. "But, I still wonder what your pa is going' to say."

●●●●●●

That night after Tom and Leone had made love for the first time as man and wife, Tom thought Leone was asleep when he folded his hands together on his chest and silently prayed:

Dear Lord, you know I'm a simple man, with simple wants. All I ever wanted was a little piece of ground to call my own, a good wife, a few kids and a little of your help with the weather. So far, except for this arm, you been mighty good to me and it's worked out pretty good.

Ever since I quit grade school knowed all I wanted to be was a farmer. I don't believe there's no better way of life than being a farmer. It's a good, honest way of living. I don't hold nothing against those that live in town and I don't believe like some do that they are all pretty much sinners. They're like us farmers, but have deprived themselves of the pure pleasure of smelling freshly plowed ground, watching green shoots come up out of the ground and grow, and seeing a wagon filled with your bounty. Ain't nothin' better than that—at least for me—and for all of it I am eternally grateful.

As far as I know, except for Grandpa down in Texas, who is preaching up a storm, there ain't never been nothin' but farmers in our family. All the way back to that old German that settled all that land in North Carolina, they have been farmers. I guess we was just made to be farmers and always will be. I know I will be.

Of course, I ain't got nothin' against being a better farmer. I hear they got some new kinds of corn they call hybrid. They somehow get the innards of different kinds of corn to mix so as to get a whole new variety. Some of them new kinds make bigger crops, some the bugs don't like and some don't need so much water. The wonders you bestow on us never cease. Soon as I can, I'm gonna get some of that seed.

And, I would like your help so's I can get a few more acres. If you could see your way clear to help with that, I would be even more grateful than I am now. What I got now is just about all me and Jim can handle, but if I had another forty or even fifty acres, I could get somebody to sharecrop it. I think that might work out real well. Leastwise, when Jim and me talked about it, it seemed like a good idea.

But, the main blessing you have sent my way is Leone. She has been the last happy straw on an already satisfied pile. I had just about given up finding a good wife and then I walked into that dance and there she was. You surely outdid yourself in fulfilling this man's dreams. No matter what happens in the future, I'll forever be grateful. She is so good natured, so hardworking. Me and her is like two peas in a pod.

It's just that her affliction, as she calls it, bothers me some. Please, dear Lord, please don't give her no more spells. Let her keep on being a regular, normal person. Oh, I know sometimes she's a little strange, but that's OK. Sometimes I guess I am, too. Whatever you do, please don't let her get no worse.

And, yes, another thing about her. She's mentioned a couple times that maybe we don't have to be farmers. Please don't bring us no strife on account of a conflict about where we're going to live. I dearly want for us to live out our days and be buried right over there in there in the Mount Carmel Cemetery. Please help her to want that, too.

Well, there is one more thing concerning me. I just don't know why I feel the need to drink too much. All the Whitener's is partial to drink, and most of the time I can have a drink or two and everything is fine. But, way too often I let it take me over and I drink way too much. And, I get mean when I get that way. Like when I hit that old boy at the dance. There wasn't no call for me to do that, and I do hope you've forgiven me for it. Leone don't say anything, but I know she don't like the drinking. I sure don't want to quit drinking entirely, but I'm gonna not get drunk any more. I want to be the best husband and pa I can be. I hope Leone and me will be having' some young'uns real soon and I sure don't want 'em to see me with too much whiskey in my belly.

Please, Lord, help me out with these thing and, please, please send us a passel of healthy kids.

CHAPTER FIVE

Tom and Leone had been married only a few months when one afternoon Tom's father's wagon unexpectedly turned the dusty corner by the pond. With Dan were Julia, Tom's nineteen-year old sister, and Gracie, Tom's eleven-year old half sister. As they approached the hitching rail, Tom came running up from the lower field where he had been hoeing cotton. He immediately noticed somber looks on all three of them. *I wonder who died,* he thought. *Or, maybe it's the cholera. I sure hope his hogs ain't got the cholera. Or, that corn blight they been talking about.*

Dan was the first to speak:

"Tom, they don't want to live with me no more. They say they want to live with you."

"That right, Julia?" Tom managed to overcome his shock to blurt out, as he pulled his handkerchief to wipe the sweat glistening on his forehead.

Julia knocked a long wisp of blondish hair off her forehead and began to answer, while Dan stared off into space, finally fixing on the weathered deer antlers nailed above the door.

"We ain't nothing but slaves there and we ain't gonna do it no more. Ever since Pa married Sallie, we ain't no better than hired help. Sallie sits around all day doing nothing and we're supposed to cook and clean and take care of her young'un. We ain't gonna do it no more. The boys don't help a bit. Grover don't lift a finger and Cal is worse. Joe helps some, but not much. And, of course, Hubert is just little, so he needs constant caring for. It's just me and Gracie expected to take care of them five boys and Pa to boot."

Cutting his eyes from the antlers to his daughter, Dan interrupted:

"Now, Honey, it ain't that bad. Sallie cooks some."

"No, she don't, Pa," Julia began, even more animated than before. "She don't cook a lick. And she's crazy. I don't know why you married her. You had a heap of young'uns when you married her. You didn't need no more. And ever since her last baby was born dead, she's been more trouble than she's worth. Just mopes around all day like she's the only one ever had a baby die. Pa, you know we love you, but we just ain't gonna stay there no more."

By this time Leone had emerged from the house, wiping her hands on an apron that had seen better days. She took Tom's arm as the visitors climbed down from the wagon.

"Hi, Pa. Hi, Julia, Gracie," she greeted. "How y'all?"

"Well, that's a Tom fool question," Dan responded, aiming a stream of tobacco juice at an ant crawling in the dirt next to the wagon. "Can't you see how messed up all this is?"

And then, turning to Tom:

"You got any whiskey, Tom? I need a drink."

"Pa, you got no cause to talk to Leone like that," Tom answered. "She just asked you how you was."

"I'm sorry, Leone," Dan responded. "I guess I'm a bit touchy these days."

"Leone, you take the girls and go on and find something for them to do," Tom said. "Me and Pa's got to talk."

"Yes, Tom," Leone answered. "Excuse me, Pa. Come on, girls. You can help me out with supper. I'll fetch a couple aprons so you don't mess up them pretty dresses."

As Leone escorted the girls to the kitchen, Tom retrieved his jug of whiskey from its hiding place under the porch. The two men sat in the rough-hewn rockers on the porch and Tom filled two Mason jars with generous amounts of moonshine. Both took healthy swigs and grimaced.

"My word, Tom," Dan said as soon as he was able, "you sure do make some fine whiskey. But, about Sallie, it ain't been all peaches and cream at my house lately, but Julia's exaggerating. Sallie ain't been quite the wife I was looking for, but she ain't all that bad. And, the baby dying like that put quite a strain on her."

"Pa, you got four of your own living there, two of 'em almost grown. And I know they don't help none around the house. Sure the girls are gonna feel put upon. And you just said yourself Sallie ain't quite all there."

Reaching the plug of tobacco out of his cheek long enough to drain the other half of his jar, Dan straightened in his chair to stare at his son and ask, "Well, you going to take them or not?"

"Pa, I don't want to. Things is going just fine here and I don't want nothing to change it. And just between you and me, Julia's OK, but it's Gracie I'm worried about. She's lazy and she's sassy to boot. You know she is. I'm thinking she and Leone might get into it any time."

"Son, I ain't never asked anything of you, but I'm asking now. I need for you to take these two girls. I don't want it that way and I'd rather they stayed home, but that's the way it is and there's just no living with them. Won't you please take them? And, if it absolutely don't work out, then after a while, I can take them back, maybe."

"Well, Pa, if you put it that way, I reckon I can. You don't have to beg me. If it's what you want and what they want, I'll do it. There will have to be some changes around here, of course, but, yeah, I'll take them."

"It ain't what I want, but I reckon I ain't got no choice in the matter. Julia's mind is made up and Gracie says she's gonna go wherever her sister goes."

"Well, then it's settled. It will all work out. We'll make it work out. Besides, it ain't like you're never gonna see them again."

"Shitfire, Tom, I know that. It's just that as a man enters his later years, he should be living in peace with all of his kids somewhere close around him. A sorry state of affairs this is."

"Yeah, Pa, you're right, but seems like life don't always go just like we would like for it to."

•••••••

While Tom and his dad had been talking on the porch, Leone and Tom's sisters had been having their own conversation in the kitchen:

"Are they gonna let us stay?" Julia said to Leone as the three of them gathered kindling for the stove from where it was stacked outside the back door.

"I sure hope so," Leone answered. "Don't you, Gracie?"

"I surely do. The situation is just about intolerable there with Pa and Sallie. Do you think Tom will let us?"

"Why, I expect he will. I think he would love to have you here. And me, too. It wouldn't be all fun and games and there's plenty of work needs doing, but we'd have time for a picnic or two and for some reading in the evening."

"Leone, we'd be ever so helpful. Before Mama died, she taught me every recipe she knew, and I've made up a few of my own. My peach cobbler's as good as any in Arkansas. Ain't that right, Gracie?"

As they piled arm loads of split pine next to the stove, Julia went on:

"We'd be just like sisters almost. You'd be the boss of course, Leone, but I just turned nineteen and you ain't but five years older than me."

"Leone, you'd be just like my mama that died," Gracie contributed.

Gracie was tall for her age, already beginning to shoot up, with little nubbins on her chest that would soon develop into something bigger. She was on the quiet side, but it wasn't that she didn't like to talk. She did. It was just that her brothers and sisters were usually so busy talking themselves that she couldn't get a word in edgewise. On those rare occasions when they gave her the opportunity to string more than two sentences together so as to express a full thought, someone was sure to say something about her like, "Don't that still water run deep?"

"Can I say something?" she finally blurted in exasperation as Leone and Julia filled the kitchen with chatter. "Can I say just one thing? Leone, I love you and if we can come to live with you and Tom, I would be just like a real daughter to you, and you wouldn't never have any trouble with me. I can't cook like Julia, but I'm a real hard worker."

"Girls, we ain't knowed each other all that long, but I love you, too. It's a real shame both your mothers died. Now, Gracie, grab that sack of string beans outside on the stump and start stringing them. And, Julia, you can go out in the garden and pick some tomatoes and okra and cucumbers and whatever else looks good. And after you've done that, one of you get me five real nice taters out of the barrel in the cellar. I'll be frying up this here chicken."

While the girls were outside, Tom left his father on the porch and came into the kitchen. He said to Leone:

"I hope you know I didn't want them here. Pa had to shame me into it."

"I figured," she answered, "but I didn't tell them that. I told them you would just as pleased as punch to have them here."

Aged and blackened from untold years of use, Leone's big black cast iron frying pan sat on the now hot stove, bubbling with hot grease. An almost empty lard can next to it would soon be replenished when Tom butchered the big sow now fattening among the others in the pig pen next to the barn.

"Gol-durn it," Leone exclaimed and jerked back as she placed the first pieces of chicken in the skillet and was rewarded with an explosion of hot, popping grease. "That smarts. Happens every time."

Returning from the garden just in time to see her sister-in-law's experience with the grease, Julia exclaimed:

"You know what mama used to do? First she'd get her a long stick and sharpen it real good. Then she'd spear each piece and put it in the skillet from far enough away so she wouldn't get burnt."

"Yeah, I guess I know to do that, but I always forget to get me a stick. Maybe I will next time. Gracie, you getting your female monthlies yet?"

"No, Leone, not yet, but I expect to anytime now," Gracie admitted with some embarrassment. "Why you asking?"

"Just trying to figure out how many females we got to make arrangements for here, that's all. I didn't mean to embarrass you."

A short silence ensued as the three of them contemplated the necessities of daily living on Tom's farm, a silence Leone broke with a question: What y'all think about your brother only having one arm?"

"Think about it?" Julia answered. "Why, we don't think nothing about it. We ain't never knowed him any other way. That's just the way he is. Not having one don't seem to hold him back much."

"Well, I think he's a hero," Leone came back. "I think he's just about the bravest man I've ever heard of. He don't never say nothing about his arm not being there. Never complains. Works from can to can't ever blessed day. And, you know his good arm is double strong on account of it having to do all the work."

"He ain't the only one who works hard," Julia answered. "We work hard, too"

"Leone, how am I gonna get to school?" Gracie changed the subject. "It's a lot further from here than it is from Pa's place."

"You're gonna have to walk, of course. We ain't got but one mule and when Tom ain't using him in the fields, usually me or him is riding him to go somewhere."

"Maybe I don't need to go to school no more. I can already read and do my numbers."

"Gracie, that's the most far-fetched thing I ever did hear. Of course you'll go to school, and graduate, too. We ain't having no uneducated young'uns around here."

••••••

Leaving the girls to put the food on the table, Leone came on to the porch and announced:

"Y'all wash up. And then come and get it or I'll throw it to the hogs."

But, before his wife could step back inside and while he was still seated, Tom reached out and gathered her onto his lap, saying:

"Pa, ain't she just about the cutest thing you ever did see?"

"Yep, you got a good one. And from the smell of that chicken, I believe she knows how to cook, too."

Pushing herself up off Tom's lap, Leone said with a laugh:

"Y'all go on. You'll say anything to get your belly fed. Now, go get that dirt off your hands and come to table. And, don't dirty my white hand towel none, either."

A few seconds later, Jim had come in from the barn and the six of them were crowded along both sides of the supper table. Tom was at the head of course, with Leone at the other end. In honor of the occasion, Leone had adorned the table with her special tablecloth decorated with borders she had crocheted herself. The tablecloth matched the curtains she had sewn to cover the bare windows she found unbearably stark when she arrived.

On the unpainted walls were several photographs of Leone's family, and of Tom's. Above the large stone fireplace occupying the place of honor hung Tom's most prized family picture. From it looked out the unsmiling faces of Tom, his father Dan, and his grandfather, The Reverend Alfred Daniel Whitener, as well as several of Tom's many brothers and sisters. The occasion for the taking of the photograph was the funeral of Dan's second wife and Gracie's mother, Louella.

As the last of them, Julia, settled in at table, without prompting they all reached out to join hands so that Tom could say grace. His heartfelt words not thanked God for their food and good fortune, but also made prolonged mention of the importance of family, and for the love and affection they all felt for each other. The concluding "amens" were loud and sincere.

The serving spoons Leone's mother had secretly given her after she married Tom started clinking against the rough crockery as soon as the last "amen" was said. However, Gracie almost immediately asked:

"Can we stay, Pa? Please can we stay?"

"I ain't none too happy about it, but Tom and me talked it over and, yes, you can stay. But you got to behave and you got to do exactly what Tom says, just like he was your pa. And, Leone, too, just like she was your ma. And you got to visit me and the boys as often as you can. That understood?"

"Yes, Pa," Julia and Gracie both responded at almost the same time with big, excited smiles.

"And, Gracie, unless Tom needs you at planting or picking time, you got to go to school. That understood, too?"

"Yes, Pa," Gracie answered with considerably less enthusiasm than she had exhibited in her first answer.

"Tom, where we gonna sleep?" Julia asked.

"We can string a blanket or something across the corner over there. That will give you some privacy until we can get another room built. We'll get another bed as soon as we can. Until then, you'll be sleeping on a pallet. Did you bring quilts?"

"Yes," Gracie answered. "Pa said we could bring two apiece. We brought good ones, ones my mama quilted."

"Come fall, soon as the crops are in, we'll add a new room or even two and turn this into a real comfortable little dogtrot."

"What's a dogtrot?" Gracie asked.

"Why, it's a two-part house with a breezeway running through the middle of it," Julia answered.

"What on earth for? Why would you want the wind blowing through the middle of your house?"

"Ain't you never noticed?" Julia answered. "For the summertime. Cools everything down, especially around a hot cook stove. Leastways if there's any breeze at all it does."

"Reckon I'll have another hunk of that cornbread," Tom said, looking at Leone. "And the butter, too. Ain't nothing like buttered cornbread to go with good fried chicken and taters."

During the meal it was obvious that Leone had been fully accepted into the Whitener family. As was evidenced by the constant chatter and good-natured kidding amongst them, they liked her and she liked them. Of course, there were soft looks and softer words exchanged between Tom and Leone, but it was already apparent that Julia and Leone were also developing a special relationship, more like two sisters than step-mother and step-daughter.

As Gracie went to the kitchen for a blackberry pie, Tom asked:

"Pa, you ain't said nothing about Sallie. How's she and that little boy?"

"She ain't so new anymore. We been married almost six years. And Hubert's doing fine. He's five and growing like a weed. But to tell you the truth, I don't think Sallie's doing so well. Ever since that baby she was birthing died last winter and then Wesley died a couple weeks later, she just ain't quite right. Even though she wasn't Wesley's mother, the two had taken a real shine to each other and his death affected her something powerful."

"What's wrong with her?" Leone asked. "She seemed OK when I was up at your place a while back."

"Doctor said it was depression. She just sits around all day and stares at the floor. Don't seem to have no energy. Oh, she cooks some, but that's about it. Seems to be getting worse."

"What do you think, Julia?" Leone asked.

"I keep comparing her to Louella. Maybe second wives is always better than third ones, but I remember Gracie's ma being real smart and a hard worker. Sallie sure ain't that. And Pa's right, she's getting worse."

Seeing that it was time to either trim the wick on the lantern or call the evening to a close, Dan elected the latter:

"Girls, that was a mighty fine dinner, good as any I ever had," he complimented as he pushed his chair back from the table. "Tom, do you mind if I spend the night. I was gonna go home, but it's getting kinda late."

"I always figured you would. While the womenfolk clean up, let's us men go back out on the porch."

"A fine idea, Tom. A fine idea, indeed."

••••••

Ten heaping bushel baskets of peaches awaited attention in the kitchen. It was to be a canning day. A day or so before, Leone and Tom's sisters had cleaned the needed Mason jars and laid out the lids that would seal them. Big pots and a fresh supply of kindling were at the ready. The peeling and slicing was to begin as soon as the sun came up.

Tom was, as usual, the first up, soon joined by Jim in from the barn. As the coffee aroma filled the room, the farm's pugnacious little banty rooster made sure everyone was done sleeping.

"Leone. Julia. Gracie. Come on, Ladies. Time to rise and shine. Got a big day coming. I'm putting some bacon on and Jim's going to scramble up a bunch of eggs. Get in here and fix some biscuits and grits to go with them."

Gradually, movement could be seen in the still dark home. Shadowy figures moved from back rooms out to the new outhouse Tom had finished building only a few days before. One by one, as they finished their morning necessities, they came to the kitchen.

Looking up from his egg skillet, Jim looked around and asked, "Where's Leone?"

"She was here a minute ago," Tom responded. "She must have gone to the outhouse."

"No," Gracie informed. "I just came back from there. She's not there. Could she have gone back to bed? I'll check."

The others continued to look around the room and out the window while Gracie returned to report, "No, she ain't there. She must have gone to the barn."

"No, she's not there. I was just there," Jim declared.

"Well, go look again. She ain't here. She must be there," Tom directed.

It took Jim only a couple minutes to run to the barn and return to report that Leone was not there.

"There only one more place she could possibly be," Tom suggested. "She must be in the cellar."

Tom grabbed the kitchen lantern from its usual place hanging above the stove, lit it and descended the stairs.

"Leone," he called as he stepped down. "Leone are you here?"

No answer.

He held the lantern as high as he could reach and called again: "Leone, Honey, are you here?"

Suddenly in the far corner, barely illuminated by the lantern, he saw a bit of the fabric of Leone's dress on the floor next to a potato barrel. Taking the few steps to the corner, he raised the lantern to see Leone cowering on the floor and looking up at him with eyes like saucers. She reminded him of a terrified young animal.

"What you doing here? Leone, why you hiding down here?"

"I'm scared, Tom," she answered in a barely audible voice.

"What you scared of? Ain't nothing to be afraid of. You got us all running around like chickens with our heads cut off looking for you. Come on upstairs now. We got canning to do."

"I don't want to. I'm scared," she continued in the same small voice.

"What got you scared? When did you get scared?"

"When I saw all them jars getting ready for the canning."

"Why on earth would you be afraid of a bunch of jars?"

"I started thinking about my accident. About when Ma and me was canning and there was that explosion."

"Honey, I don't know what happened that day, but ain't nothing going to happen here. I been canning here for nearly ten years and ain't nothing ever happened. Nothing is gonna happen. Come on now,

Honey, let's get you upstairs and you can lay down for a spell."

Shyly raising her hand, Leone allowed Tom to lift her to her feet and hold her as they went back up the ladder. The others watched in amazement as Tom led her past them into the bedroom. Returning alone after a few seconds, Tom quietly announced:

"I surely don't know what all that was about. She says it had something to do with her accident when she got hit in the head with something when they was canning peaches at her pa's. I guess we'll have to do the canning without her."

Tom and his sisters went to work and had been at it for more than an hour when Leone's drained face appeared again in the kitchen.

"Tom," she said shyly, "I'm better now. I can help some."

"Only if you want to, Sugar. Maybe you better rest some more."

"No, I'm better. I'll help," she responded, picking up a knife and sitting down next to a basket of unpeeled peaches.

Although subdued at first, by the end of the day Leone was every bit as busy as the others, fully participating in the banter and joking that always accompanied canning. No sign remained of whatever had come over her in the morning.

••••••

That night a very tired, but contented Julia lay on the pallet next to Gracie and thought:

It was good of Tom and Leone to take us in. Especially since they only just been married a few months. Sure great me and him has got such a good relationship. He's about the only one of Pa's young'uns I'm close to. I guess it was him teaching me to fish. Been close ever since.

He's the smartest of Pa's kids, of course. And I ain't tooting my horn too much to believe that I'm almost as smart as he is. Wonder why Tom and me got most of the smarts and some of the other kids didn't? 'Course, we ain't got a lot of book learning. I wonder if Tom regrets quitting school to help Pa farm? Good thing he stayed long enough to learn to read and write. But just figuring out things and knowing what to do generally you don't get out of a book. Me and him's pretty good at that.

I do wish I had gone to college like that teacher said I should. Imagine that! Me, going to college. I probably could have become a teacher myself. I think I would have liked that. Probably could have gone to Memphis or Little Rock and become a teacher. But what are you thinking about? There ain't never been no money to send a kid to college. Farming is fine. Just get college out of your head.

Tom's the one should have gone to college. But even so, he's done real well for himself. Managed to buy this here farm and everything. Working and sharecropping, I think he must have saved every nickel he earned those first few years after he left Pa's. And don't he always know how to get the best prices for his crops and stock? Especially the hogs. He can really whittle them hog dealers down to just about as low as they will go. I ain't never known him to get skinned.

And Jim. What a quiet one. A quiet, solid fella. Just does what he needs to do and goes on about his business. Sure would like to know what's in his head and why he ain't found a wife. Good looking guy like him and no steady gal even. Go figure.

I just wish Tom didn't drink so much. Sometimes he ain't so nice when he drinks. Fortunately, he don't drink that much every day, but every once in a while, he can really tie one on. I wonder what sets him off so he sometimes feels like he's got to do that. Like at the dance when he was courting Leone. Some of them are still talking about that. Jim said Tom was way out of line and that's the reason those boys beat him up. He's always sorry the next day, but that don't much help those that got to be around him after he's drunk.

And Leone, she don't never say nothing about his drinking. Wonder why she don't say something? She just goes on about her business until he either goes to bed or passes out. Then, the next day, they're all lovey-dovey again.

I would like to know why it's always men that's got the drinking problem. I ain't never known a woman who drank a lot. I heard there are such, but none of the gals who live in this neck of the woods cotton to drink all that much.

Course, Leone's got her own problems. Not all the time. Most of the time, she's normal as a regular person. But sometimes she just don't make sense or docs something crazy. Like hiding in the cellar when we was canning. A little tetched that was. Sure wish I knew how to help her.

And Gracie, too. Can't seem to get through to her. I don't know what's gonna become of her. She just don't seem to have a lot of gumption, not like most of the Whiteners do. Course she's only eleven, but already it's obvious that all she really wants to do is marry a farmer and have some kids. At least that's about all she talks about. I didn't know her mama real well. I think Louella and Pa was married only about seven years and part of that time they was separated and she was living in Texas. Wonder why she went to Texas to die? Had her three kids and left for Texas and died. Wonder why she didn't take Gracie with her? Strange, strange.

I got to tell Tom pretty soon that Washington asked me to marry him. That boy is getting real anxious. Reckon I know what's on his mind. But Tom's counting on me to help out around here. Washington ain't gonna wait forever. Got that sawmill job waiting for him down by Floral. Wonder if he'd think about moving all the way to Searcy? Leone's got a couple sisters down that way and I hear it's a nice place to live. I reckon me and Washington will be getting hitched real soon and then we might even love to move to California like he says he's got a dream of doing. Whoo-eee, California. Wouldn't that be something?

CHAPTER SIX

"Tom, if you ain't the lovingest man," Leone said as her husband leaned over her naked sunlit back and continued the sensuous massage he had begun several minutes before. Starting with her neck and shoulders, he had slowly worked his way down her back, across her milk white buttocks to her legs, and was now massaging her feet. They were in a secluded glen next to the Strawberry River, having a picnic.

The whole idea had started one night after lovemaking when he had whispered to her:

"I know a place down at the river that's all hidden away. Don't no one else know it. That's where I'm going to take you and love you all day in the bright outdoors."

Leone didn't respond, but if Tom had been able to see the coy smile on her face he would have known that the idea struck her as an extremely good one.

A day when the others were away gave them their chance. Julia and Gracie had gone to visit their father at his new farm near Denmark and Jim had gone to town for a wagon part.

As Tom continued kneading and rubbing like a trained masseuse, he said softy: "Just tell me when you want me to quit."

"Quit! You don't never have to quit. I'll just die right here. Die from pleasure."

"You're just lucky I ain't got but one hand or I could really give you a massage."

"One hand is quite enough, Tom Whitener. Just don't stop."

To get to the river, they had silently walked the better part of a mile, lost in thoughts of the pleasure that awaited them. The fresh smells of nature greatly enhanced a feeling of lightness and well-being. All was good with the world.

Leone had never been happier. Her time with Tom was turning out to be just as satisfying as she had dreamed of. Even the fact that the work on the farm was much more demanding than she had anticipated didn't diminish her feeling of completion, a feeling of completion she had never previously experienced.

As she followed Tom along the shadow of a path, even the few lapses of sanity she had experienced since coming didn't spoil her joy. Forgotten were episodes such as the one the previous week when she had compulsively insisted on spending hours gathering rocks to pile into a sort of monument she couldn't explain the significance of.

She was happy being a farmer's wife and had put aside previous hopes of someday seeing more than the backwoods of Arkansas, and perhaps even moving to the city. If anyone had asked her, she would have said that life was nigh on to perfect right where she was.

As the trail abruptly ended in an apparently impassable thicket of bushes and shrubs, Leone followed Tom as he stepped to the right behind one bush and then left behind another to access a narrow deer trail. Ducking to avoid hanging branches and vines, it wasn't but a few steps until they heard the soft murmuring of the river. Then, a white sandy beach stretched a stone's throw along the stream. It was blocked at both ends by the same thick growth that had hidden entrance to the path and ensured there would be no unwanted eyes.

As Tom spread their quilt, Leone unpacked their lunch. Potato salad and thick slabs of Tom's home-cured ham, between slices of Leone's best bread and store-bought mustard.

Tom suddenly said:

"Honey, did I ever tell you I just love your voice? The way it comes out of you like music? And the way it fits you and your personality? Did I ever tell you that? You and your pretty face and pretty voice go together like a bushel and a peck."

"Why, no, you never did. I like your voice, too. But what brought that up?"

"Oh, I don't know. I was just thinking."

Leone had hardly removed the last of the items from the poke when Tom came to her. She helped him as he lifted her dress over her head and laid it on the quilt. Then she deftly lowered and stepped out of her underwear so as to turn her full attention to the shoulder straps on Tom's overalls. Once both were naked, he took her hand and led her to the river.

"Oh, Tom, that's a might cold."

"Only at first. You'll get used to it."

And he was right. Soon the lovers were splashing and laughing like children, enjoying every moment.

After a while, though, Tom grew quiet. He said nothing as he brought his young wife to a hug to kiss her. Then, after a long sensuous play of lips and tongues, he said:

"And, now Miss Leone, I'm gonna give you the best massage you could ever imagine. Let's go lay on the quilt. I'll massage you as long as you can stand it and then we'll see what else we can do."

"What do you mean, 'what else we can do," she teased.

"You'll see, my love. You'll see."

●●●●●●

A typical day at the Whitener farm began with the first crow of the rooster, usually just as the sun was about to show itself. Tom was always first up, followed quickly by Leone. As Tom made his way to the outhouse in the gray semi-darkness, Leone shoved kindling in the cook stove and lit it. As soon as Tom returned, it was her turn to take the short walk behind the house and Tom's turn to stoke the fire.

Then, depending on what needed to be done, Tom would either busy himself on needed projects in the barn or yard. As soon as the stove wood had taken, Leone started on the hearty breakfast that would sustain a morning's hard work. Always there were eggs, bacon, grits, gravy, potatoes, vegetables of one sort or another and, sometimes, pie. About the time Leone was putting the food on the table, Julia and Gracie would present themselves, Gracie probably still rubbing the sleep from her eyes.

At table, Tom would, of course, say grace. After that, little was said. All knew what lay in front of them—another day of hard work until well after the sun had gone down. They were supported in their labor by thoughts of their evening reward: reading by lantern after the supper dishes had been washed, as well as some singing.

On this particular morning, Julia broke the accustomed silence: "Tom, why is life so hard? Why do we have to work all the time? I'm tired. I'm always tired."

Tom lifted his eyes from the strip of bacon he was about to fork, hesitated, and answered:

"Cause that's just the way it is, I reckon. We are poor farmers and there ain't no other way. Guess it's always been that way and guess it always will be."

"Tom," Leone said, forgetting her thoughts at the river, "I ain't sure that's exactly right. Farming ain't the only way to make a living."

Now thinking farming ain't good enough, Tom thought to himself. Well, I'd like to know what else she thinks this uneducated, one-armed man could do.

"What am I supposed to do, Leone? Am I supposed to want more, something different? Well, I don't. I'm just a farmer and I don't feel no dissatisfaction about it. My Pa's a farmer and his pa was a farmer as well as a preacher. All the Whiteners and Suttles and all of them all the way back have been farmers for a jillion years, I reckon. As far as I know, not one of them ever wanted to be anything but a farmer."

Not noticing Leone's increasing consternation, Tom grew red in the face as he continued:

"Am I supposed to feel not worthy because I didn't write no books and don't know nothing about churches in France and castles in Spain? Well, if I am, I reckon something is wrong with me because I don't.

"Sometimes of an evening when I look out across my fields and I see all them little plants that wasn't there til I planted them, I think it's all just the way God intended it, and I feel real good about myself. And when we sit down to supper and the table is loaded with what I grew and raised myself, I feel a powerful lot of satisfaction."

Still not noticing Leone's eyes, he went on:

"Leone, I understand that farming don't mean to you what it means to me. I understand you want something more. But that ain't me. I'm sorry I can't give you all that you crave, but that just ain't who I am. And besides, what higher calling could there be than having your own farm and raising up your young'uns?"

Finally, Tom noticed but it was too late. Leone jumped up from her chair and began running between windows to peer out, mumbling unintelligibly as she did so. As if looking for someone, she ran back and forth from one window to the other.

"Honey," Tom rose to say, "I'm sorry. I didn't mean to upset you. But what are you looking for? Are you expecting someone?"

With eyes that were on him but didn't see him, she uttered something primitive and guttural and ran to the bedroom, slamming the door behind her. When Tom went in to her, she was lying on her back, staring at the ceiling.

"Sugar, what's wrong?" he said as he laid down next to her. "Honey, are you OK?"

But there was no answer.

After a few minutes of silence, Tom grew impatient and thought to himself:

Why does she do this? There ain't a blessed thing wrong. I got things to do. I can't lay here waiting for her to say something.

Neither spoke and finally he rose and exited the room.

Leone hadn't told Tom she had been looking for the Devil. She could hardly admit it to herself. But she knew the Devil had been there, she had heard him. Maybe she had even smelled him. She heard him outside just as surely as there was birth and there was death. She wondered why he hadn't shown himself like he had the many times before. She wondered why it was only her that had been singled out for his torture.

Several hours later when Tom came back from the fields for his noon meal, his wife met him at the door with a beaming smile:

"How was your morning? I hope you got all done that you needed to. I got a good supper on the stove. Be ready in a minute."

All morning Tom had thought of little else except Leone's behavior and now she grinned and acted as if everything was normal. As she retreated to the kitchen, he stared at the knot in her apron strings and thought:

A knot. Yep, she's got me tied in a knot, just like them apron strings. Lord, why can't she act right?

• • • • • •

As with farmers everywhere, Tom was at the mercy of the weather and the sometimes severe fluctuations of the market. However, in the Bible Belt, of which Northern Arkansas was certainly a resolute part, there was one unfailing constant—the apparent prosperity of the churches. There was almost no community too small to boast of its own church. Although Baptist and Methodist predominated, the other confessions were well represented also, each of them anxious to outdo the others in building the most imposing edifices.

Having its own church and often its own full-time preacher was a luxury no congregation seemed to think could be dispensed with. It seemed that people didn't give it much thought at all. They simply built and maintained their churches as large and imposing as they could. Made possible by tithing, bake sales and charity dinners, the churches were not only impressive in appearance, they often were built to accommodate more church-goers than actually attended. They were rarely filled to capacity.

Tom, however, had questions about the entire enterprise. *I wonder why,* he thought every so often, *every no-account little town and village needs its own church and preacher. Surely folks could drive a bit and save a powerful lot of money.* Even the fact of his own grandfather being a minister, couldn't dissuade Tom of his notion that building over-sized churches and having people support ministers who didn't contribute to the secular well-being of the community was not a good idea. This belief was one reason his church attendance was a lot more hit and miss than regular.

• • • • • •

This particular year, there had been just enough summer rain to ensure that Tom's fields produced abundantly. Less rain, which sometimes happened, would have stunted his plants or made them susceptible to weevils and other pests. On the other hand, too much rain could wash them out entirely. When it was "just right," like this year, the harvest was sufficient so that day after day the women were busy in the kitchen canning more than four hundred jars of plums, peaches, okra, beans and the other bounty that would sustain them until the following year's harvest.

However, it was cotton that provided what little money they needed. Regardless of the productivity of the farm, certain items such as salt and pepper, most of their clothing, as well as all their equipment had to be purchased. Unfortunately, when the price of cotton was up, yields were down. When yields were up, prices were down—the law of supply and demand, and the bane of farmers throughout the world.

Tom also grew corn, most of which he had milled at Ruddell's Mill in Batesville. Some was used for animal feed and some to make whiskey. However, most was consumed at home in the form of corn cakes and the like.

The third main crop Tom and his neighbors grew was tobacco. The rocky local ground would not sustain the large tobacco plantations like the ones the Whiteners and Baileys had farmed in Virginia and North Carolina, but with an inordinate amount of care it would produce enough of the big leaves for personal use. Tom had a garden-sized plot set aside so that the family was kept in tobacco the entire year.

The men generally used coarse-cut leaves for what they called "chewing." However, they didn't really chew it. They placed a wad of it in their cheek, felt an immediate rush to the bloodstream and started spitting.

The women didn't use tobacco near as frequently as the men, and Leone not at all, but when they did, they preferred it cut very fine and called it "snuff." Some of them would achieve their rush by taking a little stick, chewing on the end until it was soft and then using it to paint tobacco on their gums.

Regardless of the way it was used, the constant need to spit made sure that in every room sat at least one spittoon.

As Tom and Jim returned from the mill where they had taken their corn for milling, they called for the others to come outside.

"Hey, y'all," Tom yelled, "come on out here and see what we got. We had enough harvest money to get something you're really going to like."

As the women gathered on the porch, the men were gently unloading a large carton, on every side of which, in large yellow letters, was stenciled the word, "Victrola."

"Oh, Tom," Leone cried out, "you got us one. What a blessed day. What records did you get?"

"They gave us ten. Came with the player machine," Jim answered as the men were carrying it through the front door. "We got two Scott Joplin records and a King of the Bungaloos and even a Tchaikovsky. Some old timey ones, too."

Thereafter, it was a rare evening when the family didn't listen to music after dinner. However, problems immediately arose. Each of them had their own personal favorite song which he or she wanted to listen to first. No one wanted to listen to their favorite last. After listening to squabbling for three evenings in a row, Leone finally announced:

"I've had enough of this fussing every night. Here's the way it's going to be: we're going to go strictly by age. Tonight, it will be Tom. He can listen to his favorite first. Tomorrow it will be Jim. Then me. Then Julia and then Gracie. Then we'll start over again. And another thing: no more complaining about who's going to wind the machine. If it was your night to go first, then you wind."

Tom smiled at the others and said: "I reckon that's the way it's going to be."

But the Victrola did not come without its drawbacks, mainly the demise of the singing that had been a treasured part of the evening routine. Even after the newness of the machine had worn off, the beautiful three-part and sometimes four-part harmonies perfected by frequent repetition were rarely sung.

I guess that's the price of being modern, Tom thought to himself when he considered the matter. *But I do miss the singing.*

"Hattie, I'm sure glad you came," Tom began as soon as he got down off Milly at the same intersection where Mabel had secretly brought Leone to meet him three years before. His sister-in-law had arrived just a few minutes before him and was standing under a large tree, trying to shelter from the rain.

"Well," she said as he joined her, "ain't this a real frog strangler? What do you want to talk about that's so gol-durned important we got to meet when it's pouring down rain?"

"I'm sorry you had to come out with it raining like this, but I heard you was up from Searcy and it's real important I talk to you about Leone."

"She hasn't done anything crazy has she?"

"No, nothin' really crazy. Just a lot of little things and I'm worried about her."

"Crazy little things? Like what?"

"Oh, like talking to herself sometimes. Like walking around the house naked sometimes. Or running to the windows like she was looking for someone."

"That don't sound too crazy to me. A lot of people talk to themselves on occasion. And when it's really hot, a lot of us strip down. My grandpa used to do it all the time. Used to walk around out in the fields even, naked as a jaybird. And maybe she was expecting someone."

"And there was that time a while back when she spent the whole day piling rocks. Wouldn't do her chores, wouldn't talk. Just kept gathering them rocks. Next day she was fine. Like nothing had happened."

"She is a little tetched. You knowed that when you married her. But, tell me more about this talking to herself."

"Well, she's always talked to herself some. That don't really bother me. But now it seems like she's talking to someone, someone who isn't there.

"Anyone in particular?"

"Yep, your dead Aunt Ida, your Pa's sister."

"Well, I swan. They always was close. Ida kinda took her under her wing and treated her real special, more like a daughter than a niece. And when Ida died—she was only 32 when she died —Leone took it real hard. Wouldn't leave the cemetery and then moped around for days."

"I can't make out what she's saying exactly, and when I ask her she just says, "Oh, nothin'. And if I insist, she shuts up and goes in the other room. Only thing I can make out is her saying is, 'Aunt Ida. Oh, Aunt Ida.' Over and over."

"How often does she do it?"

"Well, not all the time. Sometimes she goes for days and don't do it. Then again sometimes she'll do it twice in a day. Don't seem to be harming nothing. Most of time she's the same old Leone. She laughs and jokes. And she cooks and runs the kitchen just fine. It's just that she's doing it more often. First it was once every month or so. Then, every week or so. Now, like I say, she can do it as often as twice in a day. I don't know what to do, Hattie. I'm scared for her, and for me, too."

"Tom, like you know, you ain't always been my favorite relative. As a matter of fact, there's been times I really been down on you. But I'll do anything to help Leone and I guess helping you is part of the deal. You still moonshining?"

"I still got that little still out behind the house. Me and Jim just make it for ourselves, that's all. Why you asking?"

"Well, first of all, you need to lighten up on it. Ever since I knowed you, you've drank too much. Secondly, you need to give Leone a little bit. Think you could spare a little bit for her? For medicinal purposes?"

"Why sure, if you thought it would help. But what you're saying is against one another. First you tell me to drink less and then you say Leone should drink more?"

"Ain't nothing conflicting about it. You drink too much and she needs a little nip of an evening. A little snort might be just what the doctor ordered. Why don't you see if she won't have a little drink after dinner?"

"OK, Hattie, if you think so."

"Well, see that you do, for both your sakes."

"Hattie, as you well know, farm life is a hard one. One of the few pleasures I get is having a little snort in the evening. I don't know if I can give that up entirely."

"Tom, you ain't listening. I didn't say you needed to quit entirely. I said you need to drink less."

"I try. God knows I do. But it's hard. Sometimes I think it would be easier to quit entirely than to try to drink less. Once I have that first drink, I want another one, sure as night follows day."

••••••

By spring, much to their delight, Tom and Leone's frequent and enthusiastic love making had paid off. The others learned of it one evening as they were taking their usual places after dinner in front of the Victrola.

"Folks," Tom said, "me and Leone's got something to say. We're going to have two harvests this fall. Our first young'un will be here before Halloween."

After the couple had been duly congratulated and whooped about, Tom brought out the jug. Julia brought four glasses.

"And where's mine?" Gracie questioned.

"Ain't you a little young to be wanting whiskey?" Leone asked.

"I'm nigh on to twelve and I reckon that's old enough to at least give it a try."

"Why hell, yes, sis," Tom told Julia. "This is a special occasion. Get her a glass."

Leone looked askance, but didn't say anything.

Tom poured two fingers of the clear moonshine for each of the females, half a glass for Jim and a full glass for himself. Raising his glass, he announced:

"Here's to our beloved Leone and the healthy boy she's going to bless us with."

As Leone and Julia took small sips and made gruesome faces, they all watched Gracie drain her glass, scowl ferociously and say:

"Tom, can I have some more?"

"You most certainly cannot," Leone said. "You have had quite enough."

"Where did you learn to drink like that?" Tom wanted to know. "This obviously ain't the first time you've had strong drink."

"Only once before," she answered.

"Who give it to you?" Tom asked sternly.

"It was that wedding last fall. Some boys, I don't remember who, had a jug out by the barn and I had a sip. But just one, that's all I had, just one."

"Well, you ain't getting no more here, and see to it that you don't have no more, period," Tom said.

As Leone's pregnancy progressed, the familiar jocularity with which the members of the household treated each other was replaced by a soft deference in her favor. Both Tom and Julia made sure that Leone did not participate in the heaviest chores and that she took frequent rests, so much so that one day Leone felt compelled to say:

"Would y'all stop. I'm not sick. I'm gonna have a baby, that's all. There's work to be done around here and I reckon I can still do my share."

Rarely had a woman taken to pregnancy like Leone. Not only did she exhibit an overall radiance, but her disposition became, if possible, even sunnier. And she stopped talking to Aunt Ida and even to herself. At first no one noticed it. Then, after it hadn't happened for a few days, Julia caught Tom alone and asked:

"Tom, what's going on with Leone? She ain't talking to herself no more."

"I don't know either, but it sure is nice. Do you suppose it's the baby?"

"I don't know, but, yep, I think it's got to be being pregnant. I don't know what else it could be. Some women is just natural mothers. They was born to have kids. That's her sister, Hattie. Hattie's already got three and says she's gonna keep on having them until the Lord don't send her no more. Maybe that's Leone."

"That's fine with me," Tom said. "The more the better. But have you noticed her voice? Seems like it's changed. It's even sweeter than before. And she ain't been getting excited and yelling like she was before. All is calm and peaceful."

"Yep, she's like a new woman."

• • • • • •

The previous winter had gone well for Tom and his family. While he and Jim tended to outdoor repairs and chores in the barn, Leone and the girls slopped the hogs, fed the chickens, cooked and made sure what they had canned was properly put away. They were ready for the spring plowing and planting.

Tom had tried Hattie's suggestion that he drink less, not that he hadn't thought of it many times himself. He had. Most every day. For the better part of the last ten years, almost every time he took a drink, which was most every evening, he told himself to limit his intake to only one or two small glasses or pulls on the jug. He didn't always go on to drink himself into oblivion, but he never stopped at one or two. And even though he paid the penalty with the next morning's hangover, by evening his thirst again ruled.

As to Hattie's other idea that he give Leone a little glass of whiskey after dinner, he soon found that there was no need. Leone's demeanor had improved so much of its own accord, or more likely, on account of her pregnancy, that the suggestion was soon forgotten and he never mentioned it to Leone or the others.

And the household began to function more smoothly. Even though Julia was five years younger than Leone, the two began to work together in new ways to accomplish their chores with greater efficiency. Due to mutual respect and Julia's superior organizational skills, the two worked side by side to make the small home fairly hum with activity.

In the evening, over objection, Tom was finally able to at least delay the record playing in favor of some reading and singing. Julia's favorite songs were the hymns. She especially liked "The Old Rugged Cross" and "A Sweeter Anthem" and would take the lead, with Leone and the others joining in. For her part, Leone was partial to the old ballads, the ones she had heard since she was small, and most every time two or more farmers gathered to relax. "Barbara Allen" and "Pretty Polly" were her favorites.

"That is so pretty," Jim said one evening after the women had done a couple unaccompanied ballads. "Your harmonies are like a band of angels."

"Thank you, Jim, but it ain't nothing," Leone said. "You ever met a Southerner who couldn't sing? We all can. Yankees can't sing like we can. We got it in our blood."

"I don't know about Yankees not singing," Tom joined in, "but you're right, Southerners, and especially us Arkies, sure can sing."

"You two song birds should make a recording," Jim said. "You know, a Victrola recording. Wouldn't that be nice?"

"Why Jim," Leone said, "sometimes you don't have good sense. Why would you want to listen to a recording of us when you got us right here in person."

As to the bible reading, generally Tom would read first, then hand the book to Leone. After Leone had read one of her favorite passages, Jim or Julia would take it. Only Gracie would have to be prompted to read.

"It's good for your reading," Tom would say. "You need to practice your reading."

"But I don't like to read," she would often respond. "I don't want to read."

Then, usually it was Julia who would say something like, "That's too durn bad. Now, you go on and read, just like Tom told you to."

And she would—as briefly as she could get away with.

Losing patience with her one evening when she was particularly recalcitrant, Tom adopted his sternest tone to say:

"Gracie, I ain't got but one arm and look at all I've been able to accomplish. Me and Jim started with nothing and now look at this here farm and all we've got. But you've got two good arms. Just think about all you can do if you try. But, you got to try, and quit being so gol-durned lazy."

The girl did not respond. She just looked at Tom blankly and trundled off to bed.

CHAPTER SEVEN

"Tom," Leone said to her husband when they were alone one evening, "what would you think about me going back to Pa's to have this baby? If it ain't early, I got about a month to go and I was figuring that in a couple, three weeks, I could go down to Pa's."

"Why, Honey, why would you want to a thing like that? Julia's here to help and my Pa's new wife says she'll come over from Denmark. Why, if you did that it would make me feel like we ain't a real family even."

"I sure don't want to hurt your feelings, or your Pa's either, but I don't particularly trust that new wife of his. And I want my sister to help me. Hattie's got lots of experience helping out with babies. She's got her own and she's helped lots of neighbors and cousins and whatnot. She's durn near a mid-wife. If I was at my Pa's, Hattie could get there in just a couple hours, not have to come all the way up here. And, Pa's new wife, too. She's got some experience."

"And what about my sisters? They got their hearts set on helping you. Julia talks about it all the time and Gracie's all fixed to boil as much water as you need. No, Leone, I think you need to have this baby right here at home with us, where you belong. We could even get Carrie Shuler to come and help. From up on Sulfur Creek where she and Bill live, she could be here in an hour or so."

"It ain't like I'll be gone long. Probably, just a week or two. And as soon as the baby's born and I can tolerate a wagon, I'll come right back."

"Honey, I don't want you to do it. But you're the one having the baby and if you're set on having it at your Pa's, well, I guess I can't stop you. But you'll have to be the one to tell my sisters. I ain't gonna do it."

And so, over Tom's objection, as well as the bitter disappointment of Julia and Gracie, Loyce was born in Floral, in the very same bedroom Leone had once shared with Mabel.

The length of Leone's labor had been just right—long enough so that Hattie could get there in time from Searcy, but not so long and painful so that Leone had protracted suffering.

As soon as her labor had started, John Bell had sent a rider to fetch Tom, who, on arrival, was promptly relegated to the porch. There he and the Bailey men and boys would anxiously await the strong baby cries that would signal a healthy birth.

However, before the cries of a child, they had to endure those of Leone. As she struggled through the pain of delivery, Tom winced with every scream and whimper.

Finally, John Bell said to him sharply, "Son, you having this baby or is she? Sit still. Didn't your pa have fifteen or twenty kids and four or five wives? You must have heard lots of babies being born."

"Pa didn't have quite that many kids or wives, but that was different. Seems like having kids was about all Ma did. We got pretty used to it. But this is Leone. This is personal. It sure does bother me to hear her hollering like that."

But Tom didn't have to endure long before he was rewarded with the full-throated infant cries he had been waiting for. Soon after the new-born's first yelp, Hattie appeared holding a red-faced baby whose reaction to his new environment was outrage.

"Tom, you got you a son," Leone's older sister said with a broad smile. "A healthy baby boy. Pa, you got you a grandson."

"Boy, he sure is tiny," Tom said as he reached to take the child. "He ain't much more than a tick turd, but he sure is cute. And loud."

"Hold on Tom," John Bell interceded. "What are you doing? I didn't hold Hattie til she was more than a month old and the others maybe longer. And I got two arms."

"I ain't gonna drop him, John Bell," Tom said as Hattie relinquished her bundle to him. "I reckon he's my baby and I'll hold him whenever

I want, arms or no arms."

Ignoring the child's wails, Tom used his partial right arm to secure the child against his body while he used his left to stroke and caress him, smiling broadly all the while. After a few seconds, John Bell said, "Tom, that fussing is beginning to irritate me. Durn, but he's loud. Give him back to Hattie so she can take him in to Leone. The little fella is hungry. You other boys, go in with Hattie and see your sister. She's probably pretty tired so don't stay too long. Me and Tom will be along in a minute. We got a couple things to say."

As soon as they were alone and before Tom had a chance to sit down, John Bell started.

"I understand you're going to call him Loyce, that right?"

"Yep. Leone read it in a book and we both think it's a fine name."

"A little sissy for my taste, but I guess you didn't ask me."

"That's right, John Bell. He's our baby. You already named yours."

"Tom, glad as I am to get another grandson, this don't change my opinion of you one bit. I still don't think you'll ever make a real man."

Damn, what's it gonna take for him to respect me? Tom thought with sad disappointment. *How much do I have to do?*

"Only difference is," John Bell went on, "now you got a child to take care of. I'm gonna be watching you like a hawk to make sure you do take care of him—that boy and Leone, too. You step out of line and you're gonna have hell to pay. And Tom, leave the god-damned shine alone."

"I will, John Bell. I promise you I will. I'd be the first to admit that I probably get a snoot full a little too often, but that's gonna change. You're right, I'm a real family man now and I got to do right by my family. You'll see."

The son of a bitch, Tom thought. *Who does he think he is, lecturing to me like that? And today of all days. We'll see about the drinking. I guess I got the right to have a drink now and again.*

"Well, I hope so, Tom. I sincerely hope so. I'll be watching. Now git in there and see your wife and boy."

"Julia," Leone said to Tom's sister late one evening after Loyce had gone to sleep and the two of them had been reading to each other in a lantern-lit corner of the living room, "I just don't know what I'd do without you and Gracie here to help out. You are both truly a godsend."

"Why, it's a pleasure. Loyce is such a good baby. Helping out with him is even better than helping out with my own brothers and sisters. Maybe it's because Loyce is the only baby around. At Pa's there was always so many of 'em. Every time I think about Ma having all them kids and then Pa starting in again with new wives, it just about makes me dizzy. Always diapers to change, kids to feed, one or another of 'em bawling about something. Whew!"

"Well, you are certainly appreciated, all the same. I want you to know that. But I want to talk to you about something, just between the two of us. Honey, have you noticed I haven't had a spell lately? I haven't had a spell since before Loyce was born and he's eight months old."

"Of course, Leone. We all have. Jim was remarking on it to Tom just yesterday."

"Them spells has been the scourge of my life. They've plagued me and plagued me."

"Maybe you're done. Maybe you won't have any more."

"I wake up every day and hope that's true. I wake up every morning and pray, 'Please Lord, no more spells. If I have to have more, please not now. Let me get my kids raised up first'."

"Maybe it had something to do with having a baby. You know there's a powerful amount of something called hormones a woman's body makes when she has a baby. Maybe it was hormones cured you."

Interrupted by whimpers from the other room, Leone quickly retrieved the baby, put him to her breast and continued:

"Julia, why do you think I got the pellagra? I ain't never done nothing really bad. Oh, I might have told a fib or two when I was little and trying to stay out of trouble, but I ain't never hurt no one, or caused anyone pain. And I always try to be good. Why would God punish me like this?"

Leone wanted to go on and really open up, to tell her sister-in-law about the devil who had so unmercifully taunted and haunted her most of her life. She wanted to talk more about the serenity brought on by his continuing absence. However, to do so would have been to reveal a little more than she was presently willing to do. Perhaps she would have, had she better understood it herself.

"The Lord works in strange ways," Julia commented.

"I know, but it just don't make no sense. That girl, Ann, the one that lives down by Sandtown. She's always showing the boys her titties and charging them a penny to play with 'em. And lying all the time. She ain't got no pellagra."

"She's going to hell for sure. An eternity of fire and brimstone for her."

"But what am I gonna do if I start having spells again? What if you and Gracie ain't here? Someday you both are gonna get married and have your own families. You ain't gonna be here forever."

"Well, Honey, that brings up something I been meaning to tell you. We wasn't quite ready to announce it, but since you bring it up, now is as good a time as any. Me and Washington is going to be getting married soon. He done asked me and I said, yes. We're just waiting for the right time to tell Pa. But, no matter. Gracie's gonna be here. She'll be helping out. You got nothing to worry about."

"Why, Julia, that's wonderful news. I'm so glad for you. Of course I don't how we'll get on without you, but we'll get by. Don't you worry about us."

"That's sweet of you Leone. I was worried you might be upset. Maybe we'll name a young'un after you. I hope it won't be too long before me and Washington will have some to be naming."

"You know, Tom wants a whole herd of kids. Says he even wants to outdo his pa. Course they'd be a big help on the farm, but he just likes kids generally. You see the way he loves on Loyce."

"And, what about you? He ever think about what having kids does to a woman's body? About what having a whole bunch of kids does to her? Can't do her mind much good, either."

"Yes, we talked about that. He says he wants to keep having kids as long as I'm good for it. He says I come first. As long as I'm healthy, he wants them and if I ain't, he don't. And judging from the way it has been with Loyce, I'm good for a few, at least. I sure didn't like it while Loyce was coming out, but I guess it wasn't all that bad."

"Well, that kinda reminds me. I hope I ain't being too personal, but I been meaning to ask about you having more kids. You planning to have more right away or you doing something to try to delay the next one some?"

"The Lord's deciding. We ain't doing nothing one way or the other, but you know what a loving man Tom is. I expect I'll be in a family way again before too long."

Leone didn't say anything to her sister-in-law about her other thoughts, the ones about maybe convincing Tom to leave the farm and try something else. Even though Tom had told her more than once that he was a confirmed farmer and always would be, she still harbored a faint hope that maybe someday they could move to the city, perhaps even another state. She thought wistfully of scenes from Paris and London and Vienna she had seen in magazines and picture books. These thoughts came to her often, but as a matter of self-protection had to be willfully overridden with more practical concerns.

• • • • • •

On Saturday evening, Tom announced that the next day the family would be attending church. When asked what the special occasion was, he replied simply: "Oh, nothing. I just think it's a good idea. And, besides, we ain't been since Loyce was born. It's time we showed him off a bit."

Why you proud papa, Leone thought to herself. *You just want to go show off that young'un. Good for you. And good for me, too. Let them see what this crazy woman has made.*

Accordingly, early the next morning the whole six of them, Tom, Leone and the baby, as well as Tom's siblings, Jim, Julia and Gracie, scrubbed up, put on their best "Sunday-go-to-meeting" clothes and started piling into the wagon. However before the last of them had made it in, Tom cried out, "Whoa, wait a minute. I almost forgot," and jumped down off the seat behind Milly to run back into the house.

Returning moments later, he said to his brother, "Here you go, Jim. Here's some hair slick for us. Put a wad of that up front and rub it on back through. We got to look our best for all them sinners coming to church today to be saved."

"We got to look good for sinners?" Jim chided. "Why look good for sinners?"

"Yeah, Tom," Leone joined in, "I don't cotton to looking good for sinners. Maybe we should look really bad for them."

"That's right," Julia contributed, "let's all go back in and put on our old ragged work clothes. Let's look our very worst for them sinners. That'll teach them."

"All right," Tom came back. "I'll do it if y'all will. Y'all do it and I will, too."

"Tom," Leone reluctantly eased the smile from her face to say, "you knowed we was just fooling. Let's get going. I got me some showing off to do, and some gossiping, too."

A little while later Parson Brown was in fine form as he railed against the evils of slothfulness, drink and loose living. Even though Gracie had to lean over to whisper in Leone's ear "What's slothfulness?" all understood that if their lives were not free from these awful things, they were going straight to hell. Wrapping it up with an impassioned and almost tearful plea for God's help in avoiding sin and Satan, the entire congregation joined the minister in a rousing and heart-felt "Amen".

"A fine sermon, Parson," Tom warmly said as he shook the man's hand when it was his turn on the church steps afterward. "It was one of the finest sermons I ever did hear and I surely took it to heart."

"Why, thank you, Tom. I appreciate that. But say, we ain't been seeing much of you and Leone lately. I do hope you'll make it a point to be a little more regular in your attendance. Now that you're a family man—and your Loyce is just about the cutest little bugger I ever did see—I hope you'll be here most every Sunday. Leone, maybe you could help him out in that regard."

"I'll certainly try, Parson. I'll get him here if I can."

I wonder, Leone thought as she continued down the steps, *how often a body needs to go to church. Tom's a pretty good man already. Everybody should go to church, I guess, but except for his drinking now and again, he don't need no special help. I wonder if it would make us better people if we was here every Sunday.*

"And now Tom, take Leone and your family on over to the picnic tables. The Elders have a special treat for you. There's fried chicken, cornbread and potato salad enough for an army. After you get your fill of that, the ladies have baked a bunch of pies and cakes. I'll be over in a minute after I'm done here."

The parishioners out back had already divided into two groups when Tom and his family arrived. All the women and girls were on one side, busy preparing and setting out food, drink and condiments, while the men were on the other, centered around the nearest of several parked wagons.

As Tom and Jim walked up to the male group, warm greetings were exchanged. "Why, Sam!" Tom acknowledged a distant cousin, "I'm ain't seen you in a coon's age. How are you?"

"I been fine, Tom. Real fine. And the cotton's coming in real good. Reckon it's going to be a good year. And, I saw you and Leone come in with a new young'un."

"Yep. Loyce is his name. And he's cute a button. Hung like a stud horse, too."

"Well, don't that call for a little celebration? I knowed you to have a taste now and again. I got a jug over here in the wagon. Want a little snort?"

"Why Sam, I don't mind if I do. Just one though. Just to celebrate my new young'un," Tom grinned, without a thought for the promise he had made to his father-in-law.

"Only don't let the preacher see you. Or the womenfolk. Just pour you some in that glass there. The preacher knows we're doing it, but he won't say anything so long as we don't make a public spectacle of ourselves. He'd have a fit if we brought the jug out in public."

An hour or so later, Leone came for Tom and as soon as she noticed his condition, started in: "Tom Whitener, just look at you. You are a mess. Why do you do this? And after you told the parson his sermon was 'heartfelt'. Heartfelt, indeed. And my pa. You told my pa you wasn't gonna drink no more. You are a disgrace and a sinner."

"Why, Honey, I'm OK. I just had me a little drink, that's all."

"A little drink? You're drunk as a skunk. That's a whole lot more than just a 'little drink'. You promised you weren't gonna drink again.

Don't your word mean anything?"

"Aww, Leone."

"And you, too, Samuel. You give it to him, didn't you? You should be ashamed of yourself. Bringing a jug of whiskey onto the Lord's ground. I hope you go to hell, which you surely are. All of you. And you, too, Jim. Why'd you let him do it?"

Leaning on Jim and with his help, Tom managed to stumble to their wagon. Then, as Jim pushed and Leone and Julia pulled, the three of them finally managed to get him up. More falling than climbing into the box, he immediately laid down and passed out.

When they reached home, and as Julia was guiding Milly into the barn, Leone voiced her disgust: "Don't nobody bother trying to get him in the house. He can sleep right where he is, or over in the hog pen. I've got half a mind to throw him in with them."

••••••

Leaving her husband at home to tend their farm near Searcy, Hattie had taken the train with her three toddlers to Batesville where she met Mabel. Mabel lived just outside of town with her husband and her own toddler. Her husband, too, had agreed to remain at home while the two former Bailey women went to visit Tom and Leone.

Although Hattie was not unattractive, with her pronounced nose, a strong jaw, and half-squinting eyes, she projected a sternness entirely in keeping with her character. Certainly she was not without a sense of humor, but her default demeanor was one of seriousness. She had a certain gravitas, probably inherited from her father, respected by all.

Mabel, on the other hand, was the lighter one. Her laughing eyes and ready smile immediately distinguished her from Hattie. In this regard, she and Leone were much alike. During their years together at home, they often formed a spirited duo in opposition to their older sister and their father.

One incident still talked about, although from much different perspectives, was one in which a fresh-baked pie disappeared. John Bell and Hattie thought they knew who the culprits were and continued to accuse Leone and Mabel. However Leone and Mabel vehemently denied having anything to do with it. Yet for years afterward and almost every time they were alone together, Mabel and Leone laughed and reminded each other of how tasty the purloined pastry had been.

Since there was not a train which went from Batesville to the area where Tom and Leone lived, their father had arranged a wagon for their use as soon as they got to Batesville. They lined the rear of it with quilts, so that while Hattie sat up on the seat and drove, Mabel entertained the children in the back as best she could.

"Hattie, do you have to hit every gol-durned bump in this road," Mabel asked as the wagon hit yet another deep rut. "I'm trying to feed this young'un and he keeps losing my teat."

"Just hold your horses. I'm doing the best I can," Hattie answered, sharply jerking the reins to the left to try to keep the wheels out of a large hole.

"Hattie, you said it was only going to take four hours. I think it's been more than that now and these young'uns is getting terrible restless."

"Mabel, what do you think about Tom's sisters living with them?" Hattie changed the subject.

"Why, I don't think nothing about it. I guess every farmer needs all the help he can get. Especially at planting or harvest time."

"Don't you think it a little strange that they would leave their own pa's place where they was born to go live with their brother?"

"Well, their brother, Jim, lives there, too."

"But, that's a little different. Tom and him are farming together."

"The girls said they didn't get along with Dan's new wife. I ain't never met her, but I guess they got their reasons."

"Mabel, I think it's real strange. I think something is going on."

"Going on? Like what?"

"I don't rightly know, but I'm worried about Leone. I don't want her mixed up in no Whitener funny business. If I find out something bad is going on for Leone and her new young'un, I'll jerk them out of there so fast it will make your head swim. You know Tom's got a drinking problem and I just don't trust him or his sisters."

"Oh Hattie, I don't know why you're so down on Tom. Sure, he has a little too much to drink sometimes, but which of these good 'ol boys don't? Besides, I remember when Pa said Leone would never find a husband because of her pellagra. And now she's got Tom. He just adores her."

"We'll see how much he adores her when she starts having some really bad spells and doing something nutty."

••••••

As Hattie "geed" the horse to the right off the main road and onto the approach to the house, Tom and his family jumped down off the porch where they had been waiting and came running and shouting.

"Howdy," Tom cried out. "Y'all finally got here. We been waiting supper."

Supper was to be out behind the house where boards had been laid over barrels to create a makeshift table big enough to accommodate the six adults, as well as the several small children and babies. As Hattie and Mabel were getting situated, the Whitener women began bringing the food from the kitchen.

Knowing the disdain most of Leone's family held for him, and anxious to make the best possible impression, Tom had told Leone that they would spare no effort in providing for her sisters in the most impressive way they could. Thus, not only had Leone raided their storeroom and smokehouse for their best food and condiments, she had also taken Gracie with her to the store the previous day to use what little cash they had to buy several treats, including enough hard candy so that each could have a piece.

Although constantly interrupted by the needs of the children, the conversation at table was lively and animated. Not being in frequent contact with each other meant that the Whitener and Bailey sides of the family had much news and gossip to exchange. Expressions such as, "Well, I swan," and "I'll be durned," and "Is that so?" and even, "Well, I'll be a monkey's uncle," fairly flew. Every recent birth, marriage, death, mishap, crime and known infidelity was the subject of announcement and discussion.

Finally though, during a slight lull in the conversation and as if she had been waiting for an opportunity, Hattie turned from her seat next to Tom to say to him:

"Daddy told me your grandpa was an abolitionist. Is that true?"

"It is. It ain't no secret. Me and your pa already talked about it."

"And Pa said not only was he an abolitionist, he also didn't serve in the war because he was a conscientious objector."

"Well, he was a minister, a man of God. Of course he couldn't be killing anyone, even if they was Yankees. And by the time of the war, he already had a mess of children and his second wife depending on him."

"Did you know my pa was the Grand Dragon of the Klan there in Batesville?" Hattie said with some pride.

"Why, he never told me that. I didn't know that."

"Well, he was. He ain't now, but he used to be, and he sure don't cotton to abolitionists and the like."

"Hattie, we're talking about my granddaddy. I ain't no abolitionist. My pa ain't even an abolitionist. My pa's too busy with farming and wives so's he hardly knows what an abolitionist is. And besides, they ain't no coloreds around here. They are all on the plantations over by the river or down in the flatlands."

"The reason they ain't none around here," Hattie responded, "is because they know what would happen to them if they come around. And we aim to keep it that way. It's bad enough that a Jew family moved in down at Cave City, but we ain't having no niggers round here. Or, them that cotton to them."

Owing purely to economics, there were few African Americans in Independence, Sharp and the other counties around Batesville. The land had never lent itself to slave labor and even now the rocky ground just wasn't adequate to support more than single-family farms. Even after the Civil War the area was almost one hundred per cent white. Not that racial hatred was unknown there. The politics of race had permeated all of the South, even the backwater farms and settlements like those around Tom.

"Hattie, do you actually know any niggers?" Tom asked.

"I reckon I know enough about them to know I don't want to see none around me."

"Well, I have never known a single one, and I've only ever seen a very few. So until I've had actual experience with them, I'm withholding judgment. And I know they are not all bad. They's some pretty smart ones. Did you ever hear of Frederick Douglass? I hear he was one smart nigger."

"Frederick Douglass, that abolitionist? Surely you don't take no stock in a nigger abolitionist?"

"Hattie, I really don't want to argue with you. I'm just saying that without actually knowing about something, sometimes it's better to not have strong feelings about it."

Although Hattie and Mabel stayed for two more days, and even though he tried, there was nothing Tom could do to improve his relationship with Hattie. He catered to her every physical need and made sure conversations only centered on pleasant matters. Nevertheless, despite her warmth and concern for Leone, Hattie had at best only toleration for Tom. When the two women left, Hattie didn't even say good-bye to him.

● ● ● ● ● ●

Leone emerged from their bedroom early one gloomy, overcast morning to find Tom starting a fire in the stove. As he tore pages from an old Sears catalog to intersperse with finger-sized wood chips, she said to him:

"Did you ever see such a miserable looking day? Looks like a storm is coming."

"Honey, it's even more miserable than you know. My sister done run off with Washington. Eloped. Left us a note. It's there on the table."

"Julia? How could she do that? Wasn't a month ago she told me not to worry, that she would be here for a while.

"Read her note."

It read:

My Dearest Tom and Leone,

I am so sorry to leave you like this, but me and Washington has got to get married.

I have really liked living here with you and helping out. Especially with little Loyce. They was times you about worked me to death, but I think it says in the Bible, 'they's no rest for the wicked'. I never thought we was wicked, but we sure didn't get no rest, so maybe we are. But I ain't complaining. We all did what we had to do.

And, don't worry about telling Pa about us. By the time you read this we will have stopped by his place to tell him ourselves. Then, we're going on to Missouri. Washington has a brother there and we'll be staying with him until we can get situated and get a place of our own. Washington thinks there's lots of work in the quarries near where his brother lives.

I love and respect you all more than you know. Please give my love to Jim and Gracie and tell them to write.

And, Leone. I do so very much hope your spells are over. I think Loyce was all you needed and you won't have no more.

And Tom. I never said nothing before, but you'd be better off if you drank a little less. Especially, now that you've got a young'un to think of. But, I'll always love you regardless.

I'll write as soon as we get where we're going. And, I'll let you know whether it's a girl or a boy (I hope it's a boy).

Love, Julia.

As Leone finished reading, the tears started and her hand with the letter dropped to her side. Tom came from the stove to comfort and hug her. "Honey, don't cry. It'll be OK. We'll get by. Jim and Gracie is still here."

"No, Tom, it ain't that. I know everything will be all right. It's just that I'm going to miss her. She's become just like my own sister, not just yours. I could talk to her and tell her stuff and she always understood. And now she's going to be God knows where in Missouri and heavens knows when I'll see her again."

"Why, Honey, it ain't all that bad. First of all, Missouri ain't that far away, and second, you can always talk to me. I love to talk to you."

"Talking to you ain't the same, Tom," she continued while wiping away tears. "I could tell Julia stuff woman to woman. Stuff men just don't get."

"Leone, I don't think that's true. Just try me. Tell me something. Tell me something you think Julia would understand and not me."

"Well, it ain't exactly like that. It ain't that you don't understand the meaning of the words. It's that you don't sense the feelings behind them. Sometimes me and Julia didn't even have to talk in order to know each other's thoughts. She sometimes knew what I was going to say before I said it. Men is all about facts and figures and events and fixing problems. They think about fixing people problems like they think about fixing a broke wagon. Just make it right again. But it ain't always about fixing things. It's about feeling each other. Women do that. At least some do. They feel a connection."

"I surely do not understand."

"And Tom, that's all right. You don't have to. I love you and you love me and we're special together, like a man and a woman should be. Ain't nothing wrong between us. It's just that me and Julia is connected in a way that is special to women."

"Well, I guess I never will understand, but let me try to fix things the only way I know how. You say you're going to miss Julia so let's go see her. Soon as it's convenient for us and for Julia, maybe next spring before planting time, maybe we'll take the train and go see them. You and me and Loyce. Jim and Gracie can take care of things here for a spell. We ain't never had a vacation and I reckon we're about due. And after that, maybe she can bring her new young'un and come visit us for a bit. How would that be?"

"Oh, Tom, that would be wonderful. I love you."

He tries so hard, Leone thought, *but we ain't gonna take no vacations. I know that. Working from can to can't blamed near every day. Ain't no time for vacations.*

CHAPTER EIGHT

At supper, Tom and Leone had just told Jim and the Gracie that Leone was again in a family way, when they heard the postman yelling from atop his wagon stopped outside their house.

"Tom get out here. They's locusts coming. Billions of 'em. Eatin' everything."

"Whoa, Bill," Tom said from the porch. "What are you talking about? We ain't got no locusts around here, least ways I never seen any."

"Well, they're coming all the same. Coming from Oklahoma. Chomping everything in sight. Billions and billions of 'em. Making twenty or even fifty miles a day. They'll be here in a few days."

Alarmed, Tom asked: "What can we do? I can't let them eat my crops."

"Ain't nothing you can do. They settle in on a place and eat every blessed shoot, leaf and blade of grass. If it's green they eat it. I'd just clear out if I was you. Come back and start over after they've gone."

As the man turned his team back onto the dusty road, Tom didn't say anything. He simply started for the barn to begin his daily chores.

"Well, ain't you gonna say nothin'?" Leone asked. "What are we gonna do?"

Continuing to walk, Tom looked back over his shoulder and said that they would talk about it that evening. But, his mind was suddenly churning like a mill wheel. He thought:

As if I don't have enough problems trying to make a go of it on this no good, lousy piece of ground. Now I got to deal with a plague right out of the

Bible. Locusts. Who ever thought they was a real plague? But I'm going to make a plan. I ain't going down without a fight.

That evening at supper hardly a word was said. All were waiting for Tom to begin.

Finally, he started:

"Gracie, that was as fine a peach cobbler as I ever ate. You're becoming quite the cook. But now I got something to talk about that ain't near so pleasant. We got to fight them locusts and I think I know how to save our farm."

"Tom," Jim interrupted, "I ain't never seen a locust. What do they look like anyway?"

"I ain't never seen one, either," Tom answered, "but as far as I can tell, they's like grasshoppers, huge grasshoppers."

"What are we going to do?" an obviously frightened Leone asked. "What's the plan?"

Tom solemnly looked each of them in turn and then announced: "First of all, we ain't gonna panic and you all got to do your part. Then we are gonna build us a barrier—a barrier of smoke and fire. We'll line the entire west side of our property with brush and hay and branches and limbs and grass and everything we can find. When they start coming, we'll set it all afire. It'll be so hot and smoky them locusts will go somewhere else, they'll go around us."

"How much time we got, Tom?" Jim asked.

"Don't rightly know, but I think about a week. The postman says they's in Oklahoma now and of course they got most of Arkansas to cross before they get to us."

"How do you know this plan will work, Tom?" Leone questioned, the fear still evident in her voice. "Has a barrier like that ever worked before?"

"It's gonna work because it's got to. No, I don't know if anyone else has tried it, but we'll do it and we're gonna make it work. We'll have fire and smoke going up hundreds of feet in the air. We'll make it so's no gol-durned grasshopper could possibly get past."

Despite the confidence Tom displayed to the others, inside he wasn't nearly so sure. *Oh, sweet Jesus,* he thought more than once, *I sure hope this works.*

"And, we're gonna call it, 'Tom's Barrier'," Gracie unexpectedly piped up with a smile.

"Yes, Gracie," Leone smiled back at her. "Good for you. That's the spirit. We'll call it 'Tom's Barrier'. No bugs are going to get our crops."

Tom smiled also, but when he was tense or upset the two or three inches of the stump of his right arm that extended below his intact elbow joint had a way of quivering. Only Leone noticed that little piece of arm shivering now like she had never seen it shiver before.

Tom's west property line was the better part of a mile long and because he had not planted his crops right up to the line, it was mostly tall grass, weeds and shrubs, interspersed here and there with small stands of immature trees. The plan was to use this undeveloped area as the base of the barrier and then pile on dry branches and limbs, collected from where they had fallen on the edges and most rocky, unplowable areas of the farm. Next to it, they would pile up green stuff—grass, limbs, leaves—and hold them in reserve. After the base was pretty well engulfed in flames, they would add the greenery, hopefully to produce clouds of fire, heat and smoke.

"How long we got to keep it going, Tom?" Jim asked the next morning as they began loading axes, shovels and other tools in the wagon.

"I figure only an hour or so. I'm counting on getting the bunch out in front turned and the others following. They'll fly right around us."

"Can't they cut back in to our property once they get past the barrier?" Gracie wanted to know.

"Well, yeah, they can, but we can't do nothing about them that does that. Maybe kill a few by hand, but it's the main bunch we got to worry about. Got to get them headed off in another direction."

"Leone," Tom then turned to his wife to say, "when we get down there, you feed Loyce and then find a piece of shade to put him in. Hopefully, he'll sleep most of the time. But if he squalls some, he'll just have to do it. You work as long as you can and then go feed and change him. Then come back and work some more. We got to have you down there working. We're short-handed as it is. I hate it, too, but that's just the way it's got to be."

To himself Tom added, *And please, please don't have a spell. I need you like I've never needed you before.*

All the while Leone was thinking, *Oh my land, what am I gonna do if the Devil is in them flames. Please, Lord, protect me from that. Don't let him give me another spell.*

• • • • • •

Taking breaks only for necessary food and sleep, the four of them worked from dawn to dusk, and by the eighth day they were exhausted. However, Tom's Barrier was ready. Along the property line they had piled dry brush and branches as high as Tom and Jim could throw it. The corn and tobacco growing nearby had been plowed under so the fire could not spread to the fields, and huge heaps of greenery sat nearby. Every few yards were matches and canning jars filled with kerosene.

"Do you suppose they ain't coming?" Gracie asked Tom as she stared at locust-free skies on the eighth morning.

"Yeah, I expect they'll be here all right. But we're ready. Or as ready as we'll ever be."

But the locusts didn't come. They didn't come that day and they didn't come the next. However, when Leone rose to join Tom the morning after that, he was standing in the doorway looking down across their fields.

"Look here," he said as he felt her approach. "Look at that sun. They're coming."

"Oh, Tom. It's red like blood."

It wasn't but a few minutes until the wagon was loaded and Tom was driving down to the property line. The plan was for them to position themselves at equal distances, and when the locusts started coming Tom would fire his pistol. That would be the signal to splash the kerosene on the waiting piles and light them. Then, after the dry heaps were flaming, Tom would fire another shot and they would begin adding the greenery.

Jim was the first to be dropped off. As he hopped down, a few locusts were already arriving. He grabbed one of them of the out of the air and inquisitively examined it. Then he held it up for the others to see.

"Would you look at that," he said. "They ain't nothing but plain old grasshoppers. Maybe a little bigger than most, but just millions of durned old grasshoppers."

As the main horde flew closer, the sky took on an ominous, ever darker cast. There was no denying its fraught and foreboding message.

Having dropped the others off at their respective places, Tom parked the wagon near his end and waited. After only a few minutes, he could see beyond the advance scattering of bugs to the blackness of the main body. They were packed together as close as twigs in a pile, increasingly darkening the sky like a full eclipse of the sun.

As the pestilence came on and the locusts began to fill the air around him, Tom held his Colt .45 revolver in the air and fired. Then he began running down the line, dousing and lighting as he went. Because of rises and swales he couldn't see along the entire length of the barrier, but smoke rising from the other end told him that the others were doing the same.

Soon, the entire line was engulfed. Flames rose forty, fifty, even a hundred feet in the air. Dead, dying and singed locusts began to fall out of the sky like black hail.

Oh, Lordy, Jim thought as he lit the last of his section, *this must be what hell is like.*

But in spite of the flames, many of the bugs were getting through. Some were flying over the conflagration.

Like a general surveying a battlefield, Tom stopped and regarded the situation. After a few seconds, he again raised the Peacemaker and fired. Then, sweating and panting, he began running back along the roaring barrier, using his pitchfork to toss on large clumps of greenery. Billows of choking, blinding black and gray smoke rose up, almost blocking out what little light was left. Though barely able to see, and through almost unbearable heat, Tom threw and threw and threw.

When most of his greenery was on the flames, he continued running to help Gracie. Overcome by smoke and heat, she had collapsed on the ground, where she lay, coughing. As he dragged her away from the enveloped barrier, she managed to say:

"Don't mind me, Tom. Go do what you got to do. I'll be OK."

Rushing back to the furious inferno, Tom continued to pile on the smoke producing greenery. When he completed Gracie's section, he continued down the line to help Leone. Covered in soot and ash, she was working as best she could, but visibly faltering. Almost pushing her out of the way he yelled, "Git out of the way. Git over there and feed the baby. I'll do this part."

With almost the last of his strength, Tom worked his way along until he met up with Jim, who was similarly completing his section. Only then did Tom become aware of the fact that the grasshoppers were no longer falling. Smoke towered far into the sky and apparently none of them would, or could, fly high enough to go over it. They were going elsewhere.

Realizing that they had won, the two spent and almost unrecognizable dirty and cinder-covered men fell into each other's arms, deliriously laughing.

"Tom's Barrier worked," Jim screamed. "It worked."

Not bad for a one-armed man, Tom thought with an exhausted smile as he ran to Leone and the baby.

• • • • • •

After it was clear that disaster had been averted, it took some time for the bone-tired locust fighters to recover. First, they had to take care of the more mundane things, the foremost of which was something to eat, for themselves and for the baby. By the time Tom pulled the wagon up next to Leone, she already had Loyce at her breast. He was sucking hungrily, recovering from the distress he had so loudly voiced while waiting alone for her in the basket. Food for the adults waited for them in the wagon box, where it had lain untouched all morning while they were too busy to eat.

"Leone, Honey, soon as Loyce has had enough of your titty, git up here. I know you're exhausted. We all are. But I want to get at that food you fixed. I'm so hungry I could eat the north end out of a south bound goat."

It wasn't long until Loyce was contentedly cooing in his basket and Leone was passing out the smoked meat, biscuits and cheese. After everyone had eaten their fill, Leone stood up and put her weary arms around Tom's neck. "Tom, I am so proud of you," she said. "You did it. Not another man on this earth could have been so smart and come up with a plan that worked so well." Then, laying her head on his shoulder, she began a soft cry.

"Honey, is them tears?" he said. "What's that all about? We won. No need for tears."

She didn't answer and didn't move. With Milly slowly pulling the wagon down the dusty ash-laded road to the house, the young wife and mother continued her soft whimper all the way home.

Jim and Gracie paid no attention. They already had their tired eyes closed and lay silently in the back of the wagon.

"Tom," Jim roused to say after a bit, "maybe we could have a little pull on that shine jug even if it ain't evening yet. I got a powerful need for a drink."

"I reckon that would be a right fine idea," Tom said. "I'd be pleased to join you. Maybe even a little slug for the women folk."

"Me, too?" Gracie questioned with enthusiasm.

"Yeah, I reckon you, too," Tom responded. "You did a full woman's work today and you're entitled. But, just one, mind you. And a little one at that."

A few minutes later, the four of them had dismounted next to the house and Jim was leading Millie to the barn.

"Durn," Tom said as he looked down at his filthy overalls and then over at Gracie's sooty dress, "I don't know whether to burn these duds or let you fix them and try to get them clean."

"I don't know, Tom," Gracie responded. "Whatever you want to do. But I'm going down to the creek and see if I can't scrub some of this stuff off. It's all over me, even in my underwear."

"Well of course. We all need a good scrub. Ain't that right Leone?"

But Leone didn't answer. She was still crying. Not whimpering as before, but starting a full-on sob. Ignoring Loyce still in his basket, she jumped out of the wagon and started for the front door even before the wagon had come to a stop.

"Where you going, Honey? Ain't you gonna get cleaned up?" Tom asked.

The next sound they heard was the door to Tom and Leone's

bedroom being slammed behind her. A continuing wail could then be heard even through the closed door.

"Is she saying something? I think they's some sort of words," Tom turned to Gracie to say. "but I can't understand them."

"I think she is, but I can't make it out," Gracie responded with alarm. "It's like another language. It's like she's saying words that ain't words."

Suddenly the front door flew open and a very naked Leone came running out of the house. Had Tom not take a step sideways to block her and grab her across the waist, she would have continued out into the fields.

Leone's expression had become one of wild alarm. She had taken her hair down from its customary bun, but had neither combed nor brushed it. It flew around her head like Medusa's. As her eyes lolled wide and wantonly, an eerie cackle emerged from deep from inside her. Over and over again she grunted and growled something more akin to animal noises than human words.

Gracie, too shocked to move, stood staring as Tom threw the now-passive, but still howling Leone over his shoulder. As he carried her back to their bedroom, Tom thought, *Oh, Lord, here we go again. First locusts and now Leone. When will it ever end?*

Cradling and cuddling her as best he could, Tom lay with her the rest of the night, as her howls gradually went from body-racking to periodic screams to, finally, subdued moans.

• • • • • •

Tom's custom was to rise with the sun, or even before. This day, however, the sun had been up for hours before he opened his eyes. Looking to the side without moving his head, he saw that finally Leone was at peace. She was asleep. Gently sliding his arm from beneath her, he admired her untroubled face for a few seconds and then rose to stand next to the bed, where he took a moment to lovingly watch her slowly rising and falling chest and over-full breasts.

Oh, Honey, he thought, *just look at you. Like an angel. My lovely angel. But what are you going to be like today? Please God, please don't let her be like she was last night. She don't deserve it. We don't deserve it.*

Turning his thoughts to the baby, Tom thought he remembered Gracie bringing him in to nurse at least twice during the night and although the infant was not as yet screaming, he knew that it wouldn't be long. "Gracie," he softly called for his sister, "bring Loyce in here, please. He needs his breakfast."

When Gracie placed the boy at his mother's breast, Leone, without opening her eyes, pleasantly murmured something, turned on her side and lovingly cuddled the infant with both arms. Tom and Gracie observed for a minute and then went to the living room. They left the door to the bedroom open.

"I think she's going to be OK now," Tom tentatively offered. "Neither one of us got any sleep last night, but it seems to have worn off. She's calm now. Been sleeping for a bit. But Gracie, I'm so glad you're here. I don't know what we would have done without you. Did you get any sleep?"

"Some. In between bringing Loyce in for feedings and diaper changes."

Leone slept until nightfall, interrupted only by Gracie returning Loyce for his feedings. Tom had instructed Gracie to immediately call for him if there was need, and returned to the fields to join Jim, who was already beginning to replant what they had plowed under when the locusts had threatened the day before.

At the end of the day, and as the others were finishing the dinner Gracie had prepared for them, Leone emerged from the bedroom. She was wearing a dress and although her hair was still disheveled, she had at least taken a few swipes at it with a brush. Her face still contained traces of soot and ash. Tom and his siblings stared expectantly. She shyly looked back and then, dropping her gaze to the floor, said: "I got to get cleaned up. I'm going down to the creek. I'll do those dishes soon as I come back."

"Honey," Tom said with concern, "are you all right? Never mind them dishes. Are you OK?"

"I'm good. Is Loyce sleeping?"

He was, but by the time Leone had cleaned herself and returned, he was fussing. With an embarrassed smile, she silently smiled at each of the others in turn, and then gathered Loyce from his crib to feed him.

As she seated herself in her customary chair alongside the window, she stared out across the now-darkening fields.

"Leone, Honey,' Tom said to her after a bit, "I've got some good news. At least I hope you'll think it's good news. Pa and Sallie is coming for a visit."

"Why, of course, Tom, that's great news. When they coming? Did the locusts eat 'em out?"

"The boy that brought the news said they'd be here Thursday. Didn't say how many young'uns they would be bringing. Guess we'll have to put down pallets. If you wasn't nursing, we'd give 'em our bedroom."

"But," she persisted, "what about the locusts?"

"Missed them entirely, the boy said. They're all fine. Seems them blessed grasshoppers went south of Pa, turned and went way down by Oil Trough and near Hickory Valley."

"But Tom," Leone abruptly changed tone to say, "I've got something I've got to say about Sallie. She ain't quite right; not quite right in the head."

Oh, Honey, Tom thought, *can you really be saying this. First you start carrying on like nothing happened, like you didn't go crazy. And now you start talking about Sallie being tetched. Don't you realize what happened yesterday?*

"Tom, are you listening to me?" Leone said as she realized Tom was staring, lost in his own thoughts, and not listening to her.

"I reckon you're right. Sallie ain't quite right," he finally responded, "but she ain't bad. She and Pa had that little boy and that seems to have sobered her some, even if she was in pretty bad shape after her newborn died."

"Well, all the same, I don't want her holding Loyce. I'll tend to Loyce and she can help Gracie in the kitchen."

"Tom," Jim finally joined the conversation, "think we should hide the whiskey? The last time Pa was here, he gol-durned near drank all we had. I don't know why he don't bring his own. You know he's still making it."

"I ain't hiding the whiskey. The day will never come when I can't offer my own pa a drink when he comes to call."

Later that evening, after records were played, there was a short Bible reading and more discussion about how they had defeated the locusts, Tom and Leone excused themselves to turn in. As soon as they had closed the door, he said to her: "Honey, you didn't say nothing about what happened yesterday. Don't you want to talk about it?"

"Why I reckon we talked about it. Your barrier worked just like you said it would. You want to talk about it some more?"

"No, I mean about what happened after that. What happened with you."

"I don't remember nothing about me. Except fighting them locusts, of course. That, and I reckon we had dinner and went to bed, like we always do. Did something unusual happen? I don't recall anything unusual happening."

Baffled, Tom stared at her and then climbed into bed to lie awake pondering the situation and what he could do to help his beloved wife, and himself.

••••••

As their pa's buckboard bounced along the dry, rutted road approaching the house, Tom and Jim saw that Sallie was driving. Dan was in the back, seated along with Hubert, the couple's seven-year old son, on a pile of flour sacks.

"Pa," Jim yelled out to chide, "now I see why you keep marrying these young ones. You make 'em do all the work. Now you got this one driving."

"Yeah," Dan laughingly responded in his characteristic high whine of a voice, "but this one is only sixteen years younger. Louella, God rest her soul, was twenty-one years younger."

"Sallie," Leone appeared with Gracie to say, "don't you pay these rapscallions no mind at all. They's just jealous because they ain't as young as us. Now get down off that wagon and come on in out of the sun to where it's cooler. I got supper almost fixed."

"I ain't worried about supper," Sallie responded. "I want to see that young'un of yours. I expect he's almost walking."

As the three women headed inside the house, Hubert, no one having said a word to him, simply trailed along behind. Dan hitched his horse to the rail and the three men sauntered to the rocking chairs on the porch, where Tom had a fresh plug of his home-cured chewing tobacco lying on each one.

The first thing both groups wanted to talk about was, of course, the locusts. Word of Tom's successful barrier had already spread throughout Northeast Arkansas and beyond, and Dan and Sallie were proudly aware of how the conflagration Tom had built had driven the pests off. Similarly, Tom and Jim by the same gossip route knew that due to some fluke, the millions of grasshoppers had not attacked the area of Dan's farm, but had gone south.

After a while, having almost exhausted the meat of that conversation, Dan raised an eyebrow toward Tom and said:

"Son, that ride was mighty dusty. Long, too. I sure could use a drink."

"Why, Pa," Tom smiled, "You an elder in the Presbyterian Church, a drinking man? I have never heard the like."

"Quit your funning and get that jug out here," his father answered.

Even though Jim looked on with disapproval, when Tom returned with the whiskey, he took a short pull. However, as his father and brother traded the brown jug back and forth, he refused more and was a dour contrast to their jocularity.

Suddenly from inside the house arouse a scream, a continuing, blood-curdling scream. It was a piercing, devilish cry that all knew could only have come from Leone.

The men jumped to their feet and rushed inside to find Leone in the living room, bent over at the waist, with her arms wrapped around herself, screaming the loudest scream any of them had ever heard. Beyond Leone, in the section of the living room that acted as the kitchen, they could see a large cast iron skillet, from which were erupting almost ceiling-high flames.

Oh, no, not again, Tom thought, hoping against hope that Leone's recent episode was not about to be repeated.

Before the others could react, Sallie grabbed a box of baking soda and emptied is contents on the flames. The fire was immediately extinguished.

Seeing that the situation was handled, Tom comforted Leone. Hugging her tightly, he looked over her shoulder to ask Sallie:

"What happened? Why is she screaming?"

"Tom, I surely don't know. The skillet caught fire, like they sometimes do, and she started yelling. What's wrong with her, anyway? I put it out."

Tom took Leone to the bedroom and after a few minutes her cries had diminished and, as she fell asleep, ceased entirely. Trying to make sense of it all, Tom thought of the "spell" Leone had had on the night of the fight against the locusts. He remained with her for an hour or so and until he thought she would rest peacefully for the rest of the night.

Returning to the porch, while Sallie, Gracie and Hubert remained in the kitchen, Tom found that the jug was almost empty. While his father had consumed most of it, the episode with Leone had so distressed Jim that, against his initial firm resolve, he, too, had partaken generously. Undismayed, Tom went around the side of the house to the back and retrieved a second jug from his stash. In short order, he had "caught up" and the three men were quite drunk.

Spewing a long stream of tobacco juice which entirely missed a nearby spitoon, Dan said:

"Tom, I know you're mightily concerned about Leone. Me, too. But I got a problem, as well. It's Sallie. She ain't quite right either. I ain't never seen her act out like Leone just did, but sometimes, she just ain't quite right. Your mother sometimes did things I didn't quite understand, but Sallie can just do things that don't make no sense."

"Pa, you don't know the half of it. You should have seen Leone the evening after we drove off them locusts. She was stark raving mad. And Pa, she's going to have another young'un. Soon we're gonna have two little ones. I'm worried."

"You know what I think, Tom," Dan slurred. "I think we got us a couple fragile ones. This farming life's pretty durn hard. Especially for women, what with them having babies and all. Sometimes they just can't handle it. Me and Sallie ain't gonna have no more. Maybe you and Leone shouldn't either."

"Pa, it's a little late to be saying that."

CHAPTER NINE

Leone's pregnancy with the child they named Clifford went well, although over Tom's objection she again insisted on having the baby at her father's. She said she wouldn't feel comfortable having anyone else but Hattie help with the delivery. And from shortly after she had learned she was pregnant until after the infant was born, she had had no more serious "spells." There had been one incident with a dropped lantern in the barn, but Tom had so quickly covered her eyes and hustled her outside and away from the flames, that she hardly had time to react.

One night after the others were asleep and she and Tom were reading in bed, she abruptly put down her novel to say:

"Tom, is it right to thank the Lord that I ain't had no more spells, when he was the one who gave them to me in the first place?"

"What do you mean he gave them to you? They's some that would say the Devil gave them to you."

"Well, if God knows all and controls all, like everyone says he does, then I guess he gave them to me, just the same as he took them away. And, if they's a God, why did he let the Devil give them to me?"

"I reckon a preacher would say you got them for a reason, maybe a reason we ain't capable of understanding. Maybe you should talk to my pa about it."

"Like there's a reason for giving diseases to little babies and you being born with half an arm?"

"I don't know, Leone. I surely can't understand it all. I'm just trying to raise my crops and young'uns, and get on the best I can."

•••••••

Even though he was now more than thirty years of age, and to the surprise of everyone who knew him, Jim had remained unmarried. He continued to be an integral part of Tom's household, and not only did at least half the work, but for those times when a male perspective was needed, provided Tom with someone he could confide in and rely on for sound advice. However, he rarely volunteered anything. He was like a solid, quiet presence who was always there, but almost never called attention to himself.

Although Jim might have suspected it, Tom never told him that one of Tom's greatest fears was for the day when Jim would announce that he was striking out on his own. Tom knew it was probably coming eventually, but that knowledge didn't make it any easier to anticipate. Especially for the spring plowing, it would be hard to carry on without Jim.

As for Gracie, just entering her teen years, she certainly wasn't the most reliable member of the household, and sometimes complained as much as she worked. But she too, did her share, or almost so. But she made no secret of her desire to grow up and get married, perhaps not in that order, so she could get off the farm and into a town where she thought all real life existed.

But all in all, things went smoothly. Loyce and Clifford were strong and healthy. The weather largely cooperated, sparing the family a major flood, fire or tornado, and even the winters had been mild. There had been only an occasional dusting of snow and none of the icy rain that could freeze into sleet and be so destructive to crops, animals and transportation.

And although you couldn't prove it by Gracie's frequent complaints, it was not all hard work. In addition to visits to and from neighbors and family, as well as an occasional barn-raising, and trip to the creek to swim, the Whiteners had become quite regular in their church attendance. Every Sunday morning after Tom and Leone had shut their bedroom door to put on their "Sunday best," Leone would stop

Tom, put both hands on his face to look up at him and say something like:

"Honey, you ain't gonna drink too much today, are you? Now you promise me that you ain't gonna get drunk."

And, although he might have a quick pull or two out behind the church, he would be as good as his word and would remain generally sober.

Then the news Tom had been half-expecting, but for some reason was still surprised at. Leone was again pregnant. Loyce was not yet four, Clifford not even out of diapers and they were about to have a third.

"Well, ain't you gonna say anything?" Leone asked with some pique after she told him and he didn't respond.

"Honey, I'm just as pleased as punch, that's for sure. But I guess I just didn't expect it. I'm a little surprised."

"A little surprised?" she said sharply. "We been doing it three, four times a week. I ain't never told you, no. What did you expect? And you was the one told me you wanted a whole passel of kids. I remember it like yesterday. Those were your exact words. You said you wanted a whole passel of them."

"I know, Honey, I know," he said quietly, looking at her as gently as he could, "but what if you start having "spells" again?"

"A little late to be worrying about that now, ain't it? You should have thought of that before you was sticking it in me every chance you got."

●●●●●●

Loyce's birth hadn't changed life much for Tom and Leone. They continued to work, relax and relate to each other as before. When Leone she was not actually feeding the good-natured baby, he would sleep or play next to her while she cooked, cleaned and took care of the hundreds of details required to make their house a home. For the times when she was needed to work in the garden or fields, Tom had helped her use some old coveralls to create a sling-like carrier. With the child strapped to her front and largely out of the way, she was free to do what she needed to do.

Even when Clifford was born a couple years later, things didn't change a lot. Gracie had to help with babies more than she was accustomed to, but the only major change was the appearance of a portable pen Tom built. He called it a "young'un cage." While the baby Clifford stayed where he was put, the now-walking Loyce needed to be restrained. With the "young'un cage" Leone could drag it to where it was needed to make sure he wouldn't run off or get into mischief.

And to Tom and Leone's eternal gratitude, Gracie unexpectedly took a motherly shine to both children. Gracie almost wouldn't let Leone do anything for either Loyce or for Clifford. If Clifford began to cry while the adults were eating, it was Gracie who jumped up to see what the problem was. If Leone was feeding Clifford, and Loyce needed attention, it was Gracie who rendered it. A stranger to the home would have thought the children Gracie was cooing to and caring for were her very own. Even as to the frequent diaper changes Gracie voiced no complaint.

However, when Otto was born a couple years after Clifford, just the magnitude of caring for three little ones not only began to change the way the little farm operated, it began, imperceptibly at first, to change the family relationships. After a few months, the once frequent "please," "if you wouldn't mind" and "if it wouldn't be too much trouble" had fallen into almost complete disuse, replaced by requests which were more like commands. Now, even Gracie rarely asked anyone to do something. She told them what she wanted them to do. And of course, "thank-yous" became almost completely unknown. At the dinner table, once a place of lightness, joking and good-natured ribbing, the pervasive kidding was replaced by frequent long silences and bone-weary complaints about work not done, work not done properly or chores there had not been enough time for.

Tom was the first to comment on this.

"Y'all listen up now," he said at supper one evening after a particularly long time when no one had said anything. "I got something to say and it's important.

This family has changed. We ain't hardly a family any more. We used to be nicer to each other and we used to have more fun. I remember when I used to come to supper as much for the pleasure of the conversation as for the food. Now, I just come to eat. So, let's change. Let's go back to the way we was. I want my family back."

From her end of the table, Leone listened intently, but didn't say anything. Instead, she thought, *Be nicer to each other? What's he talking about? I ain't got no energy to be nicer. I'm tired all the time. What with these kids constantly needing attention, and chores all blessed day, I'm even too tired to read at night.*

"Well, ain't nobody gonna say anything?" Tom finally asked. "Jim, say something?"

Mirroring Leone's thoughts, Jim lowered his eyes to voice some of them:

"It's just that they's so danged much work to do. Seems like farming has become a lot harder. Seems like they's more to do. Especially since we put in more cotton. Cotton takes a lot more work. And this ground. I don't know why we got to have such piss poor rocky ground. We shoulda got us a piece over by the Mississippi."

"Jim," Tom responded sternly, "we've talked about that a bunch of times and you know we can't afford no ground over there. We was lucky enough to get the bank to go a mortgage for what we got now."

Whereupon Otto, in his crib on the side of the room, began to whimper. Before anyone could say anything, Gracie jumped up and to hold him, but he would not be comforted. His whimper turned into a full-on cry. This woke Clifford from his sleep and he, too, joined in. Even though the four-year old Loyce continued to sleep, the ear-piercing cacophony of the two others disturbed and disconcerted the already irritated adults.

Suddenly, Leone responded with her own scream. With wide eyes and unmitigated despair, at the top of her lungs she yelled, "I can't do this any more," and ran into the bedroom.

●●●●●●

When Leone ran to the bedroom, Tom immediately followed, leaving his brother and sister to care for the three little ones. Laying down next to his gently sobbing wife, he tried to comfort her. Although she threw her arms around his neck and held him close, she refused to respond to his tender words. Instead, she kept up an almost soundless soft moan which continued far into the night. Eventually, still holding Tom, she fell asleep. Tom's last thought before he, too, drifted off was that he hoped that in the morning all would be better.

But it wasn't. The next morning Leone awoke with the sun to go to the outhouse, but immediately returned to bed. When Gracie brought Otto to her for feeding, she provided her breast, but when he was done, immediately called for Gracie to come and get him. As before, she didn't respond to Tom's affirmations of love for her or assurances that all would be good again. She just looked at him with eyes that saw, but didn't communicate.

And so it went all day. She went to the outhouse as needed, fed Otto when Gracie brought him, and refused all offers of food. Even when Tom insisted that she drink from the glass he held against her lips, she took only a sip.

At noon when Jim returned home for the dinner Gracie had prepared, he asked about Leone and then said:

"Tom, I appreciate that Leone needs you, but I need your help. You got to come help me with that sow. She's having a real hard time of it."

Gracie looked at Tom expectantly as she spooned more mashed potatoes onto their plates.

"I'm sorry, Jim," Tom responded, his sad eyes attesting to his regret. "Leone needs me, and I got to be here with her. You'll just have to make do as best you can. I'll come help as soon as I can."

Returning to the bedroom to lay next to his wife and caress her forehead, Tom again began to carry on a monologue he hoped she was hearing. He had already exhausted his limited store of gossip and small talk and so instead he turned to the past.

"Remember that first night at the dance, Honey? Remember how I just walked right up and asked you to dance? And you said, 'What happened to your arm'? Remember that? And I was as nervous as a whore in church but trying not to show it. Remember that?"

Thinking he saw expression in her eyes and taking it for approval he went on. As she lay silently next to him staring at the ceiling, he recounted their entire history. He moved from the dance, to when John Bell had run him off, and eventually to when she had showed up on his doorstep. One of his fondest memories was of the time they had first gone to the river and made love in the open air. He almost started to recount that day, but suddenly caught himself and thought:

No, I ain't gonna tell that. I got a better idea. I'm just gonna take her to the river like before. It will be just like the first time.

"Honey," he said to her, "we're going to the river tomorrow. Would you like that? Just you and me. I'll get Gracie to make us some sandwiches and we'll have a picnic and I'll give you a nice long massage, just like that first time. You would like that, wouldn't you?"

Leone didn't respond, but just continued her shallow, even breathing, her eyes soft and non-committal.

By mid-morning the next day all was ready. Tom led the still-silent Leone to the wagon and helped her up to the seat. After Gracie placed the lunch and blankets in the back, she looked up at Leone to say:

"And don't you worry about a thing. I got it all handled. I got cow's milk for Otto, food for Clifford and, if he gets feisty and won't mind, a switch for Loyce. I'll take good care of them. Y'all have a good time and come back as late as you want. But look out for them chiggers. And poison ivy, too. Be especially careful of that poison ivy."

As he had the evening before, on the way to the river Tom kept up a constant stream of light chatter, voicing whatever thought entered his head. However Leone's silence continued. No matter what he said, her neutral expression did not change. When they arrived at the thicket concealing Tom's secret beach and swimming hole, Leone didn't wait to be helped from the wagon. She simply hopped down, took the picnic basket and began walking to the path behind the bushes.

During the remainder of the day she seemed to be listening to Tom and did whatever he asked her to do. When he asked for help spreading out a blanket, she immediately grabbed one end. When he asked her to take off her dress so he could lead her into the water, she quickly pulled it over her head. After a lengthy massage, she turned onto her back and willingly spread her legs. But she didn't say one word. Allen was born exactly nine months later.

During the time of her pregnancy, Leone had started out as silent and morose but as her belly grew, her ability to converse and interact with others improved somewhat. However, the old Leone was gone. Even at her best, just before Allen was born, she was a pale imitation of her former self. Rarely smiling, usually not exhibiting interest in others and speaking only when necessary or when spoken to, she did what was expected of her and little more. Even the new jokes Tom occasionally brought home from Batesville or Sandtown, eleciting guffaws from the others, produced in Leone only a wan smile. Invitations to attend church with the others were met with polite declinations.

Tom's emotional reaction to his wife's changes ran the gamut from anger to sadness to despair. One day he would be angry at her for not being the woman he had married. The next he would be angry at himself for not being more understanding. When he was sad it was with a deep sorrow which clouded his soul and colored his every thought and action. When he experienced despair, it was all he could do to get out of bed, work and keep up his facade of unfailing strength. Through it all and with all the stability he could muster, he tried to make sure that Leone never saw the lengthening cracks in his armor, that she always saw him as a pillar of toughness she could count on. There were even rare occasions of optimism when he thought that surely she would get better, that inevitably the doctors would find a cure for her.

Just before Allen was born, Leone's expectation of the new baby did infuse her with a little of her old spark, but immediately after he was born, she again withdrew inside herself. Nothing Tom or the others could do or say generated interest or excitement. As a result, Tom, Jim and Gracie took on increasingly important roles in raising the children. When one of them was hurt, he was as likely to run to Tom or Gracie as to their very own mother. If one of the boys wanted to show off a new find or accomplishment, Tom or Jim would usually be approached. But Leone didn't seem to be bothered by this. She simply looked on with seeming disinterest and went on about her business.

Naturally, word of Leone's decline got back to her father and finally after lengthy entreaties from Hattie and Mabel, John Bell was convinced to put aside his announced dislike for Tom and pay a visit. He would be accompanied by his new wife, Mattie, and their child, Leone's half-sister, Naomi.

Arriving one afternoon in a hired carriage much fancier than the plain work wagon used by Tom's family, John Bell and his new family were made welcome, offered the best chairs in the shade on the front porch, and served lemonade and iced tea.

"Well, Leone," John Bell said to his daughter after some initial small talk, "git that young'un out here. I come all this way to see my grandson and I want to see him."

"He's sleeping right now," Gracie answered for Leone. "Can you wait until he wakes up?"

"Gracie," John Bell looked at the girl, "when I address my daughter, I expect that she'll answer. No need to hear from anyone else."

"Yes sir," Gracie quietly replied, looking down at her feet.

"Leone," the older man continued, "what about it? Can I see that boy now?"

Leone's expression didn't change, and she didn't say anything. Instead she quietly rose, went into the house and immediately returned with her still-sleeping infant.

"No, I don't want to hold him," John Bell said as Leone offered the baby to him. "I still ain't all that comfortable holding these little ones."

Then, breaking into a broad smile as he looked at the baby:

"But he sure is cute, ain't he? He's cute as a button. I usually don't much cotton to babies, but this one is special. You did real good, Leone. Real good."

"And, what about me?" Tom piped up with a proud smile.

"I reckon you didn't have much to do with it except a few minutes pleasure," John Bell glared at Tom. "Leone did all the work."

Then, looking at the still silent Leone, her father softly said to her:

"Honey, why don't you take your baby and you womenfolk go on in the house. You, too, Jim. I need to talk to Tom."

When they were alone, John Bell looked intently at Tom and said:

"Is this the way she is all the time?"

"Pretty much. She just seems to go on. No enthusiasm for anything. She don't sing anymore and she don't even like to listen to records on the Victrola, like she used to."

"Did you take her to the doctor?"

"Yes. Took her to Doc Pritchard. He says she's got the pellagra and they ain't much to be done about it. He recommended frequent doses of castor oil, but that didn't seem to do any good. He said we could take her to a specialist or psychiatrist in Little Rock, but he didn't think that would help, either."

"Tom, I took her to a specialist. In Memphis. Didn't she tell you that? Years ago. Stayed at the Peabody Hotel even. Cost me twenty dollars to have some so-called expert tell me to give her laudanum. I've seen how that opium makes a vegetable out of them, and how they get addicted and can't quit. We didn't hardly do that."

"No, John Bell, she never told me about that."

"What about a sweat box? I heard the other day that maybe you can sweat it out of them."

"Yep, I asked Doc Pritchard about that, too. He said only Indians get any good out of sweat boxes. Besides, sounds like torture to me."

"But Tom, what I don't understand is what brought it on. Hattie and Mabel has grown up into fine wives and mothers. Both of 'em is even stronger than their husbands. Leone just keeps getting worse?"

"John Bell, I surely don't know. Nothing particular happened. Like we all know, she's always been a little different. But we was all just going on, working a lot, like always. We was all tired. Maybe Leone a little more so, because she was up all the time with the babies. But one day she just flew up from the supper table and ain't been the same since. Well, she's a little better than she was. Some days she's pretty much normal. But she sure ain't like she was. Got me worried sick. I just don't know what to do. And, now with four littles ones . . ." Tom's voice trailed off and his eyes glistened.

"Wipe your eyes, Tom," John Bell said not unsympathetically. "You know, Tom, I came up here half thinking that I would take my daughter and the baby home with me. Me and Mattie discussed it and she's willing. But I just can't see that me and Mattie could do anything better for her than you're already doing, except maybe one thing—how's your drinking, Tom? You still hitting the bottle?"

"Not much, John Bell and that's God's honest truth. Sometimes of an evening me and Jim will have us a snort, but that's it, just one or two. I got too much responsibility to be drinking like I used to."

●●●●●●

Got to keep my guard up. Can't let it down for a single blessed minute.

They think I don't know what's going on. Tom thinks I don't see and I don't hear, but I see and hear a heck of a lot more than they do. Got to be vigilant every second. One second is all it needs. Like that time at the supper table. I relaxed just a tiny bit and here it came, like a black, storming cloud. I ain't normal yet. I don't know if I'll ever be able to be like I was before.

Wish I could explain. Wish I could make 'em understand. Tom especially. He's the best husband a woman could ever have. He deserves a wonderful wife. I'm so sorry I'm like I am. Sometimes I think it's even worse for him than it is for me. At least I know the pellagra's got me and what I've got to do. He just thinks I'm crazy and calls it pellagra.

No! No! No! There it was again. Can't think about Tom. Got to only think about me and about it. It's like a cougar waiting to pounce any second I give it a chance.

I'm going to be strong. I ain't gonna let it get me. I'm gonna be strong so I can become a real mother to my kids again, so I can be the wife Tom wants. I'm going to spend every second staring it down. I'll look it in the eye with all my concentration and it ain't gonna get me. Then I'll get normal. I'll stare at it until it goes away forever and then I can become a real person again.

You hear that, Devil? You ain't gonna get me? I'm gonna fight you and fight you until you go back where you came from and stay there.

Yes, Leone, I am gonna get you. I'm as old as eternity and I've had millions before you. I've got forever and as long as it takes to get you.

Why me, Devil? What did I do? I never sinned.

Leone, you are a bad person. You are a bad, evil person and you belong with me. How many times do I have to tell you that?

No, I ain't. I'm good. I'm not evil.

If you was good, why would you have the pellagra?

You gave it to me.

Yes, I gave it to you, but I gave it to you because you're bad.

But, how am I bad? I was never bad before you gave me the pellagra.

Unworthiness and evil are your essence, Leone. It's got nothing to do with any good things you think you did. It don't make any difference if you're a good wife or how many kids you birth and nurture. You think going to church helps, but it don't. Church is just a comfort for folks afraid of death. It don't make no difference. Your spirit is evil and I will have you. You'll come to my side where you belong.

No, it's not true. It's a lie. I don't believe you. And God will save me.

God will save you? Leone, you should know God can't save you. You'll be mine. Fight me as long as you want, Leone, but I'll have you. You'll grow tired, and eventually you will be mine. And it's getting worse, ain't it? Your spells are getting worse and worse. Remember back to when you were young and the pellagra was just starting? Then, all you did was act a little strange sometimes. But your strangeness just got weirder and weirder. Admit it. You're getting closer and closer to my side.

No, it ain't true.

And after you, I'll have your kids. I'll get all four of them, just like I'll get you.

No, you'll never get my kids because you'll never get me. I'll keep on fighting and fighting until there ain't a breath left in me.

We'll see, Leone. We'll see. I'll see you again soon. Very soon. Now, I have others to tend to. But just remember, I'm always waiting. The first time you think I ain't there, I'll enter you like an exploding cancer and you'll be mine forever. Bye for now, Leone.

He ain't going to get them. Never. He ain't going to get Loyce, and he ain't going to get Clifford, and he ain't going to get Otto and he ain't going to get Allen. I don't care if Tom and Pa and the rest think I'm weak. I can't help it if they think I don't pay them no attention. I can't tell them what's going on. This is my fight and I've got to do it every second of every day. I'll do it for my young'uns. That Devil ain't gonna get them.

CHAPTER TEN

After the inquest and the evidence about Leone trying to burn up her own children, Tom and Jim rode home in silence, each lost in his own thoughts.

Tom's thoughts switched back and forth between rage when he remembered that she had tried kill their children, to soft remembrances of the beautiful times that had spent together—her bright, perky smile, the way she danced with her arm around him in a certain way to accommodate his missing arm, the laughter in her sparkling blue eyes. He could even hear the lilt in her voice as it rose and fell to accentuate chosen words in an unusual, endearing way. He smelled the light perfume she sparingly used because she knew there would likely be no money to buy another. He felt the freshness of her hair when it was newly washed and shining, and the softness of her skin.

Finally, Jim broke the silence to fondly remind Tom of the morning Leone showed up on the porch after having left Van Browning.

"She was like a lost kitten," he said, "wanting to be taken in and fed a saucer of milk."

"Yes, she was," Tom responded with warm remembrance. "She reminded me of that little spotted fawn we found motherless in the woods that time."

When the brothers reached home, Gracie and the children were anxiously standing on the porch. Tom saw that they expected him to say something, to tell them what had happened in court. But he wasn't up to it. He couldn't bring himself to say anything, and simply nodded to Gracie as he walked past, into the house.

Entering the bedroom which had been the place of so much joy, he closed the door behind him and sat down on the bed, lowering his head to his hand. Without tears and with unexpected calmness he began to review some of the best times of the past nine years with his beloved wife. As if thinking about Leone in happier circumstances would in some small way assuage his present grief, at random he encouraged good thoughts to occupy his head.

For no particular reason he thought of Leone's lightness and gregariousness at his father's sixtieth fifty-seventh birthday party, a few years back. More than one hundred friends, relatives and neighbors had gathered at Dan's farm for his celebration and it seemed to Tom that every one of them had commented on what a delight Leone was. Never had Tom felt prouder.

Or, on the occasion of Allen's birth, just two years ago, when he bragged to all who would listen that Leone had now given him four healthy sons, each one hung better than the previous one. Tom now smiled at the thought.

And of course no review of the best times of their marriage would have been complete without considering the wonderful times they had canoodeled and coupled, not only in their bed, but also in various other places on the farm and in the woods. Leone's passion an unexpected bonus to the lovemaking he had eagerly anticipated since the first night at the dance, Tom now relished the memories. Their sometimes furious love making, he thought with irony, made up some for the years he had spent with only his hand for solace.

Rising slowly, he took two steps to the old and battered armoire in which he and Leone stored their scant assortment of clothes. Looking to the bottom, he saw a row of shoes and boots, some with traces of field mud still on them. He looked at her best "Sunday-go-to-meeting" shoes, silently waiting for Leone to excitedly put them on to wear to some special event. Even an old pair of her work shoes elicited special feelings, as he remembered the times she had worn them to help him with the planting or harvesting.

Raising his eyes, he ignored his own well-worn work pants and shirts, and regarded Leone's three remaining dresses. The red calico print with little flowers was his favorite, and as he fingered a portion of the sleeve between his thumb and forefinger, the tears finally came. Despite the presence of loved ones just in the next room, Tom knew that he was now miserably alone.

••••••

"Damn, I miss her," Tom said to Carrie Shuler, the neighbor he had hired as a housekeeper after Leone was committed. It was a week or so after the inquest and the two sat in rocking chairs on the porch after dinner to drink and chew. As Tom sipped his whiskey, the two took turns spitting into the dirt.

"Especially her voice," he continued. "Did I ever tell you it was her voice that really got to me that first night at the dance? I couldn't seem to get enough of talking to her and just hearing her voice. Didn't make any difference what she said. I just loved the sound of her voice. I surely do miss that."

Carrie's farm was a couple miles down the road, closer to Batesville. Her husband had been was kicked by a mule and died a couple years back and Carrie continued on alone. A few days after Leone left, Carrie had brought Tom a peach cobbler, and suggested that while Leone was in the asylum, she could help out with the children.

Like her sister, Julia, before her, Gracie had suddenly eloped and Tom sorely needed help. She and Delpha Goad had one day found it imperative that they marry and strike out on their own. Typical of Gracie, the note she left for Tom said only: "Me and Delpha has run off to get married. Gracie."

Thus, Carrie's offer to come and help could not have come at a better time.

As opposed to Leone's svelte body and attractive still-youthful face, Carrie was not a handsome woman. She and Tom shared similar features—high, bony cheekbones, pronounced forehead, square jaw— however on Tom they gave him an attractive manliness, while on her they produced a coarse, unrefined visage. Even her broad shoulders and muscled arms were more similar to Jim's than they were to the more delicate of her sex. She came from hardy pioneer stock and showed it.

"And couldn't that girl harmonize?" Carrie answered while dipping her little chewed stick in her snuff, and again referring to Leone. "Goodness gracious she could sing. And when she and Gracie would sing "The Old Rugged Cross" it would just about bring tears to my eyes."

"Well, sing or not, her up and leaving like that is still a sore spot with me."

"Now, Tom, you know Gracie was almost twenty years old and already feeling like an old maid. Besides, she didn't like farm life no how. I reckon Delpha is a decent enough sort, and the two of them will do OK living in town. Besides, Leone will be home before you know it."

"Of course she will. After the inquest, the doctor told me they'll have her cured faster than green grass through a goose. He says they are doing research and coming up with new treatments all the time. Probably, just a short time until she'll be right as rain and back home again."

"Did the doctor really tell you that?" Carrie asked. "Could that be possible? She did try to burn up her own kids."

"Well, he didn't say it in so many words exactly, but something pretty close. She'll be home before Christmas, just you wait and see."

Oh, Lord, I hope that's true, Tom thought.

"I will pray for her every night and I surely do hope she'll be singing here in the kitchen soon. But just in case, I want you to know I'll be here as long as you need me. Just as long as you need me."

"You're great with the kids and every bit as good a cook as Leone, but I'm sure it will just be a short while. I'm much obliged to you no matter the time. I sure appreciate you helping out."

In spite of the apparent attention Tom was paying to his conversation with the widow, he could hardly keep his mind on what they were saying. Thoughts of Leone, thoughts of the asylum, thoughts of his house afire, thoughts of his fields and crops and animals, and, most importantly, thoughts of his children, distracted and consumed him. There was no peace. Alone and in private he had tried crying, tried screaming, tried cursing. Nothing helped.

Always there was this unfathomable hole in his soul, in his very being. More than once his thoughts turned to the big bore pistol he had used at the locust barrier.

And the longer they talked, the more he drank. Sips became swallows. Swallows became half glasses. Half glasses became long pulls directly from the jug.

Finally, seeing that further attempts at conversation were becoming pointless, Carrie mercifully suggested that it was time for bed, and padded off to the pallet she had made for herself in the back room.

●●●●●●

Leone had been gone for less than a month when Tom received the first letter from her. It read:

Dear Tom,

I am so sorry for what I did. I know I already told you that about a thousand times. I think about you and the kids and what I did constantly. I can't hardly think about anything else. I can't quit crying. I hope someday you can forgive me.

I don't know why I did it. I really don't. There was this voice in my head telling me to do it and I did. I guess I must really be crazy to have listened. There is a Devil, Tom, there really is. Now I know it for sure. But, just because there is a Devil doesn't mean I have to do what he says. I don't know why I did. I will never again be so weak. I promise.

And, I do seem to be some better. I'm getting along OK and not even as depressed as I thought I was going to be. I don't know why.

I've always loved you. Ever since the dance. You are the best man in the world for me and I adore you. I'm so sorry for the pain and hurt I've caused you. I would do anything to make it go away, to make that terrible day go away.

Things here in the asylum are pretty bad, but sometimes not so bad. They've got me in a section for the least crazy and some of the women here are real nice. Course we can hear the screams and yells from the next ward over. That's where they keep the real crazy ones. Just awful hearing them suffering like that. I'm sure glad I'm not with them.

Please come and see me, Tom. And bring the kids. And Jim and Gracie, too. Please, please, please. I'm so lonely and I miss you and the kids so much.

I'll write again soon. You write, too.
Your loving wife,
Leone

As much as he loved and missed her, Tom didn't know if he was ready to see her. He changed his mind about making the trip to Little Rock almost hourly, sometimes minute to minute. First he would remember her face, her voice, her body. When he was having those thoughts, he was ready to drop everything and fly to her. Then he would envision a flaming house and four screaming children. At those times, his hand involuntarily clinched into a fist and the muscles in his neck stood out like ties on a railroad track. He was barely able to contain his rage. The result of these swings was that indecision ruled. He just didn't know what to do and so he did nothing.

Finally, a few days after he had received Leone's letter, he wrote her back:

Dear Leone,

I'm sorry I haven't written before now. I've been pretty confused. Confused and hurt and missing you. For these past ten years, you have been the light of my life. Made it worth living. Now, without you, I'm sure that if I didn't have these young'uns, I couldn't go on. There's this huge hole in me that nothing can fill except you. Only having you back here with me can make me a real man again.

But I'm not ready to see you. Maybe real soon I will be, but not yet. As much as I try, I can't forget what you did. Sometimes I even hate you for it. I'm sorry, but that's the god's honest truth. Sometimes I think of our four little boys being burned up and I hate you.

Leone, did you ever hear the expression "star-crossed lovers"? That's us, star-crossed lovers. It means an evil star crossed our paths and brought us bad luck, a heap of real bad luck. First me with half an arm and then you with the pellagra. Then you trying to burn up the kids. Yes, an evil star.

The kids are all doing OK. They miss you something terrible. Except for

Loyce who remembers sometimes, they have all forgotten what you did and how scared they were. Well, Otto, he sometimes has nightmares. They all want to know when you're coming to be home. I tell 'em you'll be home real soon. I tell lthem the doctors are fixing you. That's right, ain't it? They're fixing you, ain't they? I sure do hope so. I think if you was all well again, and didn't have no spells, I could forget what you did.

And don't worry none about the kids. Gracie run off and got married with Delpha Goad (durn their hides, anyway) but Jim is still here, and I got Carrie Shuler (remember her? She's got that place down by Sulfur Creek) here to help out until you get well.

I pray for you every night. If there really is a devil, I pray God will smite him a mighty blow.

Your loving husband,
Tom

••••••

"Tom," Jim said late one afternoon as the two were unloading corn from a wagon, "something's on your mind, ain't it?" They had just harvested their fields and were putting it in bins in the barn. Even though the days were growing noticeably shorter, it was still warm, and they were working without shirts, the sweat pouring down their bodies and disappearing beneath their bib overalls. Large sleek muscles, grown, hardened and honed by thousands of hours in the fields glistened and strained.

"What you been thinking about? I know it ain't Leone because when you think about her, this sadness comes over you and you talk about her. You ain't said a word for a couple hours."

Tom forked a bit more corn in, dramatically stood his pitchfork on end and looked at his brother.

"What do you think they're getting for white mule in Memphis?"

"I don't know, but Prohibition starts in three or four months and the price is going to be a whole hell of a lot more than it has been."

"Exactly. What would you think if I told you I had heard that quality white mule is already bringing twenty-five dollars a gallon in Memphis and that it will be even more when all that people has got stashed away is used up? It's a seller's market."

"Prohibition is about the dumbest thing I ever heard of. Folks that voted for it ain't got a lick of sense."

"Jim, you don't understand. This is an opportunity."

"You talking about us becoming runners? Not just producing a few jugs for ourselves, but selling it?"

"You know what the price of cotton is. And corn ain't doing too good neither. Since the war ended, the whole country is in a sorry way. I don't know how we're going to make it as a family lessen we find some way to live besides farming."

"I don't know, Tom. Ain't selling the stuff a might risky?"

"I reckon. But what else we going to do? Jim, I figure that with a decent sized still we can make three gallons a week. That's purt near fifty dollars every week. Ain't that just about the most amount of money you ever heard of? How long do you think it would take us to bring in fifty dollars a week farming? We would have to have about five thousand acres and a crew of niggers to work it. You know that ain't going to happen."

"You said Memphis. Why couldn't we sell it in Little Rock? That's closer?"

"Why they's nothing doing in Little Rock. Memphis, that's where things are happening. Or, even St. Louis. Now Memphis, that's a real city even if it is right smart a piece down the road."

"And, how we going to get it there? Take four-five days to get to Memphis in the wagon."

"I been thinking on that, too. We're going to buy us a truck. Even on the back roads at night, in a truck we could be in Memphis in just a few hours and St. Louis in less than a day."

"What you going to use for money to buy a truck? You may be almost as handsome as me, but they ain't gonna sell you a truck on your good looks."

"I'll take out a mortgage on the farm. I can get a used truck for four or five hundred dollars and I got at least that much equity in the farm."

"For four or five hundred dollars you could buy a tractor. Wouldn't it be a lot better idea to buy a tractor so's we could quit using Millie? I'm plumb wore out watching her sorry ass up and down the rows every spring and fall. And farming is honest.”

"I thought about that, Jim. I figure with the crops on the added acreage we could farm using a tractor, we could bring in maybe three hundred dollars a year. And, we'd still have interest on the loan to pay the bank. Nope, I worried on it long and hard, and whiskey is a lot better deal. So, are you in or out?”

"Tom, it's agin my better judgment, but I believe and respect everything you say. If it was anybody but you, I would never do it but, OK, I will. When do we start?”

"Tomorrow morning, soon as we get this corn in. We'll go to Batesville, to the bank. Then, as soon as we have the money, we'll buy the stuff for our new still and the truck. Take us a couple days to get the still going and then we'll be cooking our first big batch.”

• • • • • •

Watch them jugs a-fillin' in the pale moonlight, the old folksong went, but Tom and Jim found that making commercial quantities of whiskey was a hell of a lot more work than just lying in the moonlight. "Stilling" a quart or two at a time was one thing, but building a still to make upwards of three gallons a week quite another.

Although Tom sorely regretted having to put a mortgage on his farm, he was known to the banker and the needed five hundred dollars obtained without difficulty. Then the boys went shopping.

It took most of what they had borrowed, but soon Tom and Jim were lurching down Main Street in a used 1915 green Packard truck with red wheels. Even though the paint was faded and chipped, and it had been a little hard to start, there was likely not a vehicle on earth that could have made the boys feel more like they were somebodies.

"Wowser!" Jim exclaimed as Tom struggled to maintain control around a corner. "Ain't we just the cat's meow. They're looking at us now.”

At the hardware store the clerk was more than willing to sell them all that they needed, but there was a glitch. They were sold out of most everything.

"Can't keep them in stock,” the man explained. "Ever since

Prohibition passed, we been selling barrels and jugs and condensers like they was going out of style."

"You reckon folks is stillin'?" Jim asked.

"Don't know what else it could be," the salesman shook his head. "There was a lot of makin' in these hills before Prohibition and while the economy was good, but now I guess a lot of folks don't know how else to get by. But we got a new shipment of stuff coming in next week and if you'll pay for it now, soon as it's here I'll put it away for you. You can pick it up in a few days."

"Well, ain't that a fine kettle of fish," Jim mused as they drove away. "Looks like we ain't gonna be the only ones with white mule to sell. I wonder what that's gonna do to the price?"

"Ain't no way to tell," Tom responded glumly. "But we ain't got much choice in the matter now, do we?"

"Tom, you got no reason to be impatient with me. I was just wondering."

"I'm sorry, Jim. It just seems like things never go right. But we'll be fine. Just you wait and see. Soon we'll be rolling in dough."

Will we? Tom asked himself. I sure hope so.

The clerk was as good as his word and the following week all that was needed for their new still was stacked behind Tom's farmhouse, waiting to be carried by hand up the little creek. The new still would replace the boys' smaller one in a secluded little clearing in the woods surrounded by maples, oaks, hickory and other hardwoods. However, that evening Tom announced another problem.

"Jim," Tom said, "I been calculating how much water we need and we ain't got enough. That little creek just ain't got enough in it to supply all we need. I don't know why I didn't think of it before, but we're going to need more water. This creek's got the finest cool limestone water I know of, but we got to get more of it."

"Well, what we going to do?" Jim asked.

"We're going to divert upstream, that's what," Tom answered with authority. "We'll go upstream to where it forks, and we'll send more of the flow to our fork and less to the other one."

"Why, Tom, that would be a job. We'd be shoveling for days."

"Unless you got some other bright idea, it's what we've got to do.

You got something else popping' into that empty head of yours?"

It took the better part of a week, but eventually the boys had dammed a portion of the other fork and had more water flowing into theirs. Enough, Tom calculated, so that both their household needs and their whiskey-making requirements would be satisfied.

Setting up the still itself took only a couple days. First, the boys had to stack flat rocks so as to create a level base on which to set the boiler. Underneath the boiler and in between the rocks, the heating fire would burn pretty much continuously. Inside the boiler, water and mash would attain the required 173 degrees and then exit as vapor. The vapor would pass out the top of the boiler into a copper tube which ran into a barrel of cold water. The tube then coiled inside the barrel several times, finally exiting into a jug or smaller barrel. It was from the end of this tube that the whiskey finally dripped after having condensed inside the tube.

The whole system was based on the fact that water boils at 212 degrees, while alcohol boils at 172. Thus, the alcohol would boil off into the coil, or worm as it was usually called, long before the water. Submersing the coil in cool water caused to alcohol vapor to liquefy and, voila, white lightning.

"You know, Tom," Jim asked as they worked. "I never did know why we use copper kettles and coils. Why is that?"

"The way Grandpa told me was that the copper attracts sulfur and other bad things the cooking produces. Them bad things attach to the copper and don't stay in the whiskey. That's the reason we have to clean the copper parts so often, so's to get rid of the sulfur and stuff."

The mash would consist of corn, of which the boys had an abundance, and, for flavor, such dried fruits as might be available. Also, they would be adding some malted barley, which would convert from sugar into alcohol. Of course, all these ingredients had to be properly prepared, which meant that they had to be chopped into smaller pieces, a task in which Tom's two older boys, Loyce and Clifford, would be required to participate.

The first batch took a week to cook, a little bit longer than their old, smaller still. Finally though, Tom summoned all hands, Jim, Carrie and the four boys, to announce:

"We got us our first jug from the new still, thank the Lord. Let's have us a little celebration drink. You first, Carrie."

Carrie took the tin cup Tom had poured half full, took a tentative sip and grimaced. "Hot dang," she finally managed to say in her distinctive gravelly voice, "if that ain't the awfullest."

At eight years already anxious to show his mettle, Loyce grinned at his dad: "I'll try, Pa. Let me try."

The adults looked on knowingly as Tom handed the cup to Loyce.

Of course the lad's reaction to the manly gulp he tried to take was immediate and severe. Fortunately, he was unable to get any of the liquid fire down before he spit, coughed and hacked it out and onto the ground. The others tried not to laugh as he stood waiting to recover, trying not to cry.

Clifford, usually anxious to follow his older brother's lead, allowed as how he, "wasn't having none."

"I reckon we won't be having no trouble with the young'uns getting in the whiskey," Tom laughed as he handed the cup to Jim.

CHAPTER ELEVEN

In 1919, the Arkansas State Hospital for Nervous Diseases in Little Rock was a large imposing building of several stories, looking down from a slight rise south of the city. With its several wings and roof cupolas, it was by far the largest building Leone had ever seen. She stared at it, numb with anxiety, as she sat beside the deputy for the ride between the train station and the expansive grounds on which the building sat. On arrival she followed the sheriff's deputy through the barred door, not noticing how her growing discomfort had moistened her palms and widened her eyes.

Inside, the intake clerk looked up from her paperwork:

"Stand right over there. I'll get to you when I get to you."

As she did as she was told, she looked around. There were three doors: the one she had just come through from the outside, one leading out the rear of the room and a third now standing open with iron bars. She stared at the oversize key now protruding idly from the lock in the barred door and thought she could already hear the solid clunk of the mechanism in operation.

The faded green walls were adorned with pictures of the president of the United States, the governor of the State of Arkansas and Jefferson Davis. Also, there was the flag of the United States, the Arkansas' state flag, and the Confederate Stars and Bars. By way of furniture, the small room contained only the desk and chair at which the clerk now worked, as well as one in front of the desk Leone assumed would be for her when summoned. Behind the clerk, stacked haphazardly on the floor and reaching far up the back wall, were hundreds of files, each one apparently for a different patient. Some looked as though they contained only a sheet or two of papers. Others were many inches thick.

Leone's sad eyes, unobserved by the busy clerk, were incapable of expressing the depth of her despair. Her thoughts rapidly switched back and forth between concern for her children and apprehension about her own fate. She knew that regardless of Tom's love for their boys, he lacked the mother's touch she alone could provide. Especially with regard to the young, Allen, now just two, she suffered with the knowledge of how much he must be missing her. She wondered if Tom had the time or patience to properly comfort him.

As to her own circumstances, they were so foreign as to be beyond her comprehension. Never having previously been outside the little farms and towns of Northern Arkansas, even passing through the City of Little Rock had been an alien experience for her. To be inside this cold receiving room and institution was like she had been picked up and placed on the moon. She read initials scratched in the fading paint and hoped that those who had preceded her had been able to quickly return to their children and loved ones.

The State Hospital now contained almost 3,000 patients, all suffering from mental illnesses of various sorts and degrees. There were separate wings in the building for men, women, and Afro-Americans, all divided into separate sections where inmates were placed based on the severity of their affliction. In addition to the imposing main building, the self-contained institution consisted of large cultivated fields, various manufacturing plants, and an assortment of laundry, health and food processing buildings.

Finally motioned to approach, Leone stood in front of the clerk as she read Leone's as-yet slim file. "Well, I swan," the woman looked up to say. "Tried to kill your own damn young'uns, all four of 'em."

Leone stared at the floor and began to sob softly.

"Can you talk?" the clerk asked. "Says here you ain't nutty all the time."

"Yes, ma'am, I can talk," she muttered.

"I'm not quite sure where to put you. Ordinarily I would assign you to a ward where they ain't all howlin' and screamin' all night, but what you did is serious. If I put you in a regular wing, someone might put a knife in you. Killing kids don't set too well with some of the gals here. We ain't had that many cases, but a couple. Now come over here to this holding cell and wait while I go talk to the warden about what to do with you."

With her eyes constantly on the cell's lock, it was all Leone could do to comply. She shuddered and covered her ears when the door clanged shut.

A few minutes later Warden Strong herself appeared outside the bars of the locked cell. The woman, tall, stout and ramrod straight, began in her normal terse and clipped manner.

"Get up and come up to the bars so I can talk to you. So, you tried to kill your own gol-durned kids. I got to deal with your assignment personally. Tell me about it? Why did you do it?"

"I'm not sure I can," Leone snuffled. "I'm scared."

"You'll get over that soon enough. Right now, you better tell me what happened. I have to decide where to put you temporarily while we make a decision about your treatment and permanent ward."

"Can't you just put me in with the regular women. I won't cause no trouble."

"And what makes you think one of them regular women won't stick a shiv in your ribs first chance she gets? There was a woman named Sarah Hartley here a few years ago. Killed her own little boy. She didn't last a month. Someone cut her throat while she was lying in her bed. Never did find out who did it. Now, quit your damn crying and answer my question. Why shouldn't I lock you up in segregation, just to protect you?"

"Segregation? You mean be all by myself. Please Warden, I don't want to go to segregation. I thought I would be with the regular women."

"Regular women? Sister you don't know much about this place, do you? Ain't no one here who's regular, at least no all the time. This is a lunatic asylum. You might not have to be segregated, but this ain't no resort. So, you'd rather be knifed someday when you was on the can?

Besides, whatever I do is just temporary until Classification decides for sure next week."

The standard process was for each inmate to be classified by a committee consisting of the head psychiatrist and two experienced staff members, each of whom had had the opportunity to observe the inmate in her interactions with others. Depending on resulting classification, housing would be according to need for greater or lesser supervision and security. The classifications ranged from "rarely psychotic and not a danger to themselves or others" to one for those who were totally out of it and deemed unable to benefit from treatment. These latter women were simply warehoused in individual cells in a wing marked by almost continuous screaming and howls, as well as the stench of urine and feces. A patient's assignment to this wing was considered a death sentence by both inmates and staff.

"Warden, I don't think anyone is going to hurt me. I'm not a bad person. I don't never cause anyone any trouble. I ain't got an enemy in the world."

"But, Leone, think about what you did. Before the sun goes down tomorrow everybody here is going to know you're a kid killer."

Leone stared at the floor.

"Leone," the warden continued, "your file says you told the judge you thought you was saving your kids from the devil, that you were going to burn them up to save them from the devil. That right? You thought you was saving your kids from the devil by killing them?"

"Warden, it's the God's honest truth. He was there."

"Well, go on. Tell me more."

"I'm embarrassed. Don't nobody ever believe me."

"Does sound pretty damn unlikely, but I won't know whether to believe you or not until you tell me."

"He was there. You've got to believe me. He was stinking and smelling of sulfur, and flames rising up all around him. He was roaring and bellowing like nothing you ever heard before. And, his private part sticking out, big as a horse's. You have never seen the like. I was screaming, but there was nothing I could do. He was gonna get them."

"And he told you to lock your kids in the house and set it afire, that right?"

"No, he didn't tell me to do it. I had to do it or he would have gotten them, he would have taken them."

"Where would he have taken them?"

"To where he lives. To Hell."

"OK, Leone, I got one more question for you and you better tell me the truth. If you don't, I'll find out soon enough and it's going to go hard for you. Before this one time, did anything like that ever happen before? Did the devil try to get your kids any time before?"

"No, ma'am, he did not. It was the only time in my life anything like that happened."

Leone knew that what she was telling the warden wasn't true. She knew that the Devil had visited her before and caused her "episodes". However, her innate sense of self-preservation told her that if she told the warden the truth, she would likely suffer consequences too terrible to contemplate.

"All right, I'll have you conditionally assigned to a light security wing. But it's conditional only. One misstep or one time somebody tries to hurt you, and I'll reclassify you quicker than a chicken on a worm. And don't forget, the final say is up to the committee."

The relief Leone felt at not being assigned to segregation was almost but not quite enough to overcome her feeling of despair and loneliness. As a guard came to take her to her assigned room, her once proud carriage continued its decline. Her former decisive stride became tentative and her eyes dominated by fear. In spite of her almost-terror, the four little boys she had left at home were constantly on her mind.

••••••

Located on either side of a large central aisle, each wing of the asylum contained approximately fifty patient rooms. Every ten rooms or so, the aisle widened into sitting areas where the women could congregate to read, talk and do craft work.

To each floor were assigned guards, at least one was always present. At each guard station there was a small table and chair, as well as a cabinet containing a bible, hand and leg restraints and a billy club. Several large coffee cans now used for cigarette butts and as spittoons sat randomly up and down the hall. On each floor there were open toilets and a large common shower.

In the center of the asylum was the main kitchen, where meals were cooked and then delivered to the dining areas on each floor. Except for severely afflicted patients and others for various reasons not allowed access to common areas, all the women were fed hot, if universally complained about, meals every day

After Leone's mandatory delousing shower and inspection of her body cavities, she was issued two standard gray smocks, four pairs of coarse wool drawers and a like number of pairs of stockings. The shoes she had arrived in were replaced by ones suitable for work in the fields, barns and manufacturing areas. She was also given two blankets, a pillow and toiletries.

It was after dinner before a guard was available to escort Leone to her assigned room. The other patients had already completed their work day and were relaxing. Many of them were congregated outside their rooms on benches or in rocking chairs arranged in circles every so often along the hallway. Leone's walk to her room was attentively observed and commented on by several women. Among the whistles and hoots, were also heard calls of "new fish on the floor," "ain't she cute" and "welcome, Honey".

"Don't mind them," the escort said. "Some of them show out like that every time a new girl arrives. You'll find most of the women here real nice."

They had not gone much further down the long hallway, when they came across a woman seated on a bench with her head hung down almost to her lap, prompting Leone to ask the escort:

"What's wrong with her?"

"I'm not sure, I ain't the psychiatrist, but probably depression or catatonia."

"What's catatonia?"

"That's when they're almost unconscious, but not quite. Won't talk. They just sit there, all day long, mostly not moving. They's a couple of them like that on this ward."

"How come it's so quiet? I hear people talking, but ain't nobody screaming or crying."

"Oh, you'll hear screaming and crying soon enough. Lots of that goes on, but just not all the time. Gals here is pretty much regular, just trying to get better and go home."

"The sheriff that brought me on the train told me there would be howling and yelling going on all day and night."

"Well, that just ain't true. More of it goes on in some of the other wards of course, but not here; sometimes it does, but not as a regular feature."

"Oh my God, what about that one?" Leone asked as they neared a middle-aged woman sitting in the middle of the aisle with her clothes neatly folded and placed in a pile next to her. She was completely naked and busily washing herself as if she were in a bathtub.

"Evening, Sallie," the escort said to her.

"Evening, Flora," the woman smiled and went on washing.

Near the end of the hall her escort stopped before a room, indicating it was to be Leone's. But, before Leone could go inside, she was attracted by a moaning sound coming from the room next door. There, through a wide-open door, she saw an attractive young woman lying on her bed, furiously masturbating. One hand was viciously squeezing one of her nipples, while the other desperately rubbed her clitoris.

"Oh, don't mind her," a tall, older patient walked up to say. "Unless she does that about four or five times a day, she ain't fit to live with. I'm Eunice Walker. The one with her finger in her pussy is Anne Hallmark. What's your name?"

Before Leone could answer, a grunting moan followed by a deep sigh and then silence emanated from "the one with her finger in her pussy." Leone stared.

"Well, answer up. Cat got your tongue? What's your name?" Eunice repeated. "I live next door. If we're going to be neighbors, we got to get acquainted. You can meet Anne, too, soon as she catches her breath."

Oh, my God, Leone thought, *what have I gotten myself into. I can't do this. And, my poor babies. Oh, my poor babies. Why do I have to be punished so? I think I wish I were dead. Oh, Tom.*

Doctor Horthamer, the State Hospital's sole psychiatrist for women, was a tall, sour, acerbic sixty-year old. His face was narrow and strained and he wore rimless pince-nez glasses. Bald on top, he cultivated the hair on the sides of his head which he combed up and over, hiding nothing. Wearing his coat and tie even on the hottest days, he justified his rumpled and stained appearance by complaining to himself that his meager salary wasn't sufficient to allow for proper cleaning or pressing. Rumor had it that some sort of scandal had necessitated his quick exit from his native Austria some years before.

"Well, I ain't got all day," he greeted Leona as she was escorted into his cluttered office for her psychiatric intake screening a few days after she had arrived. "Sit in that chair and tell me why you tried to kill your kids. Then, we'll decide what to do with you."

Leona had been looking forward to this ever since she had learned that such an interview would be part of her initial processing. Finally, she was going to get the help she needed. A real psychiatrist was going to listen to her. Hopefully, he would be of more help than the one her father had taken her to without benefit in Memphis some years before. Maybe he would even cure her completely.

Even though some of the other women she had talked to had cautioned her not to put too much faith in the doctor, Leona's hope and desire for treatment overcame what should have been healthy skepticism. Even when Eunice repeated several times that "He sure ain't helped none of us," Leona maintained her optimism. Now, confronted with the psychiatrist's brusque and impatient manner, she felt her hope begin to fade.

"So, when did your current impairment first begin?" the doctor coldly looked at her. "Your husband told the doctor there in Batesville that you've had episodes in the past."

"Well, yes. I've had them before, but never like this. Mama says I've always had them, but others say they began when some jars of peaches we was canning exploded. I don't rightly know."

"And this Devil thing. The Devil was going to get your kids so you had to fry them?" the doctor asked.

Rarely allowing her to finish an answer and frequently interrupting her, the psychiatrist went on to have Leona tell him about that fateful afternoon when she had tried to burn the house.

"My last question," he finally said:

"If we let you out, what makes you think you won't try to kill your kids again?"

But, without waiting for an answer he abruptly announced: "Obviously a classic case of pellagra. You been having diarrhea, too, ain't you? A classic case of pellagra if ever I seen one."

"Why no Doctor. I ain't had no diarrhea. Except when I eat too many prunes or green apples. I ain't hardly ever had diarrhea."

"Are you arguing with me, young woman? I'll have you know I have degrees from some of the finest universities in the world. In Vienna I studied under world-renowned pioneer psychiatrist and scholar Heinrich von Beinhoff. I have successfully treated thousands of patients. I warn you, young lady, do not argue with me."

"Oh, Doctor, I'm so sorry. I'm not arguing with you. I just want to get well. Can you help me, please?"

"Of course, I can help you. Now take off your clothes, all of them," he brusquely ordered.

Leona, too scared to remonstrate, quickly removed her clothes and placed them on a chair next to her. Adjusting his lenses to a better position on his nose, the doctor came around his desk to sit on its edge, just inches from Leona's chest.

"Now, jiggle your titties," he ordered.

And when Leona stared at him with total non-comprehension, he yelled at her: "Jiggle 'em, I said!"

Eyes wide with fear, Leona placed her hands under her breasts and began shaking them. After she had done that for a few seconds, the doctor raised his eyes, retreated back behind his desk and sternly announced:

"Diagnosis: Pellagra and schizophrenia resulting in delusions and hallucinations. Treatment begins as soon as we can work you in. Ice water baths."

After Leona dressed and was leaving the room, she disappointedly considered what she had just experienced:

Oh, my god, she thought, *what kind of a place is this. He was supposed to help me, but he just wanted to see me shake my titties. Well at least he didn't touch me. Got to be optimistic. Some of the girls say the ice water treatment helped them. Maybe kinda like castor oil. Pretty bad stuff, but I guess I can stand it.*

••••••

Leone soon learned that despite Anne Hallmark's habit of frequent public masturbation, she was a very nice person. On the outside she had been a school teacher, had never been married and had previously lived at home with her well-to-do Fayetteville family. She was well-read, courteous to a fault and loved crochet and other needle crafts. However her exhibitionism and compulsion to have sex in public with herself and sometimes with others had finally tried the patience of her family and the local judge. Five years ago, she had been committed. Despite Doctor Horthamer's best treatment (and frequent summons to his office) he had been unable to report much progress. He had diagnosed her as having schizophrenia evidenced by a psychotic compulsion, or in the catch-all rubric of the day, pellagra.

As for Eunice, she was a farmer's wife, with five now-grown children. One of the older women on Leone's ward, she was tall, portly and had been institutionalized for three years with what her local doctor and Doctor Horthamer agreed was severe depression. Like a lot of the patients in this wing, she was normal much of the time. However when one of her bouts of despondency came on, it was often completely debilitating, so much so that she sometimes could not bring herself to get out of bed. She had several times tried to kill herself. Probably due to the flatness of her chest, after her initial interview with Doctor Horthamer he had never seen her again.

Solely due to happenstance, Leone had fallen in with two of the most, when they were not symptomatic, rational and mature women in the institution. As almost a personal project, Eunice and Anne took Leone under their collective wing, introduced her to the politics and personalities of the other women, and advised her with regard to the guards, administrators and institutional procedures. In short, they immediately began to mother and protect her.

The patients on the floor ranged in age from the late teens to the late sixties and represented an approximately accurate cross-section of the Arkansas general population, i.e., most of them had been farmers' daughters and wives. Few of them had graduated from high school and, Anne being the sole exception, none had attended college. A large number of them were mothers, so that on visiting days the visiting rooms were filled with laughing, frolicking children playing chase amongst the worn and dilapidated divans and torn over-stuffed chairs.

After Anne had recovered from her orgasm and dressed herself, she sat on her bunk and smiled at Leone. "Leone, if you don't mind, please tell us all about yourself. And kindly start with your diagnosis. You're going to find that there are few secrets in here, and that almost the first thing one gal wants to know about another is what her diagnosis is. For example, mine is what they've been calling schizophrenia resulting in compulsion and disordered thinking. Eunice's is plain old depression. What's yours?"

"They been calling it pellagra, but Doctor Horthamer just said I got schizophrenia, too. That's about all I know."

"Pellagra," Eunice sneered. "That don't tell us nothing. That's just a word they use when you ain't acting right and they don't know what else to call it. The gals in here are either suffering from depression, schizophrenia or they are bi-polar. You ain't got nothing to fear from the depressed ones or, unless they're off on a really wild jag, the bi-polar ones. It's the schizophrenic ones you got to look out for. They can do some really crazy stuff. Fortunately, most of them is over in another wing."

Seeing Leone's increasing discomfort, Anne tried to console with more certainty than she felt: "You'll be all right. Just you wait and see. You'll be home again soon. But now, maybe you got some questions for us. Anything you want to ask us?"

"Well one," Leone answered. "Why is it so quiet here? I thought there would be a lot of screaming and crying? Matter of fact, most of the gals I see here is walking around and carrying on like they was at a church social."

"You'll see some fussing and crying and carrying on that's for sure," Anne responded. "Happens a lot. But, most of us is pretty normal most of the time. You see a lot more gals just depressed or in another world and just staring than you do carrying on. Most of us is pretty normal most of the time.

And they got all kinds of activities for us. Just like on the outside. Dances and bingo games and cooking classes; book clubs even, and all kinds of stuff. But I reckon we're all here for a reason, at least when they sent us here. And for the ones that's really nutty, and screaming and crapping on the floor and stuff, they ain't in this wing. They got a special wing for them."

By the time the bell rang for lights out at 10 p.m. the three women had exchanged complete personal histories. Leone felt as if she knew them and they sensed that they knew her. However more importantly, her fear was somewhat assuaged. She no longer felt as if she were alone in a universe of hostile people, places and events. Truth be known, it was quite satisfying to be in the company of two older and wiser women. She felt like they understood her, which was different than she usually felt at home, even with Tom. For almost the first time since that eventful day, she didn't cry herself to sleep.

However in the middle of the night she was rudely jerked awake by Eunice's insistent voice directly over her.

"Leone, Leone, wake up. You were having a nightmare."

"It was the Devil," the now-awake and very distraught Leone realized and sat up to say. "He was taking me. He was gonna get my kids. He was all stinky and awful and fiery. Won't I never know no peace?"

She buried her head in her hands and sobbed.

• • • • • •

It was more than a week before Leone could be "worked in" so as to begin receiving her ice water baths. In the meantime as a temporary assignment and until she could receive a permanent job, she was assigned to the farm crew. It was the farm crew's job to grow various fruits, vegetables and animals so that the asylum was largely self-sufficient. Also, sometimes the money crops such as tobacco and cotton even produced a little profit. For no particular reason Leone was able to guess, she was told she would work in the hog barns. She and Tom had always raised hogs, of course, but they had largely been Tom and

Jim's responsibility. And, she had never particularly cared for them. They were smelly, disobedient and filthy. She was glad to leave their care to Tom and Jim.

However with these pigs she found a new attraction. Especially with the little ones. With the new-borns she was want to snatch one away from a distracted mother and cuddle it like she had birthed it herself, only returning it when it cried out for its mother's.

Even though there were several experienced patients working in the hog sheds with her, trying to manage the sometimes four-hundred pound sows was a little daunting. The usually docile breeder animals could turn mean in a second, especially if they sensed what their small brains perceived as a threat to a new litter of piglets. One of the sows in particular took an unexplained dislike for Leone. It got so bad that soon Leone didn't dare go in the pen with the big animal. Even when she was outside the fence tossing over slop, the pig would look past her bucket and try to bite her. None of the other workers had any such problem with the porker.

Why me? Leone wondered with a little fear, I wonder why I'm the only one she's always trying to bite.

In any event, her time with the hogs passed uneventfully enough. As a matter of fact, in this strange place with unfamiliar people, the bovines provided an element of familiarity Leone sorely needed. Much as she had done on the farm with Tom, she began naming the more distinctive ones.

••••••

Leone fit right in with the other women. Most, if certainly not all, were usually quite normal in their behavior. Generally, they were friendly and sympathetic. The hired supervisors were not overly strict and the patients' work barely sufficient to fill their workday. Lengthy rest and lunch breaks afforded ample time for gossip, speculation about new treatments and, of course, husbands and children.

Almost all of the women had children. A remarkable number had more than ten. Most, especially if they had been institutionalized for more than a year or two, had been divorced. Only the most recently admitted talked of their husbands.

It didn't take Leone long to partially overcome her always-present depression and to guardedly respond to friendly introductions by several of the women. She immediately hit it off with two in particular, Pearl and Clara. Both were about Leone's age, had similar numbers of children and, of course, came from farm families. When their initial conversation turned to children, much to the envy of Leone and Clara, Pearl immediately produced a dog-eared and creased photograph of her three. Although the face of the youngest was blurred from movement when the shutter released, the other two were, indeed, good looking young'uns. Leone and Clara contented themselves with lengthy descriptions of how good looking their youngsters were, as well as how unbelievably early they had achieved various childhood milestones.

"Oh, my God, I miss my young'uns," Leone suddenly said after a new acquaintance had produced pictures. "I wish I had a picture. Why didn't Tom make no pictures?"

• • • • • •

On the morning of her first treatment Leone didn't go to the hog barns. Instead, she was escorted directly to the treatment rooms. From the other women she had of course heard about the various treatments and of the several, the ice baths sounded uncomfortable but not tortuous. Certainly they didn't sound as bad as others such as lobotomies, isolation and full-body restraint. And they absolutely had to be better than electroshocks, which Leone feared greatly. Thinking about how beneficial the result might be, she was almost looking forward to the freezing water.

Can't be too bad, she thought. *After all, I been cold lots of times. There was that time I got caught out in the storm and nearly froze to death. That was terrible. This couldn't be that bad. Besides, I got to get well. Got to be treated however will help me. No Devil. No Devil. No Devil. Got to get home to Tom and the kids.*

In the ice bath treatment room there was a line of eight bathtubs, a table next to each. On the tables were sheets, blankets and blindfolds.

In the back of the room were large bins, filled with ice. Eight women were being led in one at a time, given a special bathing smock to wear, blindfolded and assisted to sit in the already cold water. Then, supervised by the room manager, ice was added until a temperature of fifty degrees was attained.

Treatment for each was to be the same: Unable to see anything and in silence, the women would sit for fifteen minutes. Then, they would be helped out to lie under a blanket for ten minutes. Then, there would be a further immersion for ten minutes. At last, each woman, shaken and shivering, would be escorted back to her room for recovery.

I ain't gonna think about the cold. I'm only gonna think about Tom and the kids. Just Tom and the kids.

With curious detachment, she watched the women who preceded her being prepared and immersed. No one said a word. They had all done it before. When her turn came, she simply smiled at the attendant, put on the bathing smock and stepped into the tub. The sooner to get started with her cure the better.

At first, she was able to put the cold out of her mind. Instead, as she had so many times lately, she concentrated on all that had happened with Tom during the past ten years, on how he had welcomed her that first morning on his porch, on how she loved to see the muscles in his back flex as he washed up after a long day in the fields, on how his strong good arm would gather her in during lovemaking.

Finally, though, the bitter cold came through and despite her strongest resolve, the clear picture of Tom faded. Even his beautiful blue eyes disappeared from her mind's eye as she was overwhelmed with thoughts of how tortuously cold she was. And it wasn't just cold as an absence of heat. It was a cold with a life of its own. Even though contained inside the water, it was a cold with body and texture separate from its host, the water. It was an entity, penetrating her body much like the Devil himself had sought to do.

Had she been able to think of anything except how the unbelievable cold was numbing her body, she would have speculated on whether its penetration was reaching down inside her, deep down inside where the Devil lived. She would have hoped and prayed with all her heart that the cold was staunching and extinguishing the Devil's fires, so that she could get well and get home to Tom and her children. But she didn't have that capacity. Her mind was overwhelmed with thoughts of cold, to the exclusion of all else.

During the break she lay on the table shivering and convulsing, shaking like she had never shook before. Deep racking waves of quivers and trembling shook her body along its entire length.

Oh, my God, she thought, *I can't do this. Oh, my God. This is the worst thing ever. I can't do this no more.*

But she did. She did the second half of the treatment that day and she did the treatment the next day and the next and the next. Every time she spent hours afterward lying on her bed, half conscious and shaking. And wondering what on earth she had ever done to deserve such torture.

•••••••

A few weeks after Leone was committed, Tom's loneliness and love for her finally overcame his anger and he went to Little Rock. With him were all four children, as well as Carrie Shuler. Except for Tom, it was the first time any of them had been on a train. The young boys would talk for months afterward about what for them was one of the most exciting events of their lives. Complete with not very convincing imitations of the train's deep whistle and expansive arm gestures indicating the huge quantities of black smoke put off by the wood-burning engine, the children relived the experience over and over again, amongst themselves and to anyone else who would listen.

It had not been an easy sell for Tom to get them on the train. As soon as he told them they were going to visit their mother Loyce began strenuous objections. Even Clifford who had been the most vocal about how much he missed his mother was strangely quiet. Otto and Allen were much more excited at the prospect of riding on a train than they were at a chance to see their mother. Only Tom's repeated assurances that Leone was better now than she had been when she tried to kill them, along with graphic descriptions of what the train ride would be like, overcame their protests.

So, with a diaper bag for the two-year old Allen and a basket Carrie had filled with their best easily transported food, Tom drove his family to Batesville to catch the train for the one hundred-mile trip to the Arkansas capital. The trip south through the hilly farmlands took about four hours, a time during which Tom would repeatedly marvel at the many people who filled the world and didn't live in his "neck of the woods."

"Well, I swan," the conductor collecting tickets on the train stared at Tom. "A one-armed man with four young'uns. If this don't beat all. Mister, you certainly got your hands full, that's for sure."

Tom held out the tickets for the man and looked straight ahead.

"Why don't you mind your own business?" Widow Shuler barked. "It ain't none of your business how many arms he's got, or how many kids, for that matter."

"I'm sorry, ma'am," the chagrined trainman muttered, handing the now-punched tickets back. "I didn't mean nothing by it. I hope you enjoy the rest of your trip."

As the man continued down the aisle, Carrie said to Tom:

"All them boys come back from the war without arms and legs and different parts, and now this fool wants to pick on you. Tom, I sometimes don't know what gets into people."

Arriving at the asylum in mid-afternoon after a hired carriage ride from the train station, Tom checked in with the receptionist and confirmed that he was scheduled to have a visit with Leone that afternoon and all the next day. As he waited with others to be shown to the visiting rooms he looked around. He was appalled. He had never before in his life been in a place where human beings were confined behind concrete and steel and the experience affected him greatly.

Oh, my poor Leone, he thought, *such an awful place. Why do you have to be in such an awful place? Why do I have to bring my kids to such an awful place?*

When they entered the visiting rooms, Leone was pacing the floor waiting for them. She caught sight of Tom even before he was through the door and, tears of joy flowing, came flying into his arms. Then a scene of utter chaos as she tried to hug and kiss all of them at the same time. Even Carrie got an enthusiastic embrace. All four of the little boys, now standing at Leone's feet held their arms up for her crying,

"Mama, Mama, Mama". She took turns hoisting each up, two at a time, for turns in her arms.

The visit for the rest of the afternoon took place in a large expansive yard where, in addition to chairs and recliners for the adults, there were, swing sets, slides and toys for the children. Several families shared the area and while the children readily mixed and played together, the patients and their adult visitors, sometimes husbands, sometimes other friends and relatives, sat in separate little bunches. The patients displayed the entire gamut of symptoms of mental illness. Some sat or played with their children quite normally. Had it not been for the institutional uniforms, one could not have distinguished the patients from their visitors. However, others sat morosely staring at their feet, ignoring their loved ones. Still, a few others were quite manic, laughing hysterically and wildly gesturing.

Leone's behavior fell into the first group. After the initial tears of joy and wild hugs, there was nothing which identified her as in any way impaired. She talked to Tom about the farm, reminding him of necessary details she thought needed attending to, asked about certain friends and neighbors, and even asked him to make sure the preacher was told she would be home soon.

At one point, as she was telling him about a hog in her care she had named Randy, Tom thought to himself, *Leone, my love, why can't you be like this all the time? Just as normal as if we was having dinner with the parson.*

"I call him Randy," she explained, "because he's the randiest hog you ever did see. Them other hogs ain't got a chance and them sows just line up to have him give it to them. Didn't we have a hog like that one time?"

"I reckon as how we did," Tom laughed back. "I think we called him Joe."

"Now, Tom," she jokingly chided. "You know we didn't call him Joe. We called him Dan because he took after your Pa and ain't nobody never been randier."

However, Tom's inner being was anything but jocular. His competing emotions battled mightily as he tried to reconcile his love for Leone with the anger and hatred he felt for what she had done and for having deprived him of a wife, as well deprived the children of a mother.

And now what's going to happen? he thought, *certainly not for the first time. How am I gonna bring up these kids proper without you around? Damn you, anyway, Leone.*

Despite his continuing efforts to keep these thoughts suppressed there were occasional flashes of impatience and shortness both with Leone and with the kids. Fortunately, although those around him certainly noticed, they were able to ignore them.

Leone even went out of her way to be friendly to Carrie, saying to her:

"Carrie, thank you so much for helping out with the young'uns. Me and Tom appreciate it so much. And, I do like the way you did your hair. Maybe when I get home, you could show me how to do mine like that."

As to the children, she cuddled, talked to and threatened discipline just like any other mother would have done in a yard full of other children and adults. Although showering particular attention on her weepy two-year old, Allen, she tried to give the rest equal time.

However, Loyce, having apparently dismissed his previous anger with his mother, was the most verbal. "Momma, momma," he repeatedly asked, "when you coming home? We miss you."

"I miss you, too, sweetheart," she responded.

However, she did have a concern about being supplanted as a disciplinarian in the family.

"Tom," she said quietly during one of the few moments when the children were elsewhere, "the young'uns ain't listening to me like they used to. Did you notice that? When I tell them to do something, they look at you to see if they should mind me. They was never like that before."

Tom had noticed that, but dissembled, "Honey, you're imagining things. They mind you just fine."

In short, except for the inner tension and sorrow they both tried to hide, all went smoothly, both that day and the next. Even when it was time for Tom to take the children back to the train for the trip home, the tears were not prolonged. Leone repeatedly assured the children that she would be home soon and that she would make them banana pudding and read them lots of bedtime stories. And with imitations of the children's own arm-waving animations and guttural sound effects, she described how the smoke-belching engine would chug up the inclines and coast down the other side. After prolonged farewell hugs and kisses, she even managed a broad smile.

But, Leone was emotionally drained. It had taken all of her strength to put on her facade and repress her anger at herself for all the harm she had caused all concerned. She had summoned every last ounce of reserve in order to not to show what internally racked her every minute of the day—self-loathing, regret and depression. As soon as she got back to her room, she could maintain no longer and broke down entirely, moaning and sobbing until, exhausted, she at long last fell asleep.

CHAPTER TWELVE

By 1925 Leone had been in the institution for six years. She and Tom continued to exchange letters, although less and less frequently, and Tom still managed the occasional trip to the asylum, sometimes with and sometimes without one or more of their boys, now fourteen, twelve, ten and eight. Carrie had given up any thought of going back to her own farm and, instead, had rented it out to a family to share crop. At Tom's she had her own room next to his, took care of the household duties and tended the large vegetable garden, much as Leone, Julia and Gracie had done before her.

"Carrie," Tom said to her one evening when they were alone, "I ain't never said much about how much I appreciate you and all you've done for us. And I probably wouldn't be saying it now if I hadn't a bit of shine. But, I am. These past years we've been like two dray horses in harness together, pulling this family and everything in it where it needs to go."

"Why Tom, you are right poetic. I didn't know you had it in you. A regular Shakespeare."

"Hear me out, Carrie. I ain't done yet. I want to say that amidst all this work, you have helped me create the family I hoped to have with Leone. I'm sure sorry she's not here with me, but you've been a fine helpmate. The boys respect and love you just like you was their own mother, no thanks to me sometimes, I hate to say. I reckon you know I've always been worried about you replacing Leone because I was sure she would be back someday. Guess that's getting more and more unlikely. But the main thing is the boys. I reckon there ain't nothing in life much more important than raising up one's young'uns so they turn into proper adults. Thanks to you I think I'm going to be able to do that."

"I guess better late than never," she said. "I sure wished you had said some words like that before. Many was the day when I thought you didn't give a lick for what I did around here. Thank you for saying it now. I love them boys and I love you, too."

Tom didn't respond, but turned and walked to his bedroom, closing the door behind him.

Big strapping boys even at their ages, Loyce and Clifford had dropped out of school and were helping with the whiskey-making and farming. For a while Tom had forced them to walk to the little one-room school, but eventually, as they grew older, he grew weary of their daily complaints, and gave in.

Of course when he had informed Leone that the older boys were no longer going to school she protested strongly, but he had begun to pay less and less attention to what she wanted with regard to what went on on the farm. He even kept from her some things he knew she would have wanted to know. For example, how brisk his whiskey-making business had become, as well as some of the more serious cuts and bruises he and the boys sometimes suffered on the farm.

As to his visits to the asylum, they were happening less and less frequently. Hattie and Mabel continued to visit her often, but Tom just couldn't find the time. Almost daily he resolved to go see her the next week, but then found that the press of farming and whiskey making required his attention. Over the past years his anger had almost entirely dissipated and he mostly remembered only their good times together. Nevertheless, the demands of the farm and his still kept him from visiting as often as he should have, a fact about which she complained bitterly at every opportunity.

The whiskey business had settled into an established routine. His several reliable customers provided a steady if not spectacular income, not likely to change even with repeal of Prohibition. At times he speculated on giving up the business. He had already switched most of his fields from cotton to corn for whiskey and wasn't sure he wanted to switch them back. Cotton required more labor than did corn.

Even Leone's return home was no longer talked about much. She had become a fading presence. Although he had resisted for a long time, he had finally put all of her things, including the red calico print dress, the sight of which always brought tears to his eyes, in a box in the barn. Also, he noted with alarm that Leone's mind continued to deteriorate. It wasn't dramatic, but her sometimes jumbled thoughts and lack of ability to pay attention were increasingly noticeable. As a matter of fact, in the last of her increasingly infrequent letters, she had even confused Loyce and Otto, writing that Otto was her oldest. Her once beautiful handwriting has become so illegible that he had difficulty reading it.

This deterioration and the continuation of Leone's "episodes" were what kept her from being released. Doctor Horthamer had once told Tom that if Leone could go six months without an "episode" then he would strongly consider paroling her. However, the "episodes" seemed to be increasing in frequency, not decreasing. Most of them involved fire. Fire seemed to be her main trigger.

Of course, the staff knew to keep Leone away from flames, but there were always little accidents or mistakes. Someone would forget and leave a hot iron on an ironing board, or a worn electrical cord would short out, or something. Each time Leone would howl and rage and blubber about the Devil and her young'uns and all manner of crazy things. After some hours, or a day or so, she would gradually recover and go back to being pleasant, obedient and remorseful.

Fortunately, in the 1920s farmers like Tom were buoyed by a prosperous economy. After a fairly short depression following World War One, what were called the Roaring Twenties set in and the stock market reached record highs. Prices for his money crop, cotton, took off. Almost daily it seemed that because of market prices Tom had to change his mind about planting more cotton or more corn. As some had foreseen, the whiskey making business had turned out to be not nearly so profitable as it first appeared it would be. Jim's initial speculations had been right. Every farmer and back-woodser in the South, and indeed throughout the country saw Prohibition as an opportunity to get rich. Stills popped up where none had existed before, and the supply of whiskey was even greater than it had been before. After an initial jump, prices sunk to record lows.

But there was profit in it, and the combined income Tom received from his farming and whiskey allowed them to live a decent, if not luxurious life. There was always ample food on the table, decent clothes and even enough for hard candy for the boys when they went to town.

There was one event which made Tom think about giving up farming, in spite of what he had said so many times about always being a farmer. A huge lake of oil had been discovered in Oklahoma. The drillers were hiring every hand they could get at top wages, no experience required.

"Jim," Tom told his brother one night when they were discussing the oil boom over jars of their special product, "I sorely am tempted, but I'm a farmer and I guess a farmer is all I'm going to be. Even though we could make a pile of money at it, working on an oil rig just don't set quite right with me. I reckon we'll just keep on farming and stillin' just like Whiteners been doing for generations."

• • • • • •

Carrie Shuler was not an old widow. She had not yet turned forty when the log chain slipped and decapitated her husband. At the time, the couple was still trying to have their first child.

Like many farm women, she was long on work and short on words. Capable of laboring many hours without saying a word, when she did speak, she got right to the point, said what she had to say and quit. Although she was fond of jokes, especially off-color ones, she rarely laughed. Although she was a smart woman, that was not readily apparent. She was perfectly content to let others take the lead.

It had taken her a long time to get over the death of her husband. The couple had been very much in love, affectionate almost to a fault and had often talked of growing into their dotage surrounded by grandchildren. At times she and Tom exchanged thoughts of how much they missed their spouses, always stopping short of expressing the obvious fact that their own marriage to each other would have greatly mitigated their sorrow.

Although she had quit high school in her junior year in order to help with her own pa's spring planting, she loved to read. She read anything she could get her hands on, including the Bible, the Farmer's Almanac and, when she could get it, the newly established news magazine, Time.

Replacing Leone as a mother and household manager was a huge and difficult task, but despite some resistance from Tom, she took it on with resolve and dedication. Tom's subtle opposition was grounded in the fact that he didn't want his boys to get too close to Carrie so as to take it hard when she had to leave because Leone had returned. However, Carrie took to the boys as if they were her very own, and made sure that she read to them at least every night before bed. Also after she first arrived, it didn't take long before she had the household affairs arranged to her efficient satisfaction. Soon things were humming along just as if Leone was still managing things. Just comforting four rambunctious, if sometimes distraught boys could have been too much for a lesser person, but she not only managed it with sympathy and compassion, but also with measured discipline.

"I came to Tom's fully intending to be a mother to those young'uns and a wife to him," she later told a friend. "I guessed right away Leone was never coming home, and so I set out to replace her. It worked out pretty well, even though Tom often didn't support me like he should have. But I just never could measure up in his eyes."

Her inability to supplant Leone with Tom was not for lack of trying. Almost immediately after moving in she began to subtly, and not so subtly let Tom know that she intended to be as much a wife to him as possible. There were tender looks thrown his way, a lazy hand drawn across his arm and even softly drawn-out "good-nights" before retiring to their separate rooms at night. She even began sometimes calling him "Tommy" and occasionally "Honey."

Tom, for his part, always treated her with respect and gratitude, if not more. He rarely let his love for Leone and sorrow at her present plight interfere with their good relationship. He would never allow the boys to call her "Ma", but he did always insist that they obey her and treat her with respect.

One evening after Tom had had his usual after-dinner drinks, and had gone to bed, she went to him. Quietly closing his bedroom door behind her, she quickly drew her nightgown over her head and dropped it on the floor next to his bed. He was not yet asleep and in the faint light of the moon was captured by her flat belly and erect nipples. When he said nothing, she slipped in next to him.

The next morning an early dawn found her lying next to him with her arm across his chest. Looking wistfully into her eyes, he softly said to her:

"Carrie, I surely did enjoy that. But we can't do it no more. Leone is my wife and my love, and she'll be home someday. I don't want to do nothing to spoil my relationship with her."

And then, when she started to interrupt him to protest, he stopped her and continued:

"I will be forever grateful for what you have done for me and for my young'uns. You are surely an angel sent by God. But I love my wife. I love Leone and I always will. Maybe the Lord will forgive us for last night, but it has to be the last time."

Silently rising to gather her nightgown and return to her own room, Carrie said nothing. She knew there would be other times.

And there were other times. Every so often Tom would steal into her room and they would enjoy a night of mutual lust and passion. Or, she would catch his eye as they were going to their own rooms and later she would tip toe into his. However, each morning he would again be remorseful, tell her how much he loved Leone and resolve never to do it again.

Probably Jim and even the older boys noticed Carrie's comings and goings, but no one ever said a word.

• • • • • •

The boys' whiskey business had gradually become well-established in Tom's neck of the woods. Most everyone in both Sharp and Independence Counties, including the sheriffs and prosecutors, knew of it, but nothing was said, probably because of the prominence of some of Tom's customers. It was rumored that not only judges and politicians could often be seen taking delivery of one or more of Tom's jugs, but that even a minister or two was not a stranger to the white mule. However, with the advent of Prohibition, or more specifically, the attempted enforcement of Prohibition, their operation came under threat.

Untaxed moonshine had long been illegal in Arkansas, but no one had paid much attention to the law. Stills operated openly in complete defiance of it. But even if there had been a prosecution, where could members of an Arkansas jury have been found who would have voted for conviction?

The threat didn't come from Arkies, it came from the Federal Bureau of Prohibition, or, as its agents were universally known, "Revenooers". After it became apparent that Prohibition was being ignored by large segments of the population, especially in the South, Washington sent thousands of agents to try to enforce the law. And since violation of the Volstead Act was a Federal offense, defendants in Arkansas would be tried in Little Rock, the nearest Federal court, where there was much less sentiment in favor of the moonshiners than in the local county courts.

Another problem for Tom was the Woman's Christian Temperance Union. Although the WCTU wasn't as strong in Arkansas as in some other states, in Batesville and the surrounding area it took on out-sized power and influence almost solely because of one woman, Cleo Taylor. Mrs. Taylor was the wife of Clarence Taylor, the sheriff of Independence County and absolutely resolute in her dedication to eliminating drinking in any form. She single-handedly formed the WCTU chapter in Batesville and regularly gathered her women to seek out and destroy stills, as well as the drinking establishments sometimes called, because of the frequent condition of their exiting customers, "blind pigs." Although they certainly did carry and know how to use axes and crowbars, the ladies later claimed that the shotguns with which they were occasionally armed were never loaded.

Sheriff Taylor was a good friend of Tom's father-in-law, John Bell Bailey, and had been elected in large part because of support from saloon keepers and stillers. The fact that he had often campaigned with a drink in his hand and, in crucial districts, was wont to stand drinks for an entire bar full of voters, had severely complicated his home life. During one particularly loud argument, his wife had threatened divorce. Thus, they had called a truce. He ignored her temperance activities and she ignored his drinking and his imbibing friends.

However, there was one exception. Because of what their friend John Bell had said about Tom, both the sheriff and his wife had taken a strong dislike for him and his stillin'. Everyone in the county knew that Tom was a maker and runner and Cleo constantly insisted that her husband find Tom's still and shut it down.

Tom's greatest vulnerability came as he was transporting his goods to Memphis. The Revenooers were reluctant to go into the woods after Tom's still because they knew Tom and his neighbors were well-armed. However, when the blockaders, as the moonshiners were sometimes called because of their wont to run the Revenooers' highway blockades, were on the road, a couple cars placed across the highway by lawmen at a narrow point generally put an end to the trip.

The runners began to notice however, that blockaders with women at the wheel, or even as passengers, were rarely challenged. Perhaps owing to out-dated chivalry or maybe only as a courtesy to women, the Revenooers never stopped them. Thus, as Tom continued to hear of valuable cargoes being destroyed and even more valuable trucks and cars being seized, he got an idea. He and Jim would put Carrie behind the wheel.

Broached with the idea, she scoffed, "Me learn to drive a car? This pup is a little too old to learn that trick." However, always anxious to please Tom and unable to outlast his entreaties, she gave in. And she took to it like a duck to water.

Soon, while the men remained home, she was negotiating the back roads every bit as good as, or even better than a man. It didn't take long until their routine had become so successful that they almost forgot that what they were doing was against the law.

The stillers didn't even take particular heed when Tom came home from town one day to tell Carrie about a rumor he had just heard. Seems that Mrs. Taylor had told her husband that unless Tom was jailed, there would be no further joy in the marital bed. That threat was all it took for the sheriff to concoct a plan.

The ladies of the WCTU, accompanied by a couple of shotgun-wielding Revenooers, would stage a frontal attack on Tom's still.

The posse would arrive in force, hopefully when Tom and Jim were below in the fields, storm up the slight incline and completely destroy everything in sight. Then, armed with a warrant the judge in Little Rock had issued, they would arrest Tom and Jim.

While that was happening, the sheriff and his deputies would lay an ambush for Carrie.

It was a good plan and surely would have worked, but for two things. The first was the Arkie sense of community. Even though the farms of Independence and nearby counties were scattered and often isolated, every farmer knew his neighbor. And, owing to the tendency of grown children to settle nearby when striking out on their own, often that neighbor was a relative. Many was the farmer who could count thirty or forty actual and shirt-tail relatives who lived within twenty miles of him.

The second thing was just pure luck, thanks to Tom's cousin, Esmeralda. Esmeralda was a clerk for the judge in Little Rock and was tasked by him to prepare the warrants. However, the ink on them was still drying when she flew to get word to Tom.

As soon as Tom heard, he immediately sprang into action and before the day was out every neighbor for miles around knew, also.

The next morning before the sun was up even, a veritable army of wagons gathered behind Tom's house and listened to him announce that by the time the sun went down, they would have hauled away the entire still, garbage and all, leaving behind only Jim's red-lettered sign reading: "Welcome Revenooers and ladies of the WCTU." The taunt would remain even after the Revenooers had gone away and Tom's neighbors had brought everything back.

As to Carrie, the sheriff's look-out reported her as leaving on schedule. After that though, she disappeared. She had taken advantage of an unwatched cut-off and instead of heading east to Memphis, was roaring south to Little Rock. Nestled among her jugs was a special one to be left on the judge's porch. In the same bright red letters, Jim had written on it, "Compliments of the Batesville chapter of the WCTU and Mrs. Cleo Taylor."

By 1925 Tom and Jim's dad, Dan, and his wife, Sallie, had added a little boy, Hubert, to the many children and grandchildren populating Dan's farm. Except for the older ones who had left to strike out on their own, at home there still remained most of the thirteen children Dan had had with his first wife, Mary, as well as the three he had had with his second wife, Louella.

Owing to marriages and emancipations, as well as the occasional return, it was hard to know just who would be at the supper table on Sunday afternoon when the entire family was expected to be present. Sometimes there were as many as three dozen, other times only a few. Especially considering that several of these almost-twenty children were now having their own children and were bringing them along for visits, mealtime at Pa's house often resembled barely controlled chaos rather than a convivial family gathering.

However, when Dan and Sallie came to visit, in spite of the fact that they knew of the rigorous demands of the Tom and Jim's farming and whiskey making activities, they left all but Hubert at home. In their minds, the visit was more of a vacation for themselves than an opportunity to help out Dan's hard-pressed sons.

Dutiful sons that they were, neither Tom nor Jim voiced a single word of criticism. The visitors were waited on as royalty. Sallie did occasionally yell at one of Tom's younger boys for some minor infraction, but Dan seemed able to ignore any distraction as he set up a more or less permanent presence in a rocker on the porch. Only his visits to the table for meals, to the outhouse for necessary business and to the shelf for the jug, interrupted his "rigorous" routine. By the time the sun was setting and he was being summoned for supper, he often had had a few too many trips up the hill to replenish the jug.

After a few days of this and after she had returned from an overnight run to Memphis, Carrie could hold her tongue no longer.

"Pa," she said to Dan, "ain't you gonna do a blessed thing except sit there in that chair and chew and drink? We could use some help around here. They's wood to chop, water to be brought in, cows to milk. And Tom and Jim pert near running on empty all the time. They're exhausted every night."

But Dan just sat, smiled and rocked. He rocked and looked out across the fields, not acknowledging what she had said.

Later, when Tom returned from the fields, Carrie took him aside to complain. Hearing her out, a wry half-smile crept through his tiredness and he said: "I think I got an idea. Here's what we'll do."

The next evening at supper the main course was venison stew. However, as a part of a conspiracy known to all but Dan and Sallie, the edible pieces of the meat had been replaced by the worst gristle and fat Carrie could find. Tom and his family didn't say anything, but sat quietly eating as if it were sirloin. Dan put his first piece in his mouth, tried to chew it and said:

"Dad gum it, Tom, this is just about the boniest piece of meat I ever did have. Carrie, get in there and get me a decent piece."

"Pa," she said, "they are all the same. How's yours Jim?"

"It's just fine," he lied, barely able to get it down.

"Loyce, how's yours?"

"It's good, Carrie. It's just great."

"Pa," Tom said, "your teeth OK? Maybe you need some new choppers. Have some more taters and carrots. Surely you can handle them."

"Ain't a blamed thing wrong with my teeth. And if I wanted to be a vegetarian I would have been born a cow."

Nevertheless, Dan avoided the remainder of meat on his plate and filled up with vegetables.

Had Dan been more attentive, he would have noticed that despite their best efforts, the boys periodically had to stifle guffaws and giggles. Finally, Sallie did notice and said to Clifford:

"Boy, what you snickering at?"

Quickly recovering, Clifford placidly looked at her and said: "Oh, nothing. I was just thinking about something that happened today."

When it came time for dessert, there was berry pie. However, it was pie like had never been served in that house before. It had been made completely without sugar. Of course with the first mouthful Dan immediately loudly complained:

"That's the worst pie I ever tasted. It ain't got no sugar in it."

"That's right, Pa," Carrie said, "Some of us been putting on a few extra pounds and so I'm cutting back on the sugar."

"Cutting back!" he cried, "They ain't no sugar at all in it. I can't eat that."

As the others acted like it was the best berry pie ever, Dan sat watching them, not believing his eyes. Finally finishing almost all of his, Tom headed for his rocker on the porch. Dan followed. Seated, Tom picked up a plug of tobacco.

"Ain't you going to get the jug?" Dan wanted to know.

"Ain't no whiskey," Tom said matter of factly. "My still ain't been working right, and we done drank up all that we had. Besides, takes a lot of work to make whiskey and me and Jim just ain't had the time."

Finally, the older man caught on:

"You mean like Carrie ain't had the time to put sugar in the pie, and it was too much work to put anything in the stew but the garbage chunks?"

"You got it, Pa. That's exactly right."

Then, turning his head to the left to yell back over his shoulder Tom shouted:

"Carrie, Boys, you can bring it out now."

Tom's call was the signal for Carrie to proudly trot onto the porch carrying a dish of stew containing nothing but the most tender chunks of meat, followed by Otto with a pie as sweet as any ever made, and lastly by Loyce with a full jug of whiskey.

After uproarious laughter lasting well into the night, the next day Dan decided he would help with some chores and insisted that Carrie do her part in the kitchen.

●●●●●●

Denying to all that Leone wasn't coming home, Tom tried to keep all matters concerning his boys to himself. He was resolved not to involve Carrie if he didn't have to and insisted that he would be solely responsible for their discipline and instruction. His thinking was that when Leone returned, Carrie would leave, and Leone would smoothly resume her place as mother and wife. Of course it didn't work out exactly as Tom envisioned.

Often discipline for the boys could not wait until Tom could return to administer whatever was required. Thus, in spite of Tom's determination, Carrie took on a greater and greater role as the female head of the household.

Fortunately, they were blessed by the fact that the boys presented no serious problems. The four youngsters were healthy, strong and obedient, if at times rambunctious. Even at their young ages they seemed to innately sense that acting out was simply not in anyone's self-interest. There just wasn't time for it. They also recognized that without their strong backs, arms and good work habits, it simply would have been impossible for the adults to successfully farm and still. *And,* Tom often said to himself:

Keep 'em tired enough and they won't have energy enough to show out.

That's not to say that there weren't occasional lapses. There was the time that fourteen-year old Loyce got into the white mule. However, his father's belt and the boy's terrible hang-over ensured that it would be a long time before that happened again.

"Pa," the boy remorsefully lamented the next morning, "I ain't never gonna take another drink as long as I live." Nevertheless, as an adult, Loyce was a heavy drinker for most of his life, finally quitting for some unannounced reason when in his seventies.

And there was the fighting. Almost daily two or more of the boys got into it. Usually it was Clifford and the always feisty Otto, but the other two did their share also. So long as there was not too much blood and no broken bones, Tom ignored it, remembering the many fights he had had with his siblings as he was growing up in his pa's crowded household.

You ought to try it with just one arm, he occassionally thought but never said.

Like most parents of that era, Tom took the old adage, "Spare the rod and spoil the child" as gospel. Until the boys got too big for the belt, Tom would reward infractions with heavy and painful blows. Fortunately for the boys, because of Tom's lack of an arm, any physical resistance they might put up as they grew older was effective sooner that it might have been. But before about the age of twelve, none of the boys was a stranger to bare bottomed strappings.

Of the four boys, Clifford was the most curious and interested in schooling. He had learned to read quicker than the others, and in spare moments, of which there were not many and then only in the winter-time, he buried his nose in his mother's books. He had told Tom that when he read her books, not only did he like what he read and learned, but also it helped him remember her. Leone was becoming less of a remembered presence in their lives, and the older boys sought ways to maintain connection with her. For Clifford, Leone's books were his link to a mother he continued to miss.

But by about the third or fourth grade the boys were largely done with formal schooling. Due to planting, harvesting and other farm needs, their attendance had always been irregular. However because neither Tom or Jim had gone beyond grade school and since they both read, wrote and did arithmetic with enough competency to get by on the farm, further "book learnin" for the boys was abandoned in favor of farm chores.

None of the boys particularly cared for the Bible readings Tom insisted on each evening. Even the stories of the Old Testament couldn't hold their interest. "Them old dumb stories," Otto had called them, resulting in a quick swat from Tom and the admonition that he would tell Leone about the boy's blasphemy. So each evening the entire family sat in the light of a kerosene lamp and quietly if not fully attentively listened as Tom dutifully instructed them.

As to Allen, the eight-year old baby of the family, he was quiet, sweet and largely run over by his older brothers. He wasn't as big or as boisterous as the others, and so he was easy for them to ignore him or give a gratuitous punch to the arm or shoulder as they passed by. Allen's frequent complaints to his father that his brothers were picking on him had a standard response:

"Well, hit 'em back."

CHAPTER THIRTEEN

Preparing for bed one evening, Leone folded her thin mattress back in order to tuck in her bottom sheet and saw something she had never noticed before. Scratched almost illegibly into the bed frame was the following: "H.F. 9/15/1902". She had just noticed this when Eunice came from next door for one of their bedtime chats.

"Eunice," Leone asked, "who was H.F? Did she have this bed before me?"

"H.F," the older woman answered, "stands for Hettie Fowler. Yep, this was her room for seven or eight years."

"What was wrong with her?" Leone asked.

"I don't think anyone ever rightly knew. I guess her official diagnosis was schizophrenia or pellagra or something, but she just got more and more out of touch with reality. Towards the end, she didn't even know where or who she was."

"What happened to her?"

"She died."

"You mean she didn't never get no better and she died right here? She never went home?"

"That's about the size of it. Wasn't all that old either. I don't think they ever did figure out what she died of. She kinda gave up the will to live and just wilted away."

"Oh, Eunice, I don't want to die here. I want to get well and go home and be with my kids."

"Don't we all, Leone. Don't we all."

"The Lord will get me home again. I pray to him every day and I know he will."

"Leone, I hate to be the one to tell you this, but there ain't no God, and ain't nobody going to get you out of here except you."

"Ain't no God? What are you talking about?"

"Do you think if there really was a God, he would allow all this suffering to go on? All these wars, and diseases, and droughts and floods?

"That's the Devil doing that. It ain't God."

"Ain't God supposed to know everything, be everything, be in charge of everything? No, Leone, there ain't a God and you might as well get yourself resigned to it. I wasn't always an atheist. I was brought up a good Baptist, just like you. But the more I learned, and the more I saw, the more I came to know there could not be a God. It just don't make no sense. God is just a myth and fable to comfort people scared of dying."

As Leone was trying to digest these words she had never before heard the like of, a scream was heard from the other end of the wing: "Fire! Fire! Fire!" All the women, including Eunice and Leone, rushed to peer down the hallway.

Apparently one of the patients had, against the rules, been smoking in bed and caught her bedding on fire. It wasn't much of a fire really, and the woman's neighbors had readily jerked the bed clothes off, and quickly extinguished the flames with one of the buckets of water which sat randomly against the wall up and down the aisle. However, Leone had seen the fire.

As her eyes widened and rolled back in her head, she set up such a howling as had rarely been heard even in that institution filled with the deranged and almost so. Her deep throated scream was unique and something unto itself. For sheer volume and capacity to induce terror, even the largest African predators would have been hard-pressed to compete. The most common phrase used later to describe it by those present that evening was "like a scream from Hell."

And Leone didn't stop. When Eunice and the others tried to comfort her, she fought them off, clawing and kicking anyone who came near. Even when the guards arrived to brusquely shove her arms in a straitjacket and strap them against her body, her baying and yelping continued. Once restrained, the guards roughly threw her on a gurney, secured her there with thick straps, and hustled her off to isolation.

Two days later a much subdued and chagrined Leone found herself again in Doctor Horthamer's office. During the six years Leone had been institutionalized, it was perhaps her tenth visit there, each visit following an incident similar to the one she had just experienced.

"So, it was fire again. Devil there this time? Say, Leone, I think your outbreaks are becoming more frequent. Didn't you have one less than a month ago?"

Leone didn't answer, but stood staring at the floor.

"What we going to do with you Leone? Treatments don't seem to be helping you and you're getting worse."

"Maybe if I could get a pass to go home for a few days. I know you started giving some of the girls passes. My little one is already eight years old and don't hardly know me. My husband ain't able to leave the farming and bring the kids down here near enough. Couldn't we try that, please?"

"Yeah, you sound perfectly fine now, but who knows what you're capable of. Sorry, Leone, but someone who tried to burn up their own kids will not be getting no passes. We'll continue the treatments. Now, take off your dress. You know what to do."

• • • • • •

Well, Hattie thought to herself several months later as she was getting ready for the trip to see Leone, *I certainly do hope she ain't too crazy this time. This is sure a lot of trouble to go to just to get down there if she's having one of her episodes.*

With their constantly growing families (Hattie now had nine children and Mabel four) it had became harder and harder for them to travel. Nevertheless, they had made the trip several times during the past few years. At first their husbands had accompanied them, but now begged off, usually with the excuse of too much to do at work. Even the sisters' father and his second wife, Mattie, had visited once a year or so. For this trip John Bell, many pounds overweight and increasingly immobile, had begged off the several-hour train ride with the claim that his gout and rheumatism were acting up.

"Pa," Hattie asked during a visit to her father at Floral just before leaving for Little Rock, "is there anything you want us to tell Leone for you?"

"Tell that girl," he answered sincerely, "we love her like the dickens and are sure she'll soon be frisky as a colt and home again soon. And tell her we'll be down to see her as soon as we can."

Thanks to their father's largess, when in Little Rock the sisters and their broods stayed at the Capital Hotel, the best in town. In addition to its general grandeur, the hotel was famous for its elevator, reputedly built over-sized so that President Grant, visiting after the Civil War, could take his horse upstairs to his room with him. After Mabel had told the elevator story to her pa, he harrumphed and said:

"Probably would have, that damned Yankee."

"Or maybe they built that elevator special because they knew we'd be coming with all these kids," Mabel laughingly responded, referring to the six of her own and Hattie's they were taking with them.

On the train, Hattie reminded Mabel that because the weather was so nice, they would probably be visiting with Leone outside and that the chiggers had been particularly bad this year. Chiggers didn't seem to bother the adults so much because they usually didn't wrestle and roll around in the grass like the children did. However, many was the child who returned from a visit to the asylum's spacious lawns covered in bite swellings, a tiny chigger in the middle of each one.

Usually Hattie and Mabel would spend two days at the asylum, retiring to their hotel right after dinner the first day and returning early the next morning. The institution's administrators believed family contact facilitated recovery, and thus allowed adults to eat with their patient for ten cents each, children under twelve free. The third day, they would take the first train back to Searcy. That was their plan for this visit, as well.

However when they walked through the front door on the first day they were surprised to see that Leone was not waiting for them as she usually was. Instead, they were greeted by a long-faced guard supervisor who told them that Leone had had what she called "an incident."

As the supervisor related it, that morning Leone had been in an extremely good mood, humming and singing to herself as she prepared for the visit. She had been washing her hair, when for no reason anyone was able to perceive, she suddenly flung the water-filled wash basin aside and fell on the floor, sobbing and mumbling incoherently. Then, as the duty guard approached her, the story continued, her friend, Eunice interceded: "Let me get her to her bed," Eunice was reported to have said. "I think she'll be OK. No need to put her in isolation again."

Thus, Eunice and another woman were allowed to carry the whimpering Leone to her bed, where they towel-dried her hair, put her in a dry night gown, and installed her under the sheets.

"So," the supervisor concluded the tale, "she ain't in no shape to have a visit today. However Eunice says she's a lot better now than she was this morning. Eunice says you should come back tomorrow."

That evening in the hotel, after they had finally gotten the last of the children to sleep, Hattie and Mabel had a conversation about Leone like they had never had before. Previously, when they talked about her, many of their sentence began with, "when Leone gets well," or, "when Leone comes home." This time was different.

"Mabel," Hattie said, "Leone ain't never getting well and she ain't never coming home. You see that, don't you?"

Tears welled up in Mabel's eyes as she responded:

"Oh, Hattie, I can't admit that. I pray for her every day. I just can't believe God would just keep punishing her like this. She's one of the sweetest people on this earth. And Tom and them four young'uns needing her every single day. It's just not fair."

"Well just get over it. She ain't coming home and that's obvious. I feel bad for her, too. But, you know, I wouldn't feel so bad for her, if she wasn't so nice when she's not gone crazy. When she's OK, there's no one I'd rather be with. She just seems to shine light on everything around. But then she goes nuts, and I really do believe the Devil is inside her, inside her controlling her completely. Nothing has brought more sorrow and grief into my life, into the lives of our whole family. I would never tell another soul on earth this, but sometimes it even makes me wonder if there really is a God, that and Mattie's little baby dying.

"And, as for Tom, if he had them young'un's best interests at heart, he would divorce Leone and marry Carrie."

••••••

The next day Hattie, Mabel and their several children arrived at the asylum as soon as visiting was allowed. There, in her usual spot just inside the door stood Leone, smiling weakly.

"I am so sorry," she blurted over and over as she was hugging and kissing both sisters and all six children. "I know y'all were here yesterday, but something came over me."

"First of all, Sis," Hattie responded as they made their way to the large lawn and picnic tables, "before I forget. Tom said to be sure to tell you he'll be here for a visit soon and that he loves you more than ever. He said to tell you Otto fell and broke his arm, but it healed up just fine. All the boys send their love."

"Yes, he told me that in a letter. He made it sound like just a little thing, but I know better. A broken arm is a big deal."

Seeing her sister's face cloud with mention of an injury to one of her boys, Mabel quickly took her hand and asked: "You still look a little peaked. You sure you're better?"

"I do feel a little weak, but I sure am glad to see you. I'll be OK and I'm so glad you came. What's that you got in the basket?"

"Got our lunch," Hattie answered as she opened her large wicker basket to show Leone the contents. "I reckon you get pretty sick of the same stuff to eat every day, so we brought you some real home cooking. We got ham and biscuits and green beans and chicken and all sorts a stuff."

Before Leone could respond, their attention was demanded by the cries of a young woman screaming and running across the lawn, her light summer dress trailing out behind her.

"Get off the track!" she was yelling as she flew past. "Get off the track, the train is coming! Woooo-wooooo!"

Her arms waving like windmills, the woman continued her flight around the expansive grassy area. The many patients and their visiting families watched as she reached the far side of the enclosed area and then started back again, all the while yelling:

"There's a train acoming, I tell you! Get off the track! We're all going to be killed! Wooooo! Wooooo!"

"It's OK," Leone said to her little group. "That's just Felice Henderson. She's harmless."

Hattie and Mabel were, of course, aghast. Not so the children. They thought it was funny. As soon as the fearful woman had disappeared back inside the building, all except the oldest ones began imitating her. Around and around they ran, yelling and "wooooo-wooooo-ing."

After a few minutes of imitation, Hattie's daughter, Opal, asked her mother: "Ma, can I have some of that cobbler now?"

"Why no, you can't have none of that cobbler now. I don't care if you did make it, it ain't near supper time."

"Mabel, you didn't bring your oldest ones," Leone said as she took stock of her nieces and nephews. "Why didn't you bring Jimmie and Raymond?"

"Well, they's teenagers now, and less and less interested in family. Reckon they got friends and sweethearts that take first priority."

"And Hattie, how many did you leave home?" Leone looked at her older sister. "You got so many, I swan I can't keep track. Ain't you never going to figure out what causes all these kids?" Leone laughed and repeated for about the one thousandth time what had become a stale joke for her sister.

"Ruby and Charlie is married and moved away. You knew that. And Norene didn't want to come. She's home with Pa. So I just brought the ones I could."

Leone's feelings about the children were mixed. While she relished seeing her nieces and nephews, at the same time they reminded her of her own four little ones, so that she had to concentrate not to think of them. Even later when she played a game of mumblety-peg with the boys, it was all she could do not to cry as she wondered whether Loyce yet had his own little pocketknife with which he played the same game.

After the women had talked about the weather, as well as the latest births, deaths and marriages, Hattie grew serious and said:

"Leone, I don't know if you know it or not, but ever since Ma died, Pa and I been trying to find her relatives up in Missouri. Figured the least we could do is tell them she died. We've sent letters to the sheriff, the postmaster and anyone else we could think of. But don't seem to be anyone that's ever heard of them. We're plumb out of ideas and have give up. Her people being your relations, too, we just thought you should know that."

As Hattie waited for a response, she thought:

I sure hope that don't set her off. I sure hope Pa was right, that she deserves to know.

But Hattie needn't have worried. Leone simply looked at her with interest and said:

"That's a shame. I sure would like to know more about Ma's people. I'll bet they've left Missouri. Probably moved out west somewhere. And, a gol-durned shame they disowned Ma when she married Pa."

Shrugging her shoulders at her sister's nonplussed acceptance of what she had said about their mother's family, Hattie brightly changed the subject:

"Leone, they was a man on the train that was saying there is a book about being an inmate here. You heard about that?"

"Why sure. Everyone here knows about it. His book is called, *Jimmy Warde's Experiences as a Lunatic.*" He was in here a few years back for a while, and then he got out, and wrote a book about it."

"Is that so?"

"I read it," Leone responded. "Or better to say, I looked at it. I started to read it, but it wasn't much, and I put it down. Just a bunch of rambling about God and religion and being in here, and all. I do like to read good books about God and religion, but this one sure wasn't a good one. That Jimmy Warde could write OK, but he just said the same old things over and over."

"Well, I guess so," Mabel laughed. "What would you expect from a book written by a lunatic?"

Leone laughed for a bit, too. Then she grew serious to say:

"You know there are some pretty smart people in here. A couple of these gals has even been to college some. And, most of us is pretty normal most of the time. Just because you're in here don't mean your brain totally quit working."

Neither Hattie nor Mabel responded to their sister's statement. Instead, Mabel was reaching for her knitting when Hattie's seven-year old, Billie, looked up at Leone to say:

"They was saying you're nutty as a fruitcake. They was saying you got to stay locked up in here and ain't never getting out."

The words had hardly left his mouth when his mother strong right hand walloped him across the side of his head and sent him sprawling.

"Where did you hear that?" she screamed at him. "Who told you that?"

"Somebody," he whimpered. "Everybody. I don't remember. Ma, please don't hit me again."

"If I ever hear you say something like that again, I'll knock you three ways from Sunday. Now quit your crying and sit over there under that tree till I tell you when you can get up."

And looking at Leone: "I'm sorry, Sis. Don't pay him no mind. He don't know nothing. Of course you're coming home, Sugar. Of course you are. They're inventing new treatments all the time and the doctor himself, or his nurse anyway, told me they're about to start doing something called electroshock. Supposed to work wonders."

I suppose the Lord will forgive me for that, Hattie thought to herself as soon as she had finished speaking. *I know she ain't never coming home, never mind what Mabel thinks.*

Leone looked blankly at Hattie and then silently rose to take the few steps to a nearby bench. There she sat and, with her face in her hands, began to sob.

• • • • • •

Most of the patients worked six days per week. Those who had jobs working in the kitchen or milking cows or some such, had to alternate their days off, but for most of the women every Sunday was the Sabbath. And, it being felt that church-going and religious instruction were necessary to eventual recovery, chapel attendance was mandatory. Excused of course were those who could not be counted on to maintain decorum and not be disruptive.

In spite of the fact that the State of Arkansas' rules and regulations for the operation of the asylum specified that appropriate church services were to be provided for all patients, the State had appropriated no money with which to hire a minister. However, an ingenious warden soon devised a plan to obtain one, even if it meant a different one every Sunday.

Each week from one of the nearby churches, a different minister would relinquish his assigned pulpit in his own church come to the asylum to preach. The local ministers liked the idea because not only would they be able to reach a previously isolated group, but it would give each of them an opportunity to preach what each of them regarded as the real version of religious truth, uninfluenced by some in their own congregations with their own idea of the gospel. Thus, one Sunday the patients might hear a sermon originating in the Baptist persuasion, the next Sunday from the Methodist viewpoint, and the following Sunday based on Full Gospel beliefs. Catholics, Jews, and Muslims would have to fend for themselves.

In spite of praying regularly, Leone had never been overly religious. Of course she had gone to church all her life, but if she had been asked what was the most important part of her church attendance, she might have answered that it was singing the old hymns and socializing after services. Even when she prayed to God to be saved from the Devil it wasn't because she had a consuming belief. It was more like she had no other recourse and didn't know what else to do.

Unlike others, Leone never felt that she had an intimate relationship with the Lord. He just wasn't a continuing, always present factor in her life. Even when she was in the clutches of the Devil and begged and beseeched on a most personal level for God to save her, as soon as the episode was over, God again became a less than notable presence in her life.

"Oh, God's present in my life all right," she told her friend Beverly one day, "it's just that until I'm having one of my spells and the Devil shows up, I don't need him all that much. Then, when I'm fighting with the Devil, I need him like crazy."

"Maybe if he was more a part of your life, the Devil wouldn't show up at all. Ever think of that?" Beverly asked.

"I've tried that. I've tried praying about a hundred times a day and he still shows up. Don't seem to make no difference what I do, he just shows up."

Then, something happened in a neighboring state that caused Leone to change the way she regarded God. In the asylum, the patients had ready access to several newspapers and even radio broadcasts. Thus they followed along with the rest of the country when a school teacher named John Scopes was put on trial and convicted in Tennessee, for teaching that the origin of man as taught in the Bible was not correct. Instead, he taught that the theory of evolution as espoused by Charles Darwin had an irrefutable scientific basis and, as such had to supersede what was written in the holy book. Under Tennessee law such teachings were illegal. The trial, popularly known as the Scopes Monkey Trial, received world-wide attention and was a topic of daily conversation throughout the South, the country and the asylum.

The following Sunday after Scopes' conviction, there came to preach at the asylum one Jacob Katzner, a Pentecostal preacher from a no-longer-existent nearby little town. He was outraged. During the entirety of his sermon he fulminated against Scopes and Darwin, and what he called, "crackpot theories" such as evolution. All but foaming at the mouth, he deluged the patients with more fire and brimstone than most of them had ever heard. And Leone took it to heart.

At first she sat passively listening to Reverend Katzner's rantings. Then, as the preacher stormed, she suddenly joined several other women in leaping up and violently throwing herself to the floor. There, she thrashed about, writhing and babbling incoherently in an unknown language. She was speaking in tongues.

And God had come to her in a way she had never previously known. Abruptly and without warning God had become her personal God, one who occupied and possessed and became her, much like the Devil had on other occasions. Leone never asked why. She just started believing that from that day forward, the Devil was not going to be the sole contender for her soul.

•••••••

Sunday afternoon after church in the asylum was a quiet time for relaxation, reading and quiet conversation, followed by the best summer of the week—usually fried chicken with mashed potatoes and gravy, along with vegetables and desserts from the asylum's fields and orchards. On Leone's ward this day she sat with several other women, knitting and talking.

Nearby, two recent admittees lay on a divan, fondling each other and kissing. Elsewhere there were other pairings. Some of them were long-established with little overt signs of affection. Others, usually consisting of younger women, were more demonstrative.

No one paid them any attention.

When Leone had first arrived, she had been shocked by women being intimate with each other. *Well, ain't that something,* she remembered thinking, *I have never seen the like.* But soon she was completely at ease and even on occasion looked approvingly on their affection as a reminder of what she and Tom had shared, and what she reminded herself every day she was going to return to.

Suddenly through the front door burst the warden, followed by her assistant.

"What in the Holy Hell is going on?" she screamed. "Didn't I tell you? I told you and told you. You ain't gonna cost me my job. If you can't keep it hid, this lesbian shit is going to stop. I'll stop it if I have to put every last one of you in segregation."

All stared as she continued.

"After supper that visiting preacher and his wife wanted to take a look at where y'all live. So we come over to this ward and before I could open the door and say we was coming in, his wife peeks in the window. And what's the first thing she sees? Why, two gals fucking each other, that's what. Naked as jay-birds, laying on a bunk, licking each other's pussies."

Then it was Eunice, Leone's neighbor and friend who took center stage. Always one of the smarter and more assertive inmates, Eunice purposefully strode forward to stand before the warden and in a voice loud enough for all to hear, responded.

"Warden, you well know they ain't hardly any of us lesbians on the outside. But when you lock us in here for years at a time, we're going to take comfort where we can. Given circumstances, ain't nothing wrong with what these gals is doing."

"Don't you understand, Eunice? That preacher and his wife are going to go back and tell everyone who will listen that I'm just running a Sodom and Gomorrah here, that gals is in here loving each other every which a way. And they ain't even seen what I know goes on in your shower and who's sleeping with who. Now, I don't care that it's agin the Bible. And I know a gal who's had some lovin' is easier for me to manage. But I ain't gonna lose my job over it."

"Warden," Eunice continued, "now it's you that don't understand. Some of these women have been together for years. Don't matter how they was on the outside. In here, they are just the same as any married couple, man and women, loving and caring for each other, especially as they get older or crazier and need lots of comforting."

As Leone stood spellbound like the rest, she reflected on the several times she had been approached by women subtly, and not so subtly offering intimate companionship and even casual sex. Each time, despite her longings, she declined. Each time her thoughts of Tom kept her from the more intimate relationship she craved. However each time her resolve imperceptibly lessened.

The warden's final statement jerked her back to reality:

"Now the lot of you listen up and spread the word. I don't give a rat's ass what you do when no one ain't looking. But when there is someone besides me and my staff around, you sure as hell better keep this lesbian shit hid."

CHAPTER FOURTEEN

"Leone sure did like venison," Tom whispered to Jim as they sat in their deer blind just after dawn waiting for the large buck they had seen nearby the day before.

"Me, too," Jim whispered back. "But these bucks can get a little gamy. I like me a nice young doe. Remember that little doe we took down at Strawberry Creek last year? That was just about the sweetest and most tender venison I ever tasted."

"It sure was. I don't know why a lot of folks is always looking to shoot themselves a buck with a big rack. You can't eat them horns and their meat sometimes ain't fit for the dogs."

"What's your favorite part?" Tom asked, even though he full-well knew his brother preferred the liver.

"The liver, of course. Remember that time we put a bunch of parts in a skillet and had a tasting? We both liked the liver best. The heart and the pancreas was durned good, but for my money you just can't beat fresh deer liver."

Although Tom and Jim enjoyed hunting, it wasn't done for sport. It was done in order to put food on the table. Without much regard for a law-established season, they hunted, trapped and fished year around for whatever might be had. They eagerly harvested deer, wild boar, turkeys, squirrels, rabbits and even an occasional bear, plus all manner of flying critters, including pheasants, ducks, quail and dove. Once during a particularly lean time Tom even tried to eat a skunk, although he remarked afterward that the eating wasn't hardly worth the stink.

They fished for trout, perch, bass and crappie. However, their favorite fishing activity was "holin' catfish." Catfish as big as ten or even twenty pounds made their homes in muddy banks in holes they had created along the creeks and rivers. Tom and Jim would catch them by feeling along under the water until they came across a hole. Then they would reach in and, if a catfish was there, reach down its throat, grab hold of anything they could and jerk the fish out. Fortunately, the cats didn't have large teeth and small scratches on their arms were the only price the "holers" paid. And the meat was, Jim thought, even better than venison.

"Shhh," Tom shushed as he lowered himself even a little further behind the branches of the blind. "I see him. He's going right to the boys."

Otto and Allen were in a similar blind on the far side of a large open field. Neither of the young teenagers had previously shot a deer and Tom had positioned their blind so that it was likely that if a deer came along, it would afford them a shot. He had shot his own first deer at much less than Otto's fifteen years and Tom very much wanted him to bag his first one.

"Hot dog," Jim carefully peered out. "This is going to be good. That big 'ol whitetail is just walking right over to them."

Hardly able to talk for the tension and hope, Tom whispered, "Come on. Come on. That's it. Just keep on walking. Yep, that' right, git a mouthful of grass. Come on. Just a few feet further."

Suddenly, quicker than the blink of an eye, the buck snapped his head erect, launched himself forward and disappeared into the trees.

Tom and Jim stumbled over each other getting out of the blind, Tom yelling at the top of his lungs: "Why didn't you shoot? You had him. Why didn't you shoot?"

Tom continued to yell as he ran toward the now-emerged Otto and Allen, who were also running to meet them. As they neared each other, Tom again repeated: "Why didn't you shoot? Were you asleep?" Then he saw that Otto was crying.

"Pa, I'm sorry. I forgot to cock it. I forgot and when I did, he heard me and took off."

"Otto, I told you to cock it as soon as you got in the blind. Why didn't you do that?"

Tears continuing to flow, Otto blubbered: "I forgot, Pa. I just forgot."

Overcoming his anger and disappointment, Tom composed himself and for one of the few times in his life hugged his son. "It's alright, boy," he said. "We'll get him another day. There will be other bucks."

• • • • • •

The Great Flood as the came to call it, started in the spring in the north and in its heyday flooded the tributaries of the Mississippi from Montana to Pennsylvania. Day after day it rained and rained and rained. Then it rained some more. Even after every river, creek, dam and impoundment was full, it continued to rain. The result was the greatest flood the Mississippi drainage has ever seen. The waters spilled out across lands and farms far, far from the customary flood plain, and fields fifty or even one hundred miles from the river were covered with as much as thirty feet of muddy, stinking water. Hardest hit were the states of Arkansas, Mississippi and Louisiana.

Farmers floating by on their houses became a common sight. The corpses of people and animals were too common to count. Wrecked buildings and flotsam of every sort and description covered the surface of the flowing waters. People, animals and even poisonous snakes nervously shared every high ground.

And, it wasn't like the people didn't have advance notice. Radios had become common by this time, and even those without electricity had battery operated models to tune in to the news, soap operas and the hugely popular Grand Ole Opry. The airwaves were filled with the most dire warnings about the huge walls of water moving south. But there was little to be done. No one could be prepared for as much water as they were about to experience.

The mighty Mississippi and its tributaries had, of course, flooded for thousands or even millions of years. But those previous floods had been at a time before man had entered the picture.

When the first settlers arrived, they observed a river much different than it became. The river in the seventeenth century, and before, was bounded on both sides by wide expanses of lowlands and swamp.

Reaching as many as fifty miles from the river to both the east and the west, this alluvial land was capable of periodically absorbing untold millions of gallons of flood water.

However, the richly silted land was incredibly fertile, and the first settlers wasted no time in diking the river, cutting down the timber and planting it in cotton, corn and wheat. This not only deprived flood waters of a place to go, it also meant that the channeled water would wreak havoc when the inevitable breaks in the dikes occurred.

Although there were other causes which contributed to the magnitude of the disaster, it was the huge levees built to keep the river inside its banks that were the main reason so many suffered. These huge levees, stretching for hundreds of miles along both sides of the river, often towered high above the adjacent fields. They were fine so long as they held. However once there was a break, or a crevasse as they were called at that time, they released the full force of the water onto the lower-lying land.

During the Great Flood all the biggest rivers in Arkansas, including the Red, the White and the St. Francis, overflowed their banks for many weeks at a time. Their yellow, dirty waters even reached as far inland as Little Rock, in the center of the state. At one point, the White even ran backwards as the Mississippi overflowed its traditional channels and the water had nowhere else to go except back up its own tributary.

And the disastrous effects of the flood were not limited to just property destruction and loss of animal and human life. Victims and sometimes even their saviors sometimes became venal and vicious in their efforts to save their farms and possessions, or even to profit by the general misfortune.

Run by northern Red Cross personnel, hundreds of camps were set up across the south to shelter and feed the thousands of homeless. However, when the lifesaving supplies were delivered to local landowners for distribution, corruption often set in and receipt of something to eat was often tied to hours and hours of back-breaking levee labor.

There were several documented instances of one riparian land owner trying to save his own land by dynamiting the levee across the river, ensuring that his neighbor on the other side would be flooded and not him. Tom's farm was of course too far from the river for any such dynamiting to have immediate effect on him, but the waters thus unleashed certainly contributed to the general problem of too much water with no legitimate place to go.

Landowners desperate for levee workers sometimes arrived at Red Cross camps not only with their own guns, but also with those of National Guardsmen accompanying them in order to, temporarily at least, re-enslave black men. One black man, visiting the South from his home in the North, was charged with vagrancy and forced to work long days trying to save what had been slave-worked plantations just sixty years before.

Southerners, desperate for help, called out to the Federal government. Often they were met with the claim that the flood waters were on Southern land and that therefore it was a Southern problem. Southern assertions that the water had been Northern water until it was sent South were ignored. Coming hard on the heels of the Civil War and Reconstruction, an unneeded wedge was driven between the North and the South.

With this latest disaster many black people had had enough, and even a few of the small number who lived in Tom's area left for Chicago and other cities of the North, never to return.

For many of the farmers, black and white, who chose to stay, the flood year was simply a lost one. After the water had receded there was no way to get seeds in the ground, make a crop and get it harvested before winter set in. In order to survive many had to depend on government "dole", private hand-outs and loans from friends and relatives.

● ● ● ● ● ●

Tom had never seen a time when the high waters of the local rivers didn't drain off after a day or so. Thus when riders came to warn of the approach of a huge flood, he was confident his farm wouldn't be affected. Looking down across his fields from his porch, he told Jim:

"They're saying this flood is so big we might get washed out. How could that be? Pa's been here since just after the Civil War and he ain't never been flooded. We been farming this neck of the woods for years and we ain't never been flooded."

"I don't know," Jim shook his head. "They're saying this is the biggest flood since Noah."

"Well, even if it is, we ain't got nothing to worry about. Even if the river overflows big-time and floods those lower fields, I don't see how it could ever get up here to the house. We ain't got a lot of elevation, but we got some."

The next morning when the family gathered at the table for breakfast Tom asked:

"Where's Allen?"

"He was here a minute ago," Otto responded. "I think he went to bring that colt up. That colt was in the field down there next to the corn field."

Jim was the first one with his hat on and about to go out the door when he abruptly stopped himself and shouted:

"Good God Almighty, would you look at this."

As Carrie and the others rushed to look, they were stunned by the sight of more water than they had ever seen before, water as far as the eye could see. As the rising sun reflected off flat waters, Tom's fields had become shiny mirrors, glistening to the horizon. Except for the tops of a few isolated trees breaking the expanse, the lower reaches of the farm resembled nothing else so much as a huge lake, an endless gleaming lake. Revealing eddies and slight ripples indicated that the water was still rising and had almost reached the vegetable garden.

"Oh, that is so pretty." Carrie said, "So terrible pretty."

"Jim, Otto," Tom shouted, "get started carrying our stuff out. Get everything you can up the hill. First grab our pictures and clothes. And don't forget the bible. And our food. Don't forget the stuff in the cellar. Carrie, come with me. You got to row us to Allen."

After their last fishing trip their weathered little boat had been stored in the back of the barn, where Tom and Carrie had to wade through a foot of muddy, yellowish flood water to get to it. Tom quickly turned it right side up, Carrie threw the oars in and jumped in after them. As Tom pushed them off into deeper water, he thought to himself:

If this ain't gol-durndest thing, he thought as Carrie began to pull at the oars. *If it ain't one thing, it's another. Locusts and Leone having her spells. Julia and Gracie taking off on me. And now, maybe Allen drowned. Lord, ain't you ever going to be done testing me?*

Carrie was all but exhausted when they finally reached Allen. The boy was about a mile away, exactly where Tom thought he would be, sitting over the muddy water in the crotch of a dead oak tree. The terrified colt, tethered by the rope Allen had placed around his neck, was swimming in circles, uncomforted by the soothing words Allen repeated over and over.

"Pa," the boy cried out as soon as Tom paddled to within shouting distance, "I sure am glad to see you. I'm fine, but this here colt is plumb tuckered out. He would have been a goner for sure if you hadn't come when you did."

As soon as Tom drew near, Allen half-fell, half-jumped into the boat and Carrie regained her strength enough to start pulling for higher ground. Fortunately, only a couple hundred yards away, the top of a small hill had become an island and it only took a very few minutes before the boat was scraping in the rock-filled mud and the colt was standing out of the water. By this time the sun was well into its ascent, so that the four of them, Tom, Carrie, Allen and the little horse, were able to lie in the warm sunlight and rest.

After a while, turning on his side to examine the colt with a practiced eye, Tom said:

"He'll be OK. Give him a few minutes and he'll be good as new."

"Me, too, Tom," Carrie said. "I just need to rest a little longer."

"Rest as long as you want, but Allen's going to row us back. He ain't done no rowing today."

"That fine, Pa," the boy said. "I can row as far as you need for me to." And then, after a moment of silence and out of the blue, "Carrie is more of a ma to us than our real ma. Ain't that right, Carrie? I can't hardly remember my real ma."

Carrie's eyes widened and she looked at Tom.

"Why that ain't true," Tom responded. "We was down there just last month."

"And she didn't hardly know me. Pa, she ain't right in the head. I don't think she's ever coming home. At least Carrie is here."

"Carrie ain't your ma," Tom said.

"I know," the boy answered, "but she might as well be. She'd be a real ma to us if you'd let her."

"Your ma is coming home someday," Tom said. "You'll see, she'll be back."

"How do you know that, Pa? She's been gone so long you even took her clothes to the barn. I don't think she's ever coming back."

"Son, I've heard just about enough of that. Your ma is coming home again and that's all there is to it. Now shush up."

After the better part of an hour, the colt had not only regained its strength, but had eaten all available grass off the little island and was looking for more. That was the sign for Allen to proudly take the oars and, the colt swimming confidently behind them, row them back home, a home now lakeside.

At its maximum, the flood waters inside the house had reached a depth of four feet. It took six days before they had subsided enough so that Tom and his family could go back inside and start shoveling the thick layer of mud that had been left behind. And it was three weeks after that before the fields, crops washed away of course, were completely clear of water.

Tom and his family had spent six days and nights up the hill next to the still they had re-installed after the Revenooers' visit. Fortunately, they had been able to carry up almost all their furniture and personal items. Only the heaviest items like stoves and the armoire which had once contained Leone's dresses had been left behind. All was placed around the still's copper pot and equipment, where it was joined by various chickens, pigs and their only milk cow. Even though making for an uncomfortable sleep, mattresses were kept up out of the mud by stretching them across any available pieces of furniture, where the chickens immediately thought a dry place had been specially created for them. Keeping them off was a losing battle.

The cellar had provided enough canned goods so that the humans had plenty to eat. Only the animals suffered, as Tom and Jim, not knowing how long the little bit of food they had brought for them would have to last, rationed it out sparingly.

Drinking water was just the opposite. The animals certainly didn't mind drinking the ugly flood waters, but the radio had been full of warnings about the danger from bacteria and diseases they harbored. These warnings Tom and his family took to heart, and instead relied on whatever water had been canned along with their peaches and other fruits and vegetables. When that was finished, it was Jim who realized that the pot of their still could be used to boil their drinking water.

They had anticipated food and water problems. What they had not foreseen was the boredom situation. After they had done all they could do to secure and make their little camp comfortable, there was nothing to do. At first, they talked and sang. However, after a short while, that too grew boring. Then they started word games and played the early twentieth century equivalent of "I spy with my little eye." That didn't last very long either.

Their last resort was playing mumblety-peg with their pocket knives. Every farmer of course always carried a pocket knife, not just while working, but all the time, even though on Sunday's and other non-working days a smaller pen knife was usually substituted for their bigger working blades. For the game, Tom and Jim of course had their big Barlows, while the boys had ones made by Case Brothers. Even Carrie, an enthusiastic participant, had her own knife.

The way the game was played was to open two blades of your knife and then flip the knife a short distance in the air. If it came down so that it stuck upright in the ground on one of its blade ends, it was a point for you. If the knife didn't stick, it was a point against you. How many rounds of this were to be played, with perhaps special rules, would be agreed on in advance.

The point of the game was to acquire enough points so that the loser would have to use his teeth to remove a small peg which had previously been pounded into the ground. Depending on how far into the ground an eyes-closed rap with the back of a knife had driven the peg, this could be a very messy, dirt-spitting affair.

"I don't know how you do it," Tom cried out after about the tenth time the now-giggling Otto had bested him. "I'm been eating dirt all morning."

One particularly cold and drizzly evening after Allen had begun sniffling with misery and despair, he found his way to lean up again Carrie as she reclined on a makeshift couch. Instinctively, she wrapped him in both her arms and the two of them sat watching a sputtering kerosene lantern in need of a wick-trimming. Tom didn't notice this at first, but when he did he immediately rose from his perch on a stack of firewood to come over to them.

"Allen," he said, "you ain't no baby. I ain't having no more squalling? Now get over there where you belong and off of Carrie."

Both Carrie and Allen glared at Tom, but the boy silently obeyed.

"You ought not to be like that, Tom," Carrie said. "The boy just needs a little comfort, maybe a little loving."

"I reckon his ma will give him all of that he needs when she gets home," he said to conclude the matter.

Eventually the flood waters receded, and they were able to start carting their things back. First however, they had to clean.

"What we gonna do now, Tom?" Carrie asked as she collapsed onto a chair in exhaustion after another full day of washing and cleaning. "How we gonna go on?"

"We're gonna get this house livable again and then we're gonna replant, of course," he answered, the tiredness in his voice noticeably slowing it. "Soon as the roads is dried out and I can get to town, I'll buy more seed and we'll do it again. Have to take out another loan, but I reckon we ain't got no choice."

"We got time this year to make a crop again before winter comes?" Jim joined the conversation to ask.

"I don't know. We'll try," Tom answered, his doubt apparent.

In the pause that followed, Tom realized that in spite of the fact that Leone had been constantly on his mind as he sat in boredom at the still, he had not one time thought of her once they had started bringing their things back. Even when he saw the empty armoire, his only thought was of what it would take to clean the mud caked at the bottom of it. *Honey,* he mentally apologized to her, *I'm sorry, but you been gone a long time. I just can't think of you every minute.*

Tom was one of the lucky ones who was able to make another crop that year. He got both his corn and his cotton in and harvested it, along with the vegetables from the garden. Only his tobacco didn't have time to ripen before fall rains and cool weather doomed it. The best canned goods had been consumed long before the vegetables in the garden were ready and he had to use some of his scarce supply of money to buy tobacco, but he had shepherded his family through another year. The following spring would again plant on schedule.

This night after the others were asleep, Carrie had again crept into his bed. She had not been there for several weeks, and on the one hand he had missed her badly. Not only did he crave the physical satisfaction she brought him, but the warmth and affection she had so much of sustained and nourished him. It helped him feel that there was more to life than just day after day of hard work. On the other hand, he was sometimes glad of her absence. Without her, he felt closer to Leone and spent more time re-reading his wife's letters. The hole in his being created by Leone's absence was mostly filled when Carrie was there and he felt guilty about that. *Yes,* he sometimes thought to himself, *it's better when she's in her own bed.*

"Tom," Carrie said softly after they had both finished and caught their breath, "you know I could have made you a good wife. You know that, don't you?"

"I know that."

"And a good mother to the boys, too."

"I know that, too."

"And I been right here by your side, through good times and bad times. Fighting locusts and Revenooers, and working like a slave. Most people would think struggling together like that would have brought a man and a woman together. But you won't let me in. As much as I try, there's just this wall. I try and try. I keep house the way I think you want. I cook the way you like. I love you whenever I can. I try to mother the kids just like a real mother would. But you won't let me get close to them. You keep telling them they got to just mind you and confide in just you; always telling them their ma will be coming back, that I ain't gonna be here forever. There's this part of you I just can't reach."

And, after a long silence: "Well, ain't you gonna answer me?"

"You ain't Leone."

"Tom, she's been there for nigh on to ten years and ain't getting no better. She ain't never coming home. You need to recognize that."

"No, Carrie, I can't believe it. She's coming home. She'll get better, you'll see. They'll come up with some new treatment or something, and she'll be normal again."

"The boys don't even hardly remember her. She's been there so long, they don't know her. Even when they go to visit, which is less and less often, she has to be told what their names are. When was the last time Loyce or Clifford visited?"

"All the same, Carrie, she's my wife and their ma, and I ain't giving up on her."

This time it was Carrie who fell silent. Then, after they had both stared up into the darkness for long seconds: "Tom, I'm gonna leave you."

"Forever?" he quickly turned onto his side to look at her.

"They's a widow man lives down by Searcy. His wife died here while back and left him alone with three young'uns. I ain't never met him and I understand he ain't exactly pick of the litter. But my cousin down there told him about me, and he's willing to have me, sight unseen. Willing to marry me right away."

"Does he drink?"

"Why, Tom, what a thing to ask. You drink. Lots of times a lot more than you should."

"I want you to be with someone who's gonna treat you right."

"My cousin says he's a hard-working, God-fearing Arkie. He's got a nice little farm right on a creek. And yes, my cousin says he drinks some. But he surely ain't no worse than you. At least he don't have a still up behind his house."

"Would it make any difference if I quit drinking?"

"Why do you ask? You considering it?"

"I been thinking about it for quite a spell, and it may be time. It ain't never done me no good and, truth be told, my life's been the worse for it."

"No, Tom, I've pretty much gotten used to your drinking. It don't bother me much any more. I just can't stand the thought of always playing second fiddle to a woman that may never be back."

Again, neither of them spoke, as Tom continued to stare at her.

"When you gonna go?" Tom at last asked.

"I got some chores around here I been putting off. I want to get those done. And I want to sit down with Otto and Allen and tell them how much I love them and how I'm gonna miss them. I'll tell Loyce and Clifford, too, as soon as I can. I figure it will take me about a week."

When Tom again fell silent, Carrie whispered: "Tom, I love you."

Finally, eyes glistening, he responded: "It don't have to be."

"Yes, Tom, it does. There comes a time when I got to get my needs met, too. I got to get something back and you just can't give it."

"Carrie, I love you."

"Tom, that's the first time you've ever said that."

"Reckon it's the first time I ever allowed myself to think it. But I can't give up on Leone. I just can't."

"I understand, Tom. I really do."

"But I'll be forever grateful for all that you've done. They's not another woman on this earth who could have done what you've done. These boys is mostly raised up and looks like they's all going to grow into fine young men. Loyce and Clifford already are. And we've got you to thank for that."

"Thank you for saying that, Tom. I'll not forget."

"And maybe we could come and visit sometimes, me and the boys. After you get married and all situated, we can stop in, maybe on our way to see Leone."

"Yes, Tom, do that. Please do that."

Oh, Lord, Tom thought, *can't you give me a sign? Please, please, am I doing the right thing? Giving up this good woman and waiting on a crazy wife who might never be back. Why do you have to make it so hard?*

CHAPTER FIFTEEN

By 1930 the asylum had had quite enough of Doctor Horthhamer. After he had been exposed as a fraud with a phony degree, he and his perversions were long gone. In his place was a young psychiatrist, Jonathan Adams, recently trained in the most modern techniques. The new doctor's first official act was to eliminate the tortuous ice baths Horthhamer had insisted on, replacing them with what was called Hydrotherapy.

Hydrotherapy, a new technique, consisted of putting patients in a box-like cabinet with only their heads sticking out. Then, the temperature and humidity inside was modulated from on the coolish side to quite warm for an hour or more. These treatments were hailed as the latest thing in effective in psychiatric treatment. The entire regimen consisted of twenty-one sessions, and generally the patients thought this new therapy a big improvement over the old. They looked forward to them not only for their therapeutic benefit, but also as a time for gossiping and socializing.

The treatment was mainly reserved for incoming patients, and Leone had already been there for more than ten years. However, she so strenuously insisted that she too be treated that the doctor finally gave in and scheduled her for all twenty-one sessions.

She was in the hallway about to enter the Hydrotherapy room for the first time when a young woman she had never seen before softly asked her:

"Excuse me ma'am, I know I ain't supposed to be here, but I'm lost. Could you kindly tell me where the niggers are?"

"Why, the niggers is over in the other wing. But why you want to know?"

"That's where I belong."

"How could you belong over there?" Leone incredulously asked. "You ain't a nigger."

"Why, yes, ma'am, I certainly am. Just look at the color of my skin. And this nose. I guess I sure am."

As Leone stared at the woman's narrow aquiline nose, and then at a hand every bit as white as her own, she didn't know what to say. Her quandary was interrupted by the arrival of a guard who said:

"Harriet, now why don't you go on down the hall and leave this young woman alone. Can't you see she's got business to tend to?'

"Yes, sir. Sorry to trouble you ma'am."

As Harriet shambled down the hall, the guard said to Leone:

"Can't convince her otherwise. She ain't no nigger. Her parents come to visit all the time and they're as white as I am."

"But, if she wants to live with them," Leone asked, "why don't you let her?"

"If it was up to me, that's exactly what we would do. But when the superintendent suggested it to her parents, they went crazy themselves. Said they'd have the government, and the law, and the Klan, and I don't know what all, down here on all of us."

When Leone entered the Hydrotherapy room, she saw that along one wall was a row of eight of the cabinets, most of which were occupied by pleasantly chatting women. Three nurses were helping patients in and out of the cabinets, tucking towels in the gap between each woman's neck and the edge of the cabinet and making sure temperature and humidity were in accord with what the doctor had ordered.

Well, ain't this a lick, Leone thought to herself as she looked at each of the women in turn. *These gals just sitting there talking and gossiping like this was one of them high-falutin spas or something. Sure a far cry from the way it was when we used to get them ice baths. All that freezing and shivering and crying didn't help a bit. Good riddance. And to that quack doctor, too. I doubt this Hydrotherapy will do any good, but I ain't gonna tell them that. I want every single treatment that has any chance of helping me. And, if I don't get every last one of them, I'll pitch a hissy fit like they've never seen before.*

Leone's thoughts were interrupted by a nurse indicating that she should put her clothes in one of the little cubby-boxes along the opposite wall and enter one of the vacant cabinets. Anxious to begin the treatments, she quickly traded her dress for a bathing smock and stepped in.

After the process began, Leone turned to look at the pleasant-faced young woman in the adjacent cabinet and asked:

"What's your name? Mine's Leone. I ain't seen you here before. Are you new?"

"I'm Beverly and I ain't so new. This is my tenth treatment. Got eleven more to go."

"Is that so," Leone amiably responded. "Are they doing any good?"

"I'm not quite sure. I do seem to be having fewer episodes, but I still have some."

"What's your diagnosis?"

"Manic-depression. What's yours?"

"Pellagra. They's lots of gals here with pellagra."

"I don't understand exactly what pellagra is. What are your symptoms?"

"Sometimes the Devil takes me over and I think he's after my kids. Especially when there's a fire around I just go out of control. Afterward, I realize the devil was just in my mind, but when it's going on it's just as real as rain in the summertime. Sometimes it takes me a day or two to get back to normal. But different ones have different symptoms."

"That sounds like a hallucination to me. Why is it pellagra?"

"I don't know, and really I don't think the doctors do either. When they're not sure what you've got, they just call it pellagra."

"They's a situation I read about called pellagra where you go crazy if you don't eat enough meat and poultry and eggs and stuff. You been eating those kinds of things?"

"Why sure, and always have had. On the farm we always had enough to eat and lots of meat. Like I said, when they can't figure out what you got, they call it pellagra. Beverly, you got kids?"

But before Beverly could answer a nurse stepped in front of her cabinet and announced that her time was up. As she toweled off and dressed, she was unable to continue her conversation with Leone because she was busy answering the nurse's post-treatment questionnaire. However, as she walked toward the door, she looked back to say:

"I enjoyed talking to you Leone. And, yes, I got a couple kids. I'll look for you on the yard and we can talk more"

Finishing her own treatment an hour or so later, Leone said to her nurse:

"Well, that was quite enjoyable, but I don't feel no different."

"Sometimes it takes a while. Just wait," was the thoughtless reply.

And, Leone did wait. She waited through all twenty-one treatments, and after. But there was never any change. Her episodes came on her with ever increasing severity and frequency.

•••••

Hattie and Mabel took the train from Searcy to Little Rock. They had made the trip many times before, almost always in the summer and accompanied by several of their many children. However, this time it was the middle of winter, bitterly cold and they were alone. The women had come on business—to talk about their recently deceased father's estate.

John Bell had died a few months earlier and his assets were being squabbled over by his heirs. Margaret, the mother of Hattie, Leone, Mabel and three others, had died many years before, replaced by John Bell's second wife, Mattie. John Bell and Mattie had one child, a daughter. The six children of John Bell and Margaret were claiming the assets of the estate, as was his widow, Mattie. Mattie continued to live on the farm and said it was hers.

The crux of the situation was, of course, whether or not John Bell had left a Will. All agreed that he probably had, but no one had been able to produce one. Mattie said that she had seen a Will in his hands just a few days before he died, and that he had told her the Will left everything to her. Hattie, on the other hand, contended that her father had recently told her that his Will left everything to her and her siblings.

No lawyers had been hired yet, but allegations back and forth were growing more and more threatening. Both sides believed the other was about to sue them.

Having been found to be insane, Leone was of course legally incompetent to participate in any litigation or to inherit anything. However, she might be in possession of information which could help her brothers and sisters, and that's what Hattie and Mabel had come about.

Shown into a semi-private alcove in the long hallway in Leone's ward where the visit was to take place, Hattie and Mabel found their sister in a highly excited state. Her hair was disheveled, her eyes were wide and her stockings were bunched around her ankles. She ignored the newly-purchased rocking chairs that had been grouped together for the visit and paced back and forth, swinging her arms as she strode. Leone remained silent as Mabel began:

"Honey, don't you recognize us? It's Hattie and Mabel."

"Why sure, I know who you are," Leone quickly answered before Mabel had even finished her sentence. What makes you think I don't? What do you want? You got my young'uns with you?"

"No reason to get so excited," Hattie tried to calm her. "We just need to talk to you. And we brought you a peach cobbler. Mabel made it special just for you."

"What about my kids?" Leone ignored mention of the cobbler.

"Honey, they're doing fine. Loyce and Clifford done struck out on their own. Loyce went to Texas, and Clifford's share cropping there in Sandtown, I think. Otto and Allen's still home, helping farm."

"Oh, and before I forget," Mabel interjected, "Julia and Gracie both send their love. Julia and Washington are still farming down at DeView and they got three young'uns now. Gracie and Delpha still got their place up by Tom's pa's at Denmark. They ain't got but one young'un, but she said they're trying to get another one as soon as they can."

The fact that she wasn't going to see her children for some reason seemed to calm Leone and she finally sat. Hattie pulled another rocker so close to Leone's that their knees almost touched, and then, in her most intimate and engaging manner, began to talk about their father's funeral and the huge reception at the house afterward. As her sister spoke, Leone's demeanor quieted even more and she stared down at the floor. By the time Hattie was finished, an expression of deep sorrow had come over her and she muttered to herself:

"I love you, Pa. I'm sorry I wasn't there for your funeral. And thank you for the times you came to see me. I know what a burden I was."

Hattie allowed a minute or so of silence and then said:

"Leone, can we talk about why we're here?"

After Leone nodded her assent, Hattie and Mabel took turns explaining the situation. Finishing, Mabel asked:

"Do you have any questions?"

Leone waited for well over a minute before she fixed her gaze on Hattie and said:

"And what if I do know where Pa's Will is? What's in it for me?"

Well, she ain't too crazy, Hattie thought to herself just before saying:

"Why, Honey, I don't know what you mean. What could we do for you? You got everything you need. You say they're taking good care of you, and you look well fed."

"I want to go home," Leone stated with completely flat affect.

"Leone," Mabel interjected, "we ain't got nothing to do with that. That's up to the folks here at the asylum. That's up to the parole board."

"I know exactly what Pa's Will says and where it's at. He told me all about it the last time he was here. He wanted somebody to know, and he figured I was the only one who could be trusted with knowing the hiding place."

"Leone," Hattie quickly responded. "That don't make no sense. He would have told me or Mabel. You in here and all, he would not have told you. Not unless he told me, also."

"All the same," Leone continued in her same composed manner, "I know where it's hid and you don't. Pa was afraid Mattie would tear it up, so he buried it and told me where it was buried."

"All the same back to you," Hattie responded, her growing pique evident. "We ain't got nothing to do with having you paroled out of here. That's up to the folks here."

"Yes Hattie," Leone said after thinking about it a bit. "I see that. I guess that's true."

And then, after a long pause during which Leone stared intently at

Hattie, Leone said: "OK then, I want you to bring my kids to see me. They quit coming regularly and I ain't seen them all in a coon's age. You get them all down here to see me and I'll tell you where the Will's hid."

Well, ain't she something, Hattie thought again to herself. *Negotiating just like she was a politician or something.*

"And how do we know that you ain't just saying that, just to get your young'uns down here? Maybe you don't know nothing about no Will."

"That's just a chance you'll have to take ain't it?" Leone coldly regarded one sister and then the other.

"All right, it's a deal," Hattie looked icily at her sister to say. " We'll see what we can do. But you better know where that cussed Will is hid. We'll get them down here as soon as we can."

The next day Leone told a friend what had happened and said that she hoped she would be forgiven for the little white lie she had been forced to tell in order to get to see her sons.

••••••

It took a lot of convincing, cajoling and even begging, but eventually Hattie and Tom persuaded three of the boys to go visit Leone. Allen, however, even when told about the deal that had been made with his mother, absolutely refused.

"Pa, the boy told his father at one point, "Don't you remember what I said that time during the flood when we were out there on that little island? I told it like it is. Carrie has been a lot more ma to me that ma is. Ma can't even remember if I'm Otto or Otto is me."

Even when Hattie made a special trip to beseech Allen to go, he was steadfast, creating a permanent rift between the two. Her parting words to him were: "I ain't having nothing to do with you anymore, Allen. I will never speak to you again."

So, Tom and three of his boys, and with Hattie and Mabel, made the trip without Allen.

On the day of their visit, attendants on Leone's ward later reported that she had arisen in excellent spirits, and that as she went downstairs to see her family, she gaily greeted everyone with whom she came in contact. Seeing Tom, her boys and her sisters, her smile became even wider and she almost ran to greet them. However, half-way, she noticed that a boy was missing.

The smile rushed from her face, replaced by a scornful grimace. From her mouth started the very same mournful scream all remembered from previous episodes. She threw herself on the floor in the middle of the hallway, writhed about as someone possessed and viciously lashed out at any one who attempted to console or touch her.

Two burly attendants rushed to the scene, both pulling leather restraints from their pockets as they ran.

"It's for her own protection," one said to no one in particular as he secured Leone's arms to her side and the other tied her legs. "We can't have her hurting herself. Or, anyone else for that matter."

"We never know what sets her off," the other attendant said to Tom. "One minute she's OK, and the next she's like this. After a few minutes, or hours, or days, she's sweet as pie again, but until then..." his voice trailed off for lack of words and then concluded, "well, you see."

As Leone continued to thrash about and scream, Tom stood nearby, crestfallen.

"Oh, my God," he suddenly erupted. "I can't stand this. Can't you do anything? How come you can't fix her?"

One of the attendants looked at Tom but said nothing.

As the boys stared in astonishment, Loyce once caught his mother's eye, but it was eye-contact without connection. He might as well have sought some sign of recognition with a raging she-bear. The woman the boys called ma had become a wild, violent non-human from whom it was a stretch to feel any sort of sympathy or empathy. Tom wracked his brain trying to imagine what feelings or emotions were going on inside his wife's head. He had seen her like this previously, of course, but each time was like he had never watched it before. It's effect on him put him in a state of shock and pathos from which he, too, always required a while to recover.

With drooping shoulders and suffering eyes, Tom thought: *I ain't coming here no more. I just ain't. I can't stand seeing her like this.*

No less affected than their father, the boys, too, stared in disbelief. It was hard for them to believe that just a few minutes before they had actually been looking forward to visiting with this seething, gyrating thing that was their mother. None of them said a word, but the looks on their faces told all.

Even Hattie and Mabel were silenced by the spectacle. Hattie watched stone-faced, while Mabel was so overtaken that she had to turn away. They had seen it before, but it was impossible to become accustomed to.

Finally, more to do with total exhaustion than anything else, Leone's struggles began to slow and become less frenzied, her screams began to slacken and diminish, and her countenance started to lose its wildness. Even so, one of the attendants said to Tom that it would take a while for Leone to recover enough so that a visit was possible. They were going to take her back to her room, and perhaps another visit could be attempted the following day.

But the next day she hadn't gotten better. As reported to Tom and Hattie, the next morning the attendants entered Leone's room to find her lying on the floor, softly moaning and making sounds which might have been words. She refused to respond to their questions or to get to her feet.

Informed of the situation, Tom and the others were almost relieved. None of them had wanted to risk a repeat of what had happened the day before. As they were leaving, Loyce for the first time talked about what they had seen:

"Pa, seeing her like that yesterday was just about the awfullest thing I have ever seen. I ain't never coming back here."

"Son," Tom answered, "that's your ma. She ain't always like that. She's just sick, that's all. Sick in her mind, just like people sometimes get sick in their bodies. Don't give up on her. They'll make her well, yet. Science is coming up with new treatments all the time and one of them just has to work."

"Pa," Clifford joined the conversation, "I don't think she ever knew anything about a Will. I don't think Grandpa would tell her about his Will. What do you think?"

"We may never know. We sure ain't going to know today. Maybe another day," Tom replied, the regret heavy in his voice.

"Damn that Allen, anyway," Otto said. "If he had come, Ma wouldn't have gone off like that."

"No, son, you can't blame Allen. He never knew her as a mother and she never treated him like it when I brought him to visit. And we don't know how your Ma would have been if he had been here."

"Besides," Clifford offered, "Carrie was the one that was a real mother to us, just like Allen said. Allen got real attached to Carrie. And then when she left, I think Allen just soured on the whole deal, Ma and Carrie and family, too. He ain't never been quite the same."

Back in Batesville a few days later, Hattie, Mabel and Mattie got together to try to settle their dispute. Not having a Will meant that Hattie and Mabel didn't have strong case, but the threat that they might yet find one made Mattie more agreeable. After a full morning of negotiations and with the assistance of Sheriff Taylor as mediator, the three women agreed that Mattie could stay on at the farm for as long as she wanted. However, when she left, or died, the property would go to all of John Bell's then-living children share and share alike.

• • • • • •

It took Leone a few days to recover from the episode, but soon she was back to what was normal for her with no recollection of what had happened, or even that her family had been there. When told by others of the event, and how she had behaved, she was shamed almost to tears. Realizing there was nothing she could say or do that would undo the episode, she bore its weight alone and without comment. Even her next letter to Tom didn't mention the fact that he had been there.

And she received a new work assignment. There having been too many sexual incidents between men and women working together in the hog barns, all the women were being reassigned. Leone was to work in the laundry.

Working in the laundry had not been her first choice. She would have preferred the kind of work she was familiar with and had asked to be assigned to some sort of farming.

"Why, you wouldn't last a minute out in the field," the reassignment clerk snickered. "They's nothing but men doing the farming. One of them, or maybe a whole passel of them would have your drawers off and you spread across a bale of hay before you could say 'Jack Robinson'."

In the laundry, it had been necessary for the more experienced women to show her even the most rudimentary tasks involved in operating the big machines needed to wash and dry the hundreds of garments, sheets, blankets and other items every day. But she took to it quite well, and as releases on parole and deaths took their toll on the more experienced woman, Leone moved up and went from a menial loader and unloader of laundry to a supervisor. As supervisor, she was not only responsible for the efficient movement of items from dirty to clean, but also the arbiter of the inevitable squabbles and disputes among the sometimes less than stable patients. Many who worked with her attested that when she was not having her own problems, she was quite good at this. When complimented on it, Leone invariably said that her pa was a businessman and that she was just taking after him.

Most of the petty dust-ups among the women involved one young woman claiming another was slacking off and not doing her share. Leone's technique for resolving the matter was to counsel both women and then observe who was doing what. If she found that one really was doing less than she should be, Leone would sit down with her for an intimate talk. And, this is where her real knack came in. Especially with the younger women, she had such an engaging and confidence inspiring manner that it usually didn't take too long before the offender not only saw the error of her ways, but also became one of Leone's life-long fans.

On one occasion in particular, Leone had shown her skill at this. That was when one of the newer women raised a fuss about an older woman creating more work for the others by taking too long at dinner. Leone called the younger woman aside and quietly asked her if she knew that the older woman's knees were so arthritic that they pained her constantly. After that, there were no more complaints and Leone had a devotee.

Of course Leone's episodes, like the one she had had when Tom and Hattie had visited, interfered with her ability to supervise. Fortunately, they only lasted a day or so. In the case of the one when Tom and

Hattie visited, she was incapacitated for three days, but that was among her worst ever. Other than during than her periods of incapacitation, Leone's intellect, empathy and good-nature ensured that the other patients grew to respect her, and as she grew older, treat her much like a mother.

Thus, when Beverly, the manic-depressive Leone had met in Hydrotherapy, appeared in the laundry to report that she had been assigned there, she immediately started seeking out private times with Leone in order to confide in her and try to foster the motherly connection she had so early been deprived of. Her own mother had died while birthing her and her step-mother had been a shrew and a drunk. Leone's mother had also died at a young age and so, in addition to having children to talk about, Leone and Beverly had much in common and began to feel a close connection.

"You know, Leone," Beverly said to her one day, "our crazinesses are pretty similar. Only difference is I go up and down and you only go up. When I'm manic, I'm just flying. I can do anything. And when I'm down, nothing could be worse. I get so depressed it seems that suicide is the only answer. But you, you just go up. When you get back to normal, you don't go no lower. You just get to normal and stay there."

"Maybe," Leone thoughtfully responded. "But when I'm in an episode I certainly ain't normal. When I'm excited I think I can do anything. Usually I don't remember it, but I know from what little I do remember and from what others tell me. In that regard, I'm just like you."

Then, lowering her eyes and speaking even more softly: "I'm just trying to save me and my kids from the Devil. Afterward, sometimes I remember the Devil. The Devil and fire. Seems there's usually fire in there somewhere."

"Leone, can I ask you something real personal," Beverly said to her after a short pause. "Do you think you're getting more episodes lately. Some of the gals was talking and they seem to be keeping track."

Tears came to Leone's eyes and she was barely able to maintain her composure enough to say:

"I'm afraid that's true. Oh Beverly, I am so scared."

Seeing the sadness her question had triggered, Beverly enveloped

Leone in her arms and softly comforted:

"That's OK. Everything is going to be OK. You'll see. They'll come up with some new treatment any day now."

The welling tears beginning to overflow, Leone continued:

"I try so hard to maintain myself and have a good attitude and be optimistic, but it's so hard. I always try to be good and have a smile on my face, but inside it often ain't that way. Inside, I sometimes just want to kill myself. People who ain't crazy like us just don't understand what it's like to live their life waiting for the next episode, waiting for the next time they go nuts and do something crazy. Sometimes I just ain't that strong."

"I know, Sugar," Beverly soothed. "I know. You ain't the only one. I'm always here for you."

"And, Tom," Leone continued. "What I've done to him. And to the kids. Sometimes I think I am indeed the agent of the Devil, sent to torture myself and all those around me. What I don't know is why. What on Earth could I have done to make me such a despicable person, inflicting suffering on those I love?"

CHAPTER SIXTEEN

The 1930s were not the best years for Tom and Jim.
They continued to farm and make a little whiskey, but their
increasing ages (in 1935, Tom turned 59, and Jim, 57) as well as
outside circumstances made it increasingly hard to make a crop
and get by.

More generally, except for the Civil War period, the third decade of
the twentieth century was arguably the most trying time the United
States has ever experienced. Unlike during the time of the war between
the states when suffering was largely limited to the battlefields and
certain areas of the South, beginning in 1929 and continuing almost
until the beginning of World War II in 1941, virtually every American
was touched by the effects of two occurrences, the Great Depression
and the Dust Bowl.

As to the Great Depression, it was preceded by what came to be
called the Roaring Twenties, a period remembered for Prohibition,
gangsters, and the stock market crash of 1929. The excesses of the
Twenties were caused in part by loose money and financial regulation.
This resulted in unbridled optimism, an overheated stock market,
and such phenomena as "boiler rooms" (an office where unscrupulous
salesmen sold worthless stocks by telephone) and "blue sky stocks"
(stocks with no value, you were just buying "blue sky"). Notoriously,
Florida swamp land was sometimes sold as dry and buildable.

The government's reaction to what should have been an ordinary
trough in the business cycle made, in many instances, things worse. For

example, when no one had money to buy anything, and Washington should have been printing billions of new dollars, it printed less, causing even more unavailability. Or, when the correct thing to do would have been for the government to liberalize international trade so as to boost the economy, it imposed trade killing tariffs. Nevertheless, some good things did come of the government's efforts, including the creation of Social Security, the Securities and Exchange Commission, and many other sorely-needed regulatory and public welfare agencies.

Up in their isolated little section of Arkansas, farmers like Tom and Jim had some news of what was going on in the rest of the country, but believed they were little affected by it. They certainly didn't listen when the news announcers reported the latest developments with regard to the money supply or stock fluctuations. What they did listen to were reports of severe fluctuations in the prices they received for their crops.

Owing to the fact that they lived mostly off what they grew and raised themselves, they didn't need a lot of money. But they had to buy essentials such as coffee, salt and sugar, as well as seed to put in the ground the following spring. Thus, when what they were paid for their harvests fell, which it certainly did, they felt the effects greatly.

However, stock speculators and abysmal cotton prices certainly weren't the sole cause of Tom and Jim's problems. The Dust Bowl contributed significantly.

Beginning about 1930 and continuing until 1940 or so, Tom and Jim suffered from a lesser version of the drought which caused the rich farmlands of Oklahoma, Kansas and Texas to literally blow away, with resulting dust clouds that obliterated the sun and turned day into night. Arkansas wasn't that bad, but even so the years in the beginning of the decade were the driest the state had ever experienced, resulting in much reduced yields for Tom and Jim.

Human activities, of course, haven't always caused droughts. Historically, droughts have been a periodic phenomenon of nature, with which man's activities had little effect. However, as with the Great Flood of the previous decade, it was man's activities that turned something which occasionally happened into a disaster. It was farming practices that removed the long grasses which held the dry soil in place. Without those grasses, when the strong winds common to the mid-West came and there was no rain, millions of tons of dirt were launched high into the atmosphere, clouding and darkening half a continent.

• • • • • •

Having received just enough rain earlier in the year to get their fields plowed and their seeds in the ground, Independence Day 1931 found Tom and his youngest boys, Otto and Allen, sitting on their porch, looking down across parched fields and stunted crops. Ordinarily even on this holiday they would have been hard at work chopping the weeds that usually proliferated among the corn and cotton. But without rain, even the weeds didn't grow.

For about the thousandth time Allen asked:

"Pa, what are we going to do if it don't rain?"

"Like I told you yesterday and the day before and the day before that, it's going to rain. It always does and it's going to soon."

"But, what if it don't?"

"It's going to" Tom answered resolutely.

I just can't tell him if it don't rain some soon, we're through, Tom thought. If we don't get some rain soon, I truly don't know what we're going to do.

"But Pa," Allen persisted, "our animals is already in poor shape. We got to find a way to feed them more."

"Now, how do you suppose we can do that? Nothing is growing and to my name I think I have a total of less than three dollars."

"Pa," Otto joined the conversation, "I saw a boll weevil down in the cotton field yesterday."

Trying to lighten what was very bad news, Tom laughingly said:

"Well, I'll bet he was disappointed. Flew here from wherever he came from and ain't no more to eat here than there was there."

"Yeah," Allen giggled, "he probably high-tailed it back to wherever he came from and told them, 'Boys, whatever you do, don't go to Arkansas. Ain't nothing there and if you don't die of hunger, you'll die of thirst.'"

Spitting a stream of tobacco juice off the end of the porch, Tom cleared his throat and said:

"Boys, I want to get serious for a minute. I want to talk about your Ma."

Smiles quickly disappeared and both boys looked attentively at their father.

"She's been there more than ten years now, but we ain't giving up on her. The Whiteners ain't quitters and we ain't giving up on her, just like we ain't giving up on this farm. We ain't been going to see her as often as we should have, but while there ain't much to do around here, we're going to start. You all right with that?"

Allen stared at his bare feet while Otto dutifully answered:

"Yes, Pa."

Two days later, it did rain—a little. It rained just enough to keep the crops alive. The week after that it rained again—a little. And, so it went. Just when the green shoots and stalks were about to die, enough rain would come to keep them alive. By the end of the season Tom was able to make a crop, not a big one, but a crop. And when he sold it, he didn't receive a lot, but enough so that with the bank's help the following spring he would be able to buy seed and do it again.

● ● ● ● ● ●

A month or so later when Sister Susan Forbes' Grand Revival Experience came to town, the opening parade was led by a line of bass drums echoing like cannons. While the tubas and trumpets blared out the melody, the drums pounded out an insistent, *boom, boom, boom.* Watched by everyone from miles around who didn't have something absolutely more pressing to do, *"Onward Christian Soldiers"* and others were received with great joy and applause.

Sister Susan Forbes and her entourage were coming to town, and the advance publicity man had made sure every farmer and tradesman knew it. The throng of excited and ebullient enthusiasts trailed the musicians to a huge tent where the revival meeting was to take place.

"Hurry up," Tom told Jim as he hitched their team to the rail in front of a long line of parked wagons and carriages. "They ain't gonna be no seats left."

Sister Susan Forbes was known throughout the South as one of the most dynamic and inspiring revival preachers ever. Some even claimed she had saved more souls than anyone except Jesus himself. She would be in town for three days, preaching, saving and, for an appropriate donation to her church, offering personal consultations.

Each day would include a parade in which would march not only Sister Forbes and her entourage, but also a full complement of local politicians and clergymen, all smiling and waving. Sister Forbes would of course precede all. Wearing long white gloves despite the heat, from the back of the era's most luxurious automobile, a 1931 Dual Cowl Phaeton Cadillac convertible, she would beckon one and all to come be saved.

Her orchestra this day was made up of the combined marching bands from both Batesville and Cave City high schools, while several local churches had contributed their choirs.

The parade would end at the revival tent, which had been set up that morning in a field next to the railroad track just outside of town. The tent was festooned with multitudes of colorful flags, banners and pennants, all proclaiming the glory of God, the necessity for repentance and the holiness of Sister Forbes as God's own messenger. Beyond the tent, on an unused siding, sat Mr. Forbes's private railroad car, as well as two others which were used to transport her tent, bleachers, and other necessary equipment and paraphernalia.

Tom and Jim jostled with others being funneled into the tent and hurriedly found seats as close as they could to where Sister Forbes would be speaking. The white satin bunting which covered the elevated altar sparkled and gave prominence to the large royal blue cross in its center. On either side were places for the orchestra and choir. In the middle of all was an aisle leading to a small platform just in front of the altar on which penitents would kneel to be blessed by Sister Forbes and sprinkled with a few drops of holy water.

"Tom," Jim said as soon as they were seated and had taken it all in, "this is just about the biggest thing to hit Independence County since the Yankees was her? I wouldn't miss this for all the tea in China."

"I reckon," his brother responded, "but did you ever think about the fact that we already been baptized. And, it wasn't no few little sprinkles of water. I remember Ol' Deacon Paisley giving us the full treatment;

held our noses and under Strawberry Creek we went."

"I ain't here for the baptizing, exactly, although probably a little reinforcement couldn't hurt. I'm here to listen to Sister Forbes. And the others, too, of course, but mainly her."

Unlike in the countryside where Tom and Jim lived, the town had recently been electrified and the Grand Revival Experience took full advantage of it. Newly installed strings of electric lights illuminated every step of Sister Forbes' way as she made her heralded entrance down the aisle and ascended the altar.

She was of an almost indiscernible age, certainly not yet middle-aged, but well beyond her teen years. Her apparently guileless, almost milk white face displayed a permanent half-smile and serenity completely becoming her most pleasant demeanor. She wore a long satin, high-necked dress with a small blue cross over the heart, exquisitely complementing her shoulder length straight black hair, trimmed to bangs slightly above her eyes.

A man who introduced himself as Deacon Swanson introduced the first of two warm up preachers, both of whom went on to dazzle the crowd with descriptions of the fire and fury of Hell, as well as the rapture and euphoria of Heaven. Following that, the Deacon called on several newly saved individuals to come forward and give testimonials. All was, of course, interspersed with prayers, hymns and shouted Hosea's.

When Sister Forbes finally took the podium, she began in a quiet conversational tone and talked about the glories of God, how Jesus died for our sins and, how acceptance of him would lead to salvation.

"Pretty standard stuff," Tom whispered to Jim. "I wonder what happened to that 'fire and brimstone' shouter we heard so much about. That ol' boy up at Ash Flat has got more spunk than she does."

Later, not two people would have agreed as to exactly when her tenor changed, but everyone, including Tom and Jim agreed that it did, dramatically. Imperceptibly at first, and then with gathering force as she started talking about the Devil, Sister Susan Forbes' quiet tone went from a pleasant though high-pitched one to one with real bite in it. She grew louder, more abrasive, and, as if her voice was coming from another person entirely, a being suddenly not at all feminine or of this world.

By the time she reached full pitch, she was describing Lucifer in such realistic terms that he seemed to come to life right there in the tent. She emulated his shrieks and roars with such believability that many were sure he had in fact taken over her body. However, she came back at him just as strong, even stronger, and described the battle between good and evil, between God and the Devil.

Finally, tearing her hair and bringing all to an emotional crescendo, and as Deacon Swanson rushed to her side, she collapsed with assurances that the Devil had been defeated and the battle for the soul of man had been won. So personal and impassioned were her pleas that every person in the room, Tom and Jim included, was sure that she had been talking directly to him, and that it was his or her soul personally that had been saved. Tears flowed, as jubilant shouts of "Hallelujah" and "God bless" filled the air.

As two assistants helped the exhausted Sister down the aisle and out to her railroad car, Deacon Swanson took to the altar to assure the exuberant throng that she simply needed a few minutes to recover. She would return shortly, he said, to bless and baptize all that wanted it. In the meantime, the collection baskets would be passed.

• • • • • •

As Sister Forbes made her dramatic exit, Tom's "Hallelujahs" were some of the loudest. Without reserve and with total joy, his repeated shouts of "Praise the Lord" and "God bless" joined with those of hundreds of others, even driving out the sounds of the orchestra and choir trying to induce the singing of an as-yet-unrecognized hymn.

Finally, as the bass drum's insistent pounding at last took hold and a few of the worshipers made out the organ playing, "A Mighty Fortress Is Our God", Tom gleefully looked over at Jim. To his shock, his brother was stone-faced and staring straight ahead.

Tom reached across his body to grab his brother's arm and shouted in his ear:

"Jim, what's wrong? What's going on?"

Without changing his expression, Jim slowly turned his head to stare his brother in the eye and say:

"That woman. Sister Forbes. I ain't never seen anything like that in my life. Surely, she is heaven sent. She is the most beautiful thing I have ever seen."

Not sure Jim was hearing him above the din, Tom again shouted:

"We'll talk later. Here she comes back."

The cacophony became even louder as Sister Forbes again entered, an assistant at either arm. Her grace and stateliness making it appear almost as if she was floating rather than walking, she made her way back down the aisle and onto the little platform in front of the altar.

Seeing that the baptisms were about to begin, Jim jumped from his seat and said to Tom:

"I'm going down there. You coming?"

"Naw," Tom said, "you go on. I'll be watching."

Tom was fully caught up in all that was happening, believing at that moment that Sister Forbes was indeed an emissary from God. However, there was something about the spectacle of things that made him hold back and keep his seat. He had an unfamiliar disquiet and nonspecific anxiety, the source of which he couldn't quite put his finger on. He had previously attended revival meetings similar to this one and had experienced no such anxiety. He wondered what was not quite right, but was then distracted by the sight of his brother pushing his way through others to reach the back of the baptism line.

At the front of the line, immediately before Sister Forbes, stood Deacon Wyatt Swanson, a big, burly man, making sure that order was maintained and asking each person's name so that he could tell it to Sister Forbes. Then, as the Deacon released his hold on each person's arm so that he or she could go forward, the name would be repeated in Sister Forbes' ear.

With wide eyes, when Jim's turn came, he stepped forward to hear:

"Jim, do you take Jesus as your Lord and Savior?"

He was so dumbfounded that the Deacon had to prompt him to say yes. Jim didn't even feel the few drops of water Sister Forbes sprinkled on his head or notice the Deacon's heavy hand pushing him out of the way to make way for the next supplicant.

Returning to his seat next to Tom, Jim sat heavily, never taking his eyes off Sister Forbes.

"Well," Tom finally said after several long seconds, "Ain't you gonna say nothing about it? How was it?"

"She is divine. Surely heaven sent," Jim dreamily murmured. "I'm coming again tomorrow. And the next day. I'm coming every day."

"Whoa, boy" Tom responded. "Hold on. She sure put a trance on you. She was something, I'll grant you that. But she's just a woman and I've seen prettier. As a preacher she's durn good, but they's some others just as good. Remember that Reverend Kirkland we heard down at Floral a few years back?"

"No, Tom, she's different. She is an angel and I'll die if I don't get to see more of her."

"Well, alright, but you'll get over her. This baptizing is going to go on a while. We got a fur piece to go tonight. Let's go. You can come back tomorrow if you want."

"No, Tom, I ain't leaving until she leaves. I'm going to sit right here as long as I can see her."

More than an hour later, Deacon Swanson had hustled the last person before the sister and then announced that they were done for the evening. He reminded of the start time for the parade the next day, and again mentioned that generous donations would be appreciated. Tom and Jim stood where they were to see Sister Forbes, trailed by the Deacon and her assistants, float back outside.

Exiting the tent with the crowd, Tom and Jim turned to the right to take the path back to where their wagon was parked. However, before they had gone more than a few steps they noticed that lanterns were being held up above a large overturned freight wagon. Lying in the dusty road were four dray horses, still in harness, at least two of them with broken legs. The bleeding drivers were trying to sort out the mess, get the healthy horses on their feet, and put the others out of their misery.

"They'll be a while getting this cleared," Tom said to Jim. "Let's go around the other way, over by the train track."

The two men retraced their steps and when they got back to where they had started, took the other path. It took them through a small grove of cottonwoods and then along a path next to the siding on which Sister Forbes's train cars were parked.

As they came abreast of the small platform on the end of Sister Forbes' specially modified observation car, they heard the following:

"Wyatt, pour me a drink, will you? Better make it a double."

"Sure thing, Susan. And then how about a little fooling around? I just got to have you. Seeing you up there doing your thing, with all your beauty and power, sure turns me on."

"No, Wyatt. How many times do I have to tell you? Not just after a meeting. It makes me feel base."

"Well, you weren't feeling too base the other night when we had that white mule and had to replace the sheets, were you?"

"Wyatt, I told you. You can wait until the meetings are over, and we get out of this sorry little excuse for a town. Then, as long as there aren't any meetings, you can have me all you want."

In the dark Tom and Jim couldn't see each other's faces and didn't say anything. However, as soon as they retrieved their wagon and were on their way home, Jim opened up:

"Why, that hussy. She's just a heathen, an outright heathen. Acting all pious and saintly, like she's better than Jesus Christ himself. What a faker!"

"Not so fast, Jim. Just because her and the Deacon is drinking and loving each other don't mean what she's saying ain't true. It don't one bit lessen what she's got to say. She's circulating God's word. She's doing good."

"They ain't married. She ain't his wife. All that preaching today about sinning and lust and all that, and she's doing it herself. That ain't right."

"Jim, if every man and woman that wasn't married and was loving each other was condemned, I don't reckon there would be many folks left. I know what the Bible says, but what it says and what people are doing can be two different things."

"And me thinking she'd just come down from heaven with a band of angels."

"Jim, I don't think her personal life, even though she's for sure going straight to Hell for it, detracts one bit from her preaching. She's preaching truth and gospel and you'd best listen to it."

Jim didn't respond, and after a while Tom said:

"You heard what she was preaching about drinking, about it being the way of the Devil. That all really got through to me. I been thinking on it a long time, and she's right. I'm gonna quit."

"What do you mean, you're going to quit? I wouldn't be sorry to see it, that's for sure, but she ain't nothing but a drunk herself. You heard her."

"And what of it? What she said got right through to my soul. I been drinking too much most of my entire life and I ain't gonna drink no more. As of right now, I'm done."

And he was. To the end of his days he never took another drink. Nor did either of the two men ever again mention Sister Susan Forbes.

● ● ● ● ● ●

The previous three presidents having been almost completely ineffective in ending the depression and restoring prosperity, Franklin Roosevelt took office in 1933 determined to adopt whatever measures, no matter how unorthodox, to do it. With more than thirteen million unemployed, the country was ready for what only a few years before would have been dismissed as the product of socialism or communism. Allen, still in his teens, was able to take advantage of one of Roosevelt's more radical measures.

Although he needed his father to fudge his age by a year, Allen signed up for the Civilian Conservation Corps (CCC)a program designed to put money in the hands of people who desperately need it. Tom's family wasn't on relief as were most of the others with boys in the CCC, but conditions in Northeastern Arkansas were so bad that the Whitener family's status as needy was never questioned.

The way the enterprise worked was that teams of enrollees were set to work somewhere in the country building and improving things. The projects included such things as parks, bridges, roads and trails, flood control structures, arbors, stream beds and banks, as well as airport landing fields. For this work, the boys would be paid thirty dollars each month, twenty-five of which would be sent to the family. The remaining five the boy could spend as he saw fit.

Returning from signing up, Allen was putting his horse away when his father greeted him:

"Son, I want you to know this is a good thing you're doing, and I certainly appreciate it. It's a damn shame it's come to this. Me almost sixty years old and never before took a nickel of welfare. But I think Roosevelt is gonna get us out of this. Thank God he created the CCC for you to go into."

"It's OK, Pa. I don't mind. I like it. It's going to be an adventure. I'm really looking forward to seeing more of the world. I leave next Wednesday. Got to be on the train at 10 a.m. They're shipping me to a camp in Monterey, California."

"Woo-eee, ain't that something! To California. I ain't never been out of Arkansas and you going all way to the Pacific Ocean. Maybe you'll even get to Hollywood and see them making moving pictures. How long did you sign up for?"

"Six months. That's the most you can sign up for. But, after that I can sign up for another six months. I figure I'll keep on signing up for as long as you need for me to."

"Well, that is surely appreciated, Son. What they going to have you doing?"

"The man in town didn't know. He said they ain't even finished building the camp, yet. But he said there's lots of trees and forests in Monterey and so maybe we'll be doing something with them. As long as we get our money each month, I guess I can do most anything."

"I wish your brothers would do it, too. It's a shame all three of them is so stuck on their girlfriends that they think they can't live a little while without them. Ain't none of the three doing anything but farming, not that that's so bad, but you couldn't get Clifford out of Arkansas with dynamite, and the other two say they ain't going nowhere but Texas."

"They're OK, Pa. I'm not sure Otto is going to make a farmer, but all three of them is as hard-working as they come. And they ain't dumb, neither."

"Son, I just got two pieces of advice for you. Number one, don't be doing no gambling, and especially don't be shooting no craps. They's a way to rig those dice so's they always come up a certain way, and you can lose your shirt, leastwise your five dollars for the month. And number two, stay away from those women of easy virtue. You don't want to be catching something you can't get rid of. Oh yeah, and a third thing. Always remember your family and the good Christian way you were brought up."

Then, hitching up his overalls, Tom snickered as he thought of his other boys and said:

"I'm just glad Clifford's gal ain't named 'Jewell'. Loyce married a 'Jewell,' Otto married a 'Jewell' and three 'Jewells' would be at least one too many."

Then, more seriously: "You know, Allen, it's gonna be real lonely around here. I guess I'll be seeing Clifford pretty regular, but with Loyce and Otto down in Texas, I don't know when I'll see them. Especially if they marry their 'Jewells' and start families there. And I don't know why they think Texas is all so hot anyway. My granddad did OK there, but he was a minister and I reckon his congregation pretty much provided for him."

"Well, it must have been pretty satisfying with all them young'uns he had."

"Yep, twelve of 'em, with three wives. He kept outliving 'em."

"Well Pa, you still got Jim. And I'm glad you and him ain't making too big a crop, not that you could sell it for growing costs if you did. And, them knees of yours ain't going to let you farm too much longer."

"I'll be OK. Don't worry about me. But what about your Ma? Any chance you would go down to Little Rock with me to see her? You got almost a week before you report, and we could take a couple days to go visit her."

"I don't know, Pa. Why don't we go see Carrie? You know I cotton to Carrie. And besides, the last time I was at the asylum, Ma didn't hardly know me and was talking a bunch of gibberish. And that was a while back. Don't reckon she'd know me at all now. Does she still know you? When was the last time you visited?"

"I was there not too long ago. I don't go as often as I should, that's true, but I go. And sure she knows me. Like I keep saying, don't give up on her. There are new medicines and treatments being invented all the time. She'll get well yet, you'll see."

Allen had been gone to the CCC camp for a few weeks when Jim had to take the tractor to the mechanic in Batesville for repairs. As he returned and drove into the barn, he found Tom pitch-forking hay into the loft. Jumping down from the tractor, Jim said:

"Durn, Tom, I still don't know how you do it. Pitch-forking with one arm as good as most men do with two. But, take a little break and let's have a chaw. I got something I need to tell you."

As the two sat on a hay bale and took turns using their teeth to tear hunks of tobacco from a plug, Jim started:

"Tom I'm afraid I got some bad news for you. You ain't gonna like it, but it's something I got to do."

Turning back to Tom after launching a brown stream into the dirt, he couldn't find words. He just looked at him.

"Well, what is it?" Tom asked impatiently. "What you got to say?"

"This is hard. Give me a second," Jim said with a quivering chin and quavering voice. And then, after looking down at his well-worn work boots for a long second, he said:

"Tom, you know I love you something fierce. There's almost nothing I wouldn't do for you. Living here with you and farming is all I've ever done, and I guess farming is about the best life a man could have. But it's time I struck out on my own. It's time I become a man and quit living in your shadow. Yeah, I know, I'm too old to do anything else. That may be, but I got to try."

Tom continued to listen attentively, but his pulse quickened, and it was all he could do to process what his brother was saying. *Of all the gol-durned luck,* he thought. *How on this earth am I going to go on without him?*

Only vaguely aware of the distress he was causing his brother, Jim continued to look down at his boots and went on, while Tom never took his eyes off him.

"When I was in town this morning," Jim said, "I ran into Elmer Smith and his daughter, Jennie. You remember meeting them several times. They live part of the time on their place up in Missouri and part of the time on a ranch they got down in Texas. They stay in Batesville a few days every time they pass through. He's got a brother here, I think. Anyway, we was just talking, kinda shooting the breeze, and out of the blue Elmer says he wants to talk to me, privately. We step aside where Jennie can't hear, and he says he's got a proposal for me.

"Well, me and Jennie been seeing each other just about every time she comes through, and every time we get along real good. And, I've had supper a couple times with her and her pa. They's fine people. But when Elmer tells me she's taken a real shine to me, you could have knocked me over with a feather. I had no idea. And she wants to marry me. Can you imagine that? Wants to marry me.

"She ain't much to look at and is almost as old as me, and I guess Elmer recognized those as pretty big drawbacks because he says if I marry her, he'll give us a piece of ground down by his place at Clinton, Texas. He says it will be kind of like a dowry. He says it's good ground, too, both for farming and ranching. This is just about the biggest thing that's ever happened to me. The Lord sure must finally be looking out for me."

"You love this gal?" Tom finally said forcing himself to ignore his own needs in favor of Jim's.

A stunned expression came on Jim's face and after a thoughtful pause he said:

"Well, I don't know. Love her? I never thought about that. Do I have to love her?"

"It's up to you, Jim. You'll always be my brother no matter what you do, but if you're going to marry a woman, seems to me you need to love her."

"I'm pretty sure I could learn to love her."

"That ain't the same, is it?"

Jim didn't answer, but again looked down at the straw strewn dirt.

"I already told them I would probably do it, but that I needed to talk to you first."

"That's fine. You're talking to me. But now what are you going to do?"

"I don't know, Tom. You know a lot more about love than me. What can I do? I can't let this slip away."

"I think I know a way so you can not do anything you ain't proud of, you can keep your self-respect and maybe, just maybe, you can do what your mind is telling your heart you want to do."

"I'm willing to try just about anything."

"OK, here's what you do: get on back to Batesville and tell Elmer and Jennie you really want to marry her, but that you got to love her first, and you can't love her unless you get to know her a little better. Then suggest that you and her take a couple days and get better acquainted. Cousin Alfred there in Batesville will let you stay at his place for a couple nights, and during the day you can take Jennie around to see the local sights. Take her to see the cave there at Cave City and you can take her swimming in the river and to church tomorrow morning and just whatever else you can think of. And the two of you just talk and talk and talk."

"I get it. You're thinking if we spend some time together, we can fall in love. But what if we don't?"

"In that case, you're no worse off than you are now. Then, you'll have what Preacher Rowe calls a moral dilemma. Then you'll have to decide if you'll violate your principles for some pieces of silver, so to speak."

Tom didn't say anything more, and he gave no sign of the pain he was feeling. Instead, he went back to pitch-forking the hay and thought:

Another test. Well, I been tested before and I ain't give in yet. I got more sand in my craw than that.

But Jim didn't have to violate his principles. He did exactly what Tom said, and three days later roared up in front of the house with a woman sitting next to him on the wagon.

"Tom," he yelled with a smile as big as a full moon, "get out here and meet Mrs. Jennie Whitener, your new sister-in-law. We are in love and done got hitched. We're going to Texas."

Why, she ain't bad looking, Tom thought to himself as he came out the front door. *Sturdy looking gal. Probably make a fine farmer's wife. But I guess I done outfoxed myself. Maybe I should have told him just to tell her no, that if he wasn't in love with her, he couldn't accept the offer. It surely would have been better for me. Oh well, I guess I'll sleep better for it, even if I don't know what I'm going to do to keep on farming.*

Tom rarely thought about his missing arm and never lamented its lack. But as Jim was helping his new bride down off the wagon he did. Belying the grin on his face, his thoughts continued to be troublesome:

A one-armed man all alone trying to farm some no-account, rocky ground. Oh, Jim-boy, you are definitely leaving me in a heap of trouble.

"Well, how-de-do and welcome, Mrs. Whitener," he brightened to enthusiastically greet his new sister-in-law.

••••••

Jim and Jennie were staying over a few days before going on south and Jim was helping Tom behind the house when the postman arrived with a letter. As soon as Tom saw that it was from the State Hospital, he said to Jim:

"Why don't you go on in the house and help Jennie with some firewood or something. I want to read this letter."

Slowly making his way to his rocker on the porch, he put on his glasses and sliced the envelope with his pocket knife to read:

Dear Mr. Whitener:

I am sending this missive for the purpose of advising you concerning the present condition of your wife, Leone.

First of all, it has been reported to me that you recently visited with her, and that even though the visit didn't go as well as you might have hoped, it went without incident and benefited her somewhat. I am also told that you said to a member of my staff that you would soon visit again, perhaps in the company of one or more or your sons.

I want to assure you that during these many years Leone has been with us she has received the very best of care and treatment the State of Arkansas has to offer. We have always kept abreast of the latest advances in psychology and psychiatry, and Leone has been afforded whatever at the time was in her best interests and most likely to yield beneficial results. Most recently, when modern science developed various drugs that empirical trials had shown to yield promising results, the most appropriate were prescribed for her.

However, despite our best efforts and notwithstanding these state-of-the-art medications, she has continued to decline. Nothing we have done seems to have affected her deterioration in any way whatsoever. Thus, even after your recent visit, her condition has worsened, dramatically so, I must report.

To conclude, I feel compelled to advise you that you are welcome to visit Leone at any time convenient to you, commensurate with the Hospital's rules and regulations, of course, but that you should not expect that she is in the same condition as when you last visited. She is much worse.

Her condition has varied from catatonic to hysterical. At times, she simply sits, apparently lost in whatever thoughts she may yet have left to her. At other times, if not restrained, she flies around the room, screaming and shrieking and seeking hard objects with which to assault herself or anyone nearby.

Thus, in all honesty, I do not know what good would be served by further visits. As I say, you are welcome to visit if you want, but you are forewarned that your time with her will probably not be of benefit to either of you.

Should her condition at in any time in the future change, for better or worse, you will be immediately advised."

Tom didn't notice when the letter fell from his hand and lay looking up at him from beside his chair. Instead, he thought of the whiskey jug. It had been a long time since he had been tempted to have a drink, but now he was. He felt like a mule had kicked him in the stomach, and he desperately wanted anything that would soften the pain. It took him long, pensive minutes before he banished whiskey from his mind and once again thought, *Well, all the same, I ain't giving up on her.* With renewed resolve he stood and went to the kitchen where his brother and Jennie were preparing supper.

"Jim," he said, "grab that pitcher of lemonade, won't you, and come on out to the porch. I need to talk to you."

By the time Jim was sitting next to him reading the letter, the sun was almost down to the tops of the trees at the furthest extreme of the farm, near where Allen had saved the colt. Wistfully, Tom looked out on lengthening shadows and saw an unexpected little zephyr come up and lift and handful of dust high into the air.

"Jim," he said as soon as the younger man had finished reading the letter. "She's been in there almost twenty years and I'm tempted to give up hope."

When Jim tried to interrupt him to comment, Tom said:

"No, Jim, don't say anything. Just let me talk. Let an old man remember.

"In spite of all the bad times, me and Leone surely did have some good ones. I'll never forget when we met at the dance. Her and her big ol' eyes and her saying 'I ain't never danced with a one-armed man before'." I think I started loving her right then. Truth be told, that's the Leone I'm still in love with. That little innocent gal with the big eyes. Or that morning she ran away from Van and showed up on the porch. This same porch where we're sitting right now. She was laying there in the morning like a lost kitten. Or, the first time we made love down at the river. And how lovely she was there in the sunlight. Oooh-weee, those were some happy times. Or the locusts. Remember the locusts?"

"I surely do," Jim smiled as he remembered.

"Millions and millions of them. And us burning them up. And you and me and Leone and Gracie piling on the leaves and brush. Lordy, what a battle it was.

"And our first young'un. She was so proud of that big ol' Loyce. Like to have killed her, but she said she was doing it for me. And three more fine babies now growed into fine young men.

"But now I'm alone, Jim. All alone."

Jim started to say something, probably to say how sorry he was to be leaving their farm, but again Tom stopped him.

"No, Jim, don't say nothing. You don't need to say a word. Just let me have my time.

"Sure seems like it's been a whole lot of people leaving me. I guess Julia was first. Can't blame her. Can't blame anyone. Everyone's entitled to they own lives. That don't mean it don't hurt. But I understand.

"And Carrie. I probably miss her as much as Leone. If I had known how things was gonna turn out with Leone, I don't know if I could have resisted marrying her. She is a good woman and was a good mother to the boys. But she did what she had to do. She was right, no future for her here with me.

"And Pa. I surely do miss him. Ma, too. He was a good man. Too bad he didn't have a little better luck with women. Maybe you and me could go over to Mount Carmel tomorrow and put some flowers on their graves.

"And Jim, I guess you know how I'm gonna miss you. When we first started farming together I was ready for you to leave most any time. We was young then, and I figured some little gal would turn your eye, and away you'd go. But when it didn't happen, I guess I just reckoned you'd be here forever. Surely did enjoy the years you being here."

"I'm sorry, Tom," Jim said with glistening eyes.

"It's OK, Jim. It really is. I wish you and Jennie all the luck in the world. Besides, I'll be getting down to Texas to visit, you'll see. Maybe next time I visit Leone, I'll just continue on down to your place in Clinton.

"That's it, Jim. That's all I wanted to say. Now let's go see if Jennie's got them vittles ready."

CHAPTER SEVENTEEN

In the more than fifteen years Leone had been in the asylum, her appearance had changed. Her once coal black hair, still pulled back in an easy-to-manage bun, was now streaked with gray, and her face was beginning to crease deeply. Shadows of her former beauty were still present, although as a mature woman she had lost that feline innocence Tom had found so captivating. Dressed in a baggy and unflattering asylum-issue dress, it was hard to notice that she was much thinner than previously. As with Tom, her posture had deteriorated and she wore wire-rimmed glasses.

As usual she arrived at the bustling laundry this day a little before the normal start time. But before she could begin the day's work, she was told the supervisor wanted to see her. Leone and Mavis Smail had long been more than just civilian supervisor and patient, and had become friends. Over the years they had almost naturally used their friendship and mutual trust to relegate themselves to separate areas of expertise. Mavis dealt with administrative tasks in the office, while Leone, no doubt because of comradery created by her status as a fellow patient, was very successful in supervising the women and operation of the laundry itself.

"Sit down," the woman warmly greeted Leone as she walked in. "Would you like some coffee?"

"No, thanks, Mavis. And remind me to talk to you before I go about washer number seven. It's started acting up something terrible."

"Leone," the supervisor took on a more serious countenance, "These years we've been working together, you know how close we've become. You're a better friend to me than most of my friends on the outside. I have really enjoyed your company and we talk to each other like a pair of magpies. But I'm afraid I've got some bad news for you. I just can't cover for you any more, and you can't work here. It's too dangerous for you and for the other women. That gal getting scalded yesterday was the last straw."

Then Mavis paused, waiting for Leone to respond. But she didn't, not verbally. Leone's face of course expressed all. Her expression of quiet confidence and geniality disappeared, replaced by one of consternation and sadness. Her eyes growing wider, she stared at the supervisor, who went on:

"You and I have talked about this several times and you admitted yourself that your spells are getting worse and they are coming more frequently. Every time you have a spell you do something crazy, break something, get into it with one of the other gals, or somebody gets hurt. And every time, you need a while to recover. Sometimes you need three or four days. Especially now that the whole damn country is in the midst of a depression and they keep cutting the asylum's funding, I just can't afford these disruptions. It's hard enough to make this laundry function without you being a problem. I've got to have someone I can depend on."

Continuing to stare at the supervisor across the desk, tears quietly began to roll down Leone's face.

You knew it was coming, Leone said to herself. *You knew she couldn't go on letting you be such a problem. Every time you hope it's the last, but they just keep coming. And she's right, they're worse. And what am I going to tell Tom? It's really going to make him sad. Him and his optimism and me just getting crazier and crazier. And my boys. Won't none of them be coming to visit if they think I'm having spells every day. Can't blame them much. Who would want to visit their crazy ma in an insane asylum?*

"Leone, I'm sorry. I really am," the supervisor said with heartfelt compassion.

"Mavis, tell me straight. Do you think there's any hope for me? They've tried all kinds of different treatments and I just keep getting worse. Do you think I'll ever get better?"

"I've seen a lot of gals come and go and the worst thing any of them could do for themselves was to give up hope. Once they gave up hope it was pretty much downhill. But those who never gave up hope, a lot of them, did get better. A few gals no one ever thought was going to get better did get well and paroled out of here."

"Yes, Julie did. I miss her. I was sure glad for her when she paroled home, but next to you and Eunice she was just about my closest friend. Even Anne Hallmark finally paroled home. Seems like everyone paroles but me."

"Just don't give up hope."

"You know, Mavis, I thought the Lord was going to save me. I've always been a Christian woman and I truly did think that one day the Lord would make me well again. When we had that visiting preacher a few years back, and he was preaching about the Monkey Trial and I started talking in tongues, I really did think me and the Lord was connected. But, nothing come of it. Maybe I should have made him more a part of my life. I just keep getting worse. And, all my prayers every day. Looks like just a waste of time."

"The Lord works in strange ways," Mavis said, trying to comfort.

"When I first met Eunice all that long time ago, she told me she was an atheist. I'd never met an atheist before and just didn't understand how anyone could be one. She never tried to push it on me and we never said anything more about it. But I'm beginning to think maybe she was right."

"Leone," Mavis said, "don't ever give up hope."

Again Leone went within herself to consider what Mavis had said: *Hope, she says. We ain't never had nothing but hope. And what good has it done? Just made the disappointment worse. All these gals getting better and paroling home. Good for them, but it don't give me no hope. Just makes me want to die.*

"Oh God, Mavis," she said, "the thought of never going home and dying in here terrifies me. I can't imagine anything much worse."

"Just keep on doing as best you can. Keep on with whatever treatments they come up with. That's all you can do. And maybe say your prayers regularly and hope for some luck."

Taking a few moments to compose herself, Leone changed the subject:

"Is this going to change my classification?"

"It don't have to. I spoke to the superintendent about it and she says it's up to you. You can stay where you are and be idle all day while the other women are at work, or you can change to a ward where no one works."

"A ward where no one works?" Leone calmly repeated the supervisor's words back to her. "You mean where the real crazies are? Where there's just screaming and crying all day? Why, that ain't no choice."

"Like I said, you can stay right where you are. But whatever you choose, the superintendent said the doctor is going to be talking to you about some new treatments. The hydrotherapy didn't seem to do you any good, but there's some new things they want to try."

"I'm going to miss you."

"And, I'm going to miss you, too, Sugar. Women come and women go, but you're like a fixture here, like part of the institution. But we'll still see each other. I'll drop by."

Suddenly Leone bent her head into her hands, letting deep convulsive gasps and sobs overtake her. As she silently sat and wept, Mavis came around the desk and hugged her.

●●●●●●

Nervously rubbing her hands together, Leone sat by herself in one of three uncomfortable wooden chairs waiting for Doctor Adams to call her in. She could hear the woman he was with crying.

When the door to the doctor's office opened a smallish middle-aged woman emerged. Doctor Adams's arm was around her shoulders, and he was saying something to her Leone couldn't quite make out. However, when the two reached the exit door and the doctor stopped, the woman turned to look up at him and with pleading eyes said:

"God bless you, Doctor. Thank you for all you've done. I'll try to do exactly what you said. I'll parole out of here, yet?"

As the woman turned back toward the exit door, the Doctor held out his hand to Leone and said:

"Pleased to meet you, Leone. I'm Doctor Adams. I'm very sorry we haven't previously had occasion to meet, but there just hasn't been time to work you in. Because there are so many women needing to see me, I can only see the most critical or those I have the best chance of helping. Did you know that soon we'll have more than one thousand women here? We need ten psychiatrists, not just me."

As they stepped into his office and seated themselves, he continued:

"I see as many as I can, but the day only has so many hours in it. I keep telling them that more patients need to be treated in the county where they came from, but that never happens. They just keep sending them to Little Rock. Cheaper, I guess."

Seeing little likelihood that the doctor would ever quit talking, Leone finally interrupted him to say:

"Doctor, I heard about the insulin comas and I don't want them."

"OK, I heard you, but let's talk about it. Hear me out and then we'll decide.

"As you know, modern science isn't really sure what causes mental illness. There has been a lot of speculation and different theories, but there's just no certainty. And, because no one knows the causes, a lot of different treatments have been tried, most of them completely ineffective. Years ago, they were trying incantations, exorcisms and all manner of voodoo stuff. More recently some psychiatrists thought isolation was the way to go. Sometimes they even locked the patient up in a dark room while they were restrained and bound hand and foot. Still more recently, as you yourself have experienced, ice baths were in favor. Even though those freezing baths sometimes induced heart attacks, it was then felt that the benefits outweighed the risks. And it's true, some benefited. However, the vast majority, including you I read in your file, did not."

Although the room was well-lit and quite warm, as the doctor had droned on Leone had pulled her cardigan close up around her neck, wrapped both arms around herself and begun to rock. *Does this man ever quit talking?* she thought to herself. *Why don't he tell me something I don't know?*

"And," the doctor continued, "that brings us to the present. Hydrotherapy is still being used, but it's being phased out. Probably some were helped by hydrotherapy, but most were not."

"That's right, Doctor," she interrupted. "It didn't help me a bit."

"That's true, you don't seem to have benefited. But others have, probably more because of the socialization during treatment than by the baths themselves. In any event, you went through all twenty-one sessions and the result was not positive."

"So what does that leave us with?" she asked.

"A lot of hope and not much demonstrated result, I'm afraid. There is a technique being perfected as we speak called prefrontal lobotomy. A lobotomy is a surgery into the patient's brain during which the connections to the prefrontal cortex from the main part of the brain are cut. Initial results are quite promising, but there have been some set-backs. While the most dramatic manifestations of mental illness have been curtailed in many patients, the improvement has often been accompanied by what otherwise would be called catatonia—the patient's affect becomes completely flat, with neither expressions of joy nor sadness. Thus, the jury is still out on lobotomy and I am not using it."

"Doctor, we know about lobotomies. We hear about all the latest developments. I ain't having no lobotomy. Ain't no one going to cut into my brain."

"That's right, Leone. As I said, I don't do lobotomies. But there is another promising treatment that's being perfected. It's called electro-convulsive therapy, or ECT for short, or sometimes, shock therapy. It involves administering strong jolts of electricity to the brain, so as to induce convulsions. In ways we don't fully understand, the disruption of the normal electrical activity of the brain can cause it to realign in more normal and beneficial patterns. This treatment is so new and has been tried on so few people that I haven't yet tried it on any of my patients. I want to see more results first.

"Are you with me so far, Leone?"

"Yes, Doctor. I'm listening to every word."

"And there is one other option—Insulin Shock Therapy. We've been using IST here for the last few years and you've no doubt heard of it. Maybe you even know patients who experienced it. It has had mixed results. Over a course of several weeks, we administer a huge dose of insulin which causes the patient to go into a coma. Then after an hour or so, we inject the patient with glucose which terminates the coma. The vast majority of patients who benefit from this treatment have been diagnosed as schizophrenic. You're not schizophrenic, and so it's never been prescribed for you. However, I'm now suggesting it. We just don't have any other options."

"Yes, Doctor, we all know about it, but what about drugs? Gossip on the ward is that they's new drugs coming that will cure us all."

"Yes, it's true that researchers are working on several new drugs which might be effective in treating mental illness. However, these drugs won't be available for years. They have to be perfected. And in view of the many different forms that mental illness takes, I hardly think it likely that one drug, or even a few of them, will cure all.

"So, it's up to you, Leone. ECT and IST is all I have to offer you. In view of your continually worsening condition, I'm recommending IST. I can't promise you a good result, but there's minimal risk involved, and it might help. And if it doesn't work, we can always try ECT."

Oh my God, Leone thought as she was leaving, *please, please let one of these work. They've just got to.*

• • • • • •

When Tom arrived at the asylum for his next visit with Leone, it had been two months since her final ECT treatment, which had come after a series of unsuccessful IST sessions. Nothing had helped. In her more lucid moments Leone had of course asked the medical people why they had not worked for her, but each time was met with the same answer:

"We just don't know. Sometimes they help and sometimes they don't."

When she slowly walked into the visiting room, her ten-year age difference with Tom wasn't readily apparent. They both looked old. As with him, she had aged dramatically. She looked much more than her fifty plus years. With her stooped gait, narrowing shoulders and white paper-thin skin, one would have guessed at least seventy.

As to Tom, the hard years on the farm had taken their toll on him, as well. Once proud, tall and erect, he now shuffled as much as he walked. His failing back and painful knees had reduced him to leaning heavily on the sycamore branch he had carved into a cane. Although his deep blue eyes hadn't lost their sparkle, their acuity was gone and he, too, wore glasses. His many years in the fields under the hot Arkansas sun had turned his skin leathery, wrinkled and marked with brown blotches.

Now the oldest couple in the asylum, Tom and Leone were known to most all. Other patients were older than Leone, but not one of them had a spouse who had continued to visit. Usually, the spouses visited for a few months or a year or so, and then tapered off to not coming at all. The Whiteners were treated with respect and deference by staff and patients alike.

The spacious visiting room Tom entered was used mostly during inclement weather. It could accommodate more than one hundred patients and their guests, but when there were a lot of visitors, it was crowded. A diverse collection of old and new chairs, tables, divans and rockers filled the room and scattered throughout were old and dented spittoons, which doubled as ash trays for the few smokers.

Some of the patients had only one visitor, while others sat with whole families. Two of the visiting women were nursing their infants. Others had filled tables with their patient's favorite snacks, entrees and desserts, almost all of them home made. As Tom looked to the door at the other end of the hall where he knew Leone would enter, he was oblivious to the low din of conversation coming from the other patients and their families. He thought only of his wife.

When Leone finally arrived, he broke into a broad smile and hurried toward her. Pulling her against him with his still strong arm, he felt her arms go lightly around him. Then with surprise he realized she wasn't raising her head for the kiss he had so yearned for, the touch of those ever-soft lips he had so treasured through the years. Even as he reached under her chin to try to raise her head, she stubbornly kept her head tight against his chest.

"Honey," he said, "Ain't you going to kiss me?"

And, as she stood silent, "Honey, ain't you going to answer me?"

Seeing what was going on, the supervising attendant came over and quietly said in Tom's ear:

"She ain't been talking much lately. Why don't you sit over there on that empty divan and maybe she'll come around?"

As they seated themselves on a large well-worn couch looking out on a window filled with rain and storm clouds, Leone said to Tom:

"Tom, would you get me a drink of water?"

"Why, sure I will, Honey."

When she had finished the water, she handed the glass to Tom, put her hands in her lap and looked down at them.

Leaning her way and putting his hand on hers, Tom overcame his growing distress to say:

"Sugar, did you get my letter? The one about the boys getting married."

"No, Tom, I don't remember no letter."

"Well I wrote you one. I don't know why you wouldn't get it. I told all about Loyce and Otto and Clifford, all three of them getting married. Happened real sudden. Loyce and Otto both got married and headed out for Texas. And they hadn't no more than got gone when Clifford decided he wasn't going to be outdone and he got married, too. Otto and Clifford both married gals named Jewell. Ain't that a lick, now we got two daughters-in-law both named Jewell. And, Lola. Loyce's wife is named Lola. Jim's down in Texas, too. Him and his new bride, Jennie.

When his wife didn't respond, Tom asked sharply:

"Well, ain't you gonna say something? Three of our boys get married and Jim moves off to Texas and you don't say anything. Leone, you're scaring me. Don't you care about our family no more?"

"That's nice, Tom," she answered flatly.

Then, his consternation grew to irritation:

"And Allen's in California in a CCC camp. Do you remember me writing you about that?"

"Oh, that's nice, too" she answered, her voice as bereft of affect as before.

Then, calming, Tom continued:

"Clifford's Jewell is five years older than him and anxious to start a family. Did I tell you that? They's farming down around Sandtown."

"That's nice," was the almost expected reply, followed by:

"Tom, is it almost time for lunch?"

"Honey, it's still morning. I just got here. Lunch won't be for another couple hours. Can I get you a snack? Maybe they got an apple or something I can get you."

"Them folks over there is having lunch. Why can't I have lunch?"

"Sugar, they're just having a snack. They brought it from home. I didn't bring no snack."

Finally raising her eyes from her lap, she glared at her husband and in a voice that was not of this world shouted:

"I want my lunch. I want it right now."

Hearing Leone's almost-scream, the supervising attendant hurried over and in her most consoling voice said:

"Leone, we'll get you some lunch. Them people over there got a whole ham and some fresh bread. How about a ham sandwich? I'm sure they would be willing to share."

The excited Leone disappeared as quickly as she had appeared. The calm Leone answered:

"With mustard, if you please."

When Leone had finished about half of the thick slices of bread and ham, she put the remainder on her plate and again stared at her lap.

Tom reached over to put his large calloused hand on top of her much smaller ones and said:

"Honey, did I tell you that fox got in the hen house again? I thought I had it fixed so's nothing could get in, but he did it. Ate every egg and killed a couple hens just for fun. Did I tell you that?"

"That's nice, Tom."

Finally, not knowing what else to say or do, Tom sat looking at his silent wife until the visitation supervisor announced that visitation was ending. As they stood up, he gathered her to him, held her with tears in his eyes and when she failed to respond, kissed the top of the head and left.

• • • • • •

"Well, I must say, this is one of your better days," one of the three women breakfasting with Leone said to her a few days after Tom's previous visit. You ain't talked this much in a month of Sundays."

"Yes, I am feeling better today," Leone answered without elaboration. "Would you please pass the grits?"

As usual, breakfast at the asylum was substantial. Consisting of pancakes, eggs to order, bacon, sausage, grits, gravy and biscuits, it was designed to be one of the main meals of the day. After such a breakfast many of the patients skipped lunch entirely, eating again only at supper.

"Leone," one of the other women said, "I don't know how you don't get fat. You eat like a horse and just sitting around all day you don't do nothing to work it off."

Leone said nothing as she spooned more grits onto her plate and doused them in gravy.

"You never did tell us what your husband had to say," the third woman said. "Any news from Batesville?"

Before Leone could answer, the first woman broke in:

"Y'all ever heard of something called a conjugal visit? I just read in a magazine that some people are in favor of giving prisoners overnight visits with their spouses and calling them conjugal visits. I reckon us and our spouses would like that just as much as any convicts would, and I don't see why we can't have them."

As the others nodded and clucked with approval at the idea of possibly again having marital relations, Leone put the first spoonful of grits and gravy in her mouth. But, she said nothing. Finally, one of the women asked her:

"Leone, why don't you answer her? Any news from home?"

But it was too late. Leone wasn't answering. She was gone. She just sat eating her grits and looking absently across the room. Having seen this behavior in her before, the others quietly got up and left.

After she had finished eating, Leone moved to a rocking chair in the hall and sat knitting. She didn't speak and didn't acknowledge greetings. An attendant had to tell her several times when it was time for lunch.

Placing her knitting on the floor, she quietly rose to walk the short distance to the dining room where she picked up a tray to start down the serving line. However, something caught her eye and she stopped.

"Okra," she said so quietly that no one heard her. Then when the woman behind her said that she should move along, she repeated more loudly, "Okra."

"Come on, Leone," the woman said, "you going to stand there or get some food?"

"Okra is the Devil's food. It's the reason he's green. Green and fire red."

"Leone, you better watch yourself. You're going nutty again."

Spinning to abruptly face the woman, Leone almost shouted, "Okra. We had fried okra yesterday. I ain't eating no more okra."

"Well, you don't have to eat the gol-durned okra," the woman barked back. "Eat something else. Or, don't eat at all, I don't care. But move along."

At this Leone hysterically threw herself onto the floor, and with flailing arms and far-away eyes continued to shout over and over:

"Okra. Gol-durned okra. I ain't gonna eat no more okra. Tom don't like okra. My boys don't like okra. Devil's food. No more okra."

The senior patient in the dinner room, a woman who had known Leone for years, came over to her and leaned down to say:

"It's OK, Honey. It's OK. You don't have to eat no okra. Come on, let's go to your room. You can lie down for a while. You'll feel better."

Mollified enough to cease her hysteria, Leone allowed the woman to help her to her feet and escort her to her room, where she remained until supper.

When it was time for supper an attendant finally noticed that Leone had not come and went looking for her. Opening her door, the attendant stopped, shook her head in disgust, and stared.

Leone was lying on her bed completely naked, methodically cutting all the hair from her body with a small pair of round-nosed sewing scissors. She had already cut her pubic hair, and was now closely cropping the hair on her head. The entire front part was completely bald, and she was working her way to the rear. As she cut a few strands at a time, she very carefully stretched them out and laid them on her body. Her neck and most of her breasts had disappeared beneath a hairy mass of gray.

"Leone, what on earth are you doing?" the attendant blurted.

When Leone turned her head to the side to answer, it was obvious that whatever answer she might give would be extraneous to the world of the sane. Her mouth was pulled into a menacing sneer, her eyebrows were stretched half way up her forehead and her wild eyes were like saucers filling most of her face.

"I'm building a barrier," she half growled. "That Devil ain't going to get my young'uns. I'm building a barrier just like we did for them locusts. And when the Devil comes, I'm going to light it. Going to burn him up, just like he wants to do to us."

Whereupon, Leone launched into an eerie, howling laughter which went on and on. Even after she was transferred to the ward for those deemed beyond help, it went on.

CHAPTER EIGHTEEN

After Jim left, Tom tried to farm on alone, but the long years of toil had so taken their toll that it wasn't long until he just was no longer able to do it. Even though his spirit never flagged, increasingly arthritic knees and problems with his back made it physically impossible to continue.

"I ain't quitting," he told anyone who would listen. "I'll soon be back at it, you'll see. As soon as they come up with something to fix these knees, I'll be making crops with the best of them."

But, of course "they" never did, and except for the vegetable garden which grew smaller each year, Tom's fields lay fallow, covered in weeds. Most days, weather permitting, he could be found in his rocker on his porch, awaiting a friend or relative with a cooked meal and companionship. To most any visitor he began to repeat himself over and over, telling the same stories and reminiscing about how Leone's father had "run him off," how Leone had been "pretty as a June bug on a string" and what fine young men his boys had become.

In spite of the superintendent's letter advising that further visits would not be happy ones, and how unsatisfactory the previous one had been, Tom did make one last trip to Little Rock to see Leone in the asylum. Accompanied by a cousin who helped him on and off the train and made sure his cane was always at hand, the men were ushered into a small visiting room in the wing of the asylum maintained for those who were beyond hope.

Leone sat alone at a small table. She was wearing a plain blue dress, no make-up and stared at her lap. Seated in a chair against the wall was the required visitation supervisor, a large middle-aged woman, who said to Tom as he entered:

"I washed her face and combed her hair. I tried to get some lipstick on her, but she wouldn't sit still for it. She probably won't talk to you. She don't talk to anyone. She just sits. Sometimes we even have to feed her."

"Honey," Tom said as he uncertainly lowered himself onto one of the chairs, "It's me, Tom, your husband."

Leone didn't move.

Looking at the top of his wife's bowed head, Tom leaned forward and lay his arm across the table, stretching for but not quite reaching the edge.

"Honey, don't you recognize me? I come all the way from Sidney, won't you talk to me?"

"I told you, Mr. Whitener," the supervisor interjected, "that's the way she is all day, every day."

Ignoring the supervisor, Tom continued:

"Honey, I got news from home, news about our young'uns. Don't you want to hear it? Allen got married and is headed for California. And Clifford's doing just fine. He's still farming there in Sandtown. Honey, please look at me. Won't you say something?"

But, she never did. Tom prattled on for the better part of an hour relating everything he could think of, but nothing roused her. She never lifted her head.

Finally, the supervisor again interrupted:

"Mr. Whitener, we can stay here all day if you want, but you're just not getting through to her. Can't you see it's just no use."

"I may stay here all night, too," Tom snapped as he threw his head back to glare at the women. "This is my wife and I'll stay as long as I gol-durned please."

His expression reverting to one of love and compassion as he again looked at Leone, Tom said nothing. He had run out of things to say.

After a few silent moments, he looked over to the supervisor and said:

"Would it be OK if I came around the table and held her? Maybe if

I hugged her, she would like it."

"I wouldn't recommend that, Mr. Whitener. She don't like nobody touching her. It was all I could do to get her ready to see you. You touch her and she's likely to fly into a rage."

Oh, Lord, Tom thought as he sat, *I have asked you so many times why you have done this to us. Why, oh why, oh why? Why have you forsaken us?*

Never taking his eyes off his wife, Tom rose and backed across the room to the door. Burying his face in his hand, he exited.

The next day when Tom returned home, he immediately went to the picture of Leone he kept next to his bed, the one that had been taken even before they were married. Holding the picture in his lap and looking down at it, he talked to the wife he remembered from so many years ago:

"Honey, if you ain't the cutest. You are pretty as a peach and surely the best wife a man could ever wish for. I loved you from the first time I saw you and I still do. I'll always love you."

EPILOGUE

With his knees and back getting worse and worse, Tom stayed on his farm as long as he could. Eventually though, it had to be sold and he had to leave. Clifford and Jewell in Sandtown of course took him in, even though with their growing family it was a stretch to make room for him. Tom died in 1943 and was buried in the Mount Carmel Cemetery near his parents and two of his siblings.

Leone never left the asylum, finally dying there in 1960. She had been there for forty years.

Tom and Leone are buried next to each other beneath a marker which reads, "A devoted father and mother."

The four boys turned out every bit as good as their parents had hoped, leading long and productive lives. Loyce and Otto lived out their days in Texas, Clifford in Arkansas and Allen in California, leaving many children of their own. Tom and Leone's many descents are scattered throughout the United States, from Alabama to California to Montana and elsewhere.